MW01265625

THE
LIGHTS
OF
ISARN

BY NAOMI KING

First edition.

This book is a work of fiction. Names, characters, places, and incidents are the product of the author's imagination or are used fictitiously. And resemblance to actual events, locales, or persons, living or dead, is coincidental.

Text copyright © by Naomi King 2021

All rights reserved. This book or any portion thereof may not be reproduced or used in any manner whatsoever without the express written permission of the publisher except for the use of brief quotations in a book review.

To all my crazy, amazing, ridiculous friends.

I couldn't have chosen a better Squadron to fly with.

PROLOGUE

Y ou can't do this!" he shouts, his voice breaking the stillness that fills the room of politicians.

"We already have," one says. "You've shown too much reckless behavior to be given the title. We're protecting Isarn, it isn't personal."

"That's *exactly* what this is! You know I'm the only person capable for this job. You can't handle change, that's what it is."

Several of the nine Beacons stand up. He doesn't back down. He stares over the faces across the table.

"I won the election! *I'm* what the people want. They want me to be their leader. Their Vire. And you all know it. Instead you're putting a-"

"Enough!" The man at the end of the table stands. "Our decision is final. You have been overruled for reckless behavior, Malco Score will take your place as Vire."

He smashes his fist on the table. "This isn't fair!"

"Call security," one says.

Men rush in and take him by the arms.

"Escort him out."

"I can let myself out," he snaps, jerking his arms out of their hold and storming out of the room.

She waits for him outside the door. As soon as he comes through she stiffens. "What did they say?"

He says nothing.

"Daken. What did they say?"

Anger breaks into his vision. "I'm going to kill them."

"They rejected you?"

He meets her eyes. "And they're going to die for it. The Board of Beacons, Malco, all of them."

She looks up at him and nods. "They don't see it."

"But I do."

"We do."

He stands tall and leaves the building. He'd make them see it. He'd show them they couldn't keep all the power in their own hands. That power belonged to the people. They proved that today.

"Call the others," he says. "We've wasted enough time playing fair."

NINE YEARS LATER

CHAPTER ONE

Looks like *someone* fell asleep at their desk again. Really Skye, I expected much better of you."

Skye groaned and lifted her head from the desk she sat at. Wires and device chips scattered around her. Had she fallen asleep while working again? She rubbed her face with her hands and looked up at the smirking boy.

Her younger brother Locke stood at her workbench, holding his school tablets, doing his homework completely last minute.

He crossed his eyes. "Look I can finally do it!"

Skye rolled her eyes at him. "VACA, what time is it?" she asked, looking back down at her work from last night.

"Voice Activated Control Algorithm loading," the program on her laptop buzzed. "Good morning Skye, it is 7:27."

Skye groaned and pushed herself up from the desk. "Where's Mom and Dad?" She asked her brother.

A shout of excitement from the other side of the basement made Skye's head jerk up.

She looked over at Locke. "That would be Dad. Mom left for work."

"And you're not going to go see what the yelling is about?" Skye cast a glance at where the yell had come from.

"I am *terribly* busy with this extremely important school work." He flipped the screen around to show the doodles he'd made around the homework. "Look I made you." He pointed to the sketch of a figure with buck teeth and a unibrow.

Skye sighed and pushed him to the side as she headed out of her workroom in the corner of the basement. The rest of the room was her dad's laboratory. The poorly lit room was filled with tables covered in vials, beekers, and test tubes. Each one was filled with some crazy chemical or medicine.

"Dad?" she called, unable to find him in the mess.

Her dad came out from behind a stack of beekers. "Skye! Come here, I need to show you something." He led her to the contraption where a green vial sat on the table.

"Is that the-" Skye was definitely awake now.

He nodded with enthusiasm. "Yes. The cellular fusation serum is done." He looked practically giddy. He'd been working on it for months.

"Have you tested it yet?" she asked, grabbing a pair of safety glasses like the ones her father was wearing and leaning down to get a closer look at the green serum.

He shook his head. "No, not yet. I *just* finished it, I haven't had time to test it yet."

"How are you going to do that?" Skye asked, thinking of ways to do it in her head, and not liking any of the ways they turned out.

He rubbed the back of his neck. "The best way I can think of doing it, is to separate the cells, that way the serum has something to work with."

"Are you saying you want to cut yourself open?"

"That depends on whether or not your mother is home."

"Why don't you do it on a test animal or something?" Skye's brow started to etch with worry.

"That would take a considerably long time to get a test animal, plus, how bad could it be? If everything works as planned, the serum will seal whatever cut I give myself, and fuse the cells back together."

Skye crossed her arms. What was he *thinking?* "You could infect yourself with the serum and die. Are you seriously willing to risk your life for a science experiment?"

"Skye, this serum could save millions of lives, I might as well try." He sat down at the desk. "Can you grab me the sterilization rub from the bathroom?" He eyed her worried look. "Don't worry, it'll barely be a nick."

Skye did as she was told and came back a minute later with the liquid and a swab.

He rubbed it on his hands and sterilized a small blade.

He paused. "You're sure Mom's not home, right?"

"Locke said she just left for work. Why?"

He gave a nervous laugh. "Because she would absolutely kill me if she saw this."

Skye looked away as he pressed the miniscule blade into his hand. This could go *so* badly.

"Pass me a syringe, will you?"

She grabbed one from the table and handed it to her father, trying to look anywhere but the small pool of blood forming on his palm.

Her father used the syringe to suck a few drops from the green vial. He gave her a stressed smile, then pushed the back of the syringe, sending a few drops of the serum onto his cut.

Nothing happened.

Skye leaned in closer. The serum wasn't working?

Her father's eyebrows were pressed in frustration. "It should've worked," he mumbled. "I had everything right."

"Have you had any effects from the serum yet?" Skye asked.

He studied his hand. "There's a slight burn, that's all I can tell right now."

"You should wipe that stuff off," she said, handing him a towel.

He nodded and wiped away the green liquid. "I thought I had everything right…" He shook his head with a disappointed smile. "Thanks for your help, Rivet."

Skye smiled at the use of her father's nickname for her. "No problem, it was, uh…"

"Fun?" he guessed.

"Not sure I would say that."

He laughed. "You excited for today?"

Skye swallowed hard. Not really. Not at all. It was Finals day.

She didn't want to leave. Even just the thought of it made her stomach flip. *Tons of teenagers go through this*, she told herself. The thought didn't bring her much comfort.

She shrugged in reply. "I don't know."

She wanted to remind herself that she would become a great Light and protect Isarn. That she would fight side by side with a Squadron. That she would be assigned to an amazing Mentor to teach her everything she needed to know. But her mind only wanted to focus on the part where she would be a *soldier*. A teenager being trained so that one day she could help shape the world.

Her dad placed a hand on her shoulder. "How are you doing, Rivet?" There was a sort of concern in his voice that made it hard for Skye not to cry.

"I'm fine."

"It's okay to be nervous."

She sighed. "I know… it's hard not to be."

"You'll do great. And not just in the Finals, you'll make an amazing Light. I'm sure you will. I know how hard it is to leave, but you're going to be fine. You'll get a great Mentor, you'll be a part of a Squadron, they'll become like family. Trust me."

Skye nodded. She was looking forward to that at least, but she didn't know about the rest…

She hesitated on speaking the thought she'd had last night. "Should I do this?" Skye finally asked. "What if I become a Light and something happens to me? What if-"

He rubbed his hand over her arm. "You should never not try. It would be so easy for you to fail on purpose and never worry about it. Look, I can't promise nothing bad will happen, I hope more than anything in the world it won't, but at some point in your life, you've got to face your fears." He paused. "I can't tell you what to do, but I know you'll do what you know is right. No matter what you choose, I'll be here for you."

Skye swallowed a choked up gulp of tears and nodded. "I know."

Dad smiled and looked up over the mess. "I should clean this up. You better get going, you don't want to be late for the Finals."

She nodded and went back into her workroom to grab her backpack where she had left it last night.

Locke dropped his head onto the table and let out a long groan.

"You better hurry up, you've got to leave soon-"

His groan got even louder.

"Okay then." Skye grabbed her commscreen and headed upstairs. "Have fun."

"Life is miserable," Locke mumbled as Skye shut the door.

After getting ready Skye headed out into the cool morning air. The day was crisp from the end of winter and the cool wind blew Skye's auburn hair wildly. Her bright turquoise eyes showed more hints of green his time of year, as her skin turned a tone lighter. For a sixteen year old, she was about average height, she was maybe a little thinner than most of the other girls, but mostly she lacked upper body strength.

Skye slipped on her gripped gloves, and sped down the street on her hovercycle. She always loved these types of days; the days where she could ride through the streets in the cool air and not worry about whether or not she would pass the Finals and leave home.

She had little doubts that she wouldn't pass the Finals. She'd gotten perfect scores on almost every exam they'd been given that year. What if she didn't make it? But what if she did? She wasn't exactly sure which one she wanted more.

She shook her head. She needed to get her mind off of the Finals. She slipped in her ear piece and blasted music from her commscreen as loud as it would go. The music brought a calming sensation with its melodies, letting her stressed mind relax.

Skye soon pulled into the school parking lot. She slowed her hovercycle to a stop in front of the two-story gray building. She shoved the keys in her pocket and ran inside.

Final exams, Skye thought as she walked into the classroom she'd been instructed to go to.

There were about twenty other teens already sitting down. Most of them were on their commscreens, some were talking to their friends, but Skye could tell they were all nervous.

She took a seat near the back of the class. She didn't know many of these kids. She recognized a boy from her chemistry class, but everyone else were strangers. It figured, the City District was one of the biggest Districts in Isarn. A Spark could go an entire 10 year education here and never know every student.

"Hey."

Skye turned to see who had spoken. "Uh… hi?"

A girl Skye didn't recognize sat next to her. She was leaning over so she was as close to Skye as possible while still in her seat.

"Isn't this so crazy?" she asked, sounding like they'd been friends forever. "I can't believe we're graduating! Well, trying to anyway. I think I have a pretty good shot, how about you?"

The girl's bright blue eyes were spread wide as she waited for an answer.

"Um, I think I'll do good."

She studied Skye. Her freckled nose scrunched up as she nodded. "You will. You seem smart."

"Thanks…"

"Class!" the teacher called, "I'm sure many of you are nervous, but let's try to remain focused for today, shall we?" She waited for the class to answer, but no one spoke up. "I'm sure you must be excited to see what you will be doing, so please give a warm welcome to Principal Maxwell, he'll explain how this will all go down.

The screen behind her flashed with a recording of the principal. "Congratulations class for making it through the year. As you know, you will be given a final test. This will determine whether or not you will become a Light. Your answers will also determine your Guild. Intelligence, Agility, Ingenuity, Stealth, or Leadership. There is more than one answer to most of the questions, and some of these will surprise you. This exam is not just testing your knowledge, it's testing *you*."

Wait. What?

"Good luck students, may the Eagles fly with you."

The screen flashed black.

CHAPTER TWO

A crisp white sheet of *real* paper slid onto Skye's desk. Not a tablet like she'd been using her whole life. No. Paper. No one even used paper anymore.

One of the students pointed it out.

"This way we'll be able to tell if you erased something," the teacher said, giving them each a pencil.

"Are we not allowed to erase and rewrite the answer?" a student asked.

"You are. Your new answer will still count."

"Then what's the point of using paper if changing the answer doesn't affect our score?" she asked.

"This way we know if you doubted your answer."

Uneasy chatter filled the room.

"You have two hours. Good luck." The teacher started a timer and left the room.

Skye flipped over the page and read the first question.

1. *Only one color, but not one size. Stuck at the bottom, but easily flies. Present in sun, but not in rain. Doing no harm, and feeling no pain. What am I?*

"What the-" This was a *riddle*. This was supposed to be a real exam. She was supposed to answer questions on math and science, not on kids games.

The whole point of this is to test us.

She looked back over the question. This was like one of the games she and Locke had played when they were younger. There had to be a logical way to answer this.

"If I take the variables from each part and cancel them out it'll make it a lot easier," she whispered to herself. She had a bad habit of talking out loud when her brain got too busy to hold all of her thoughts.

"Only one color, but different sizes..." She drummed the page with her pencil. "It can fly, but is stuck on the ground. What only shows up in the sun? Rainbows are only in the sun, right? But that's more than one color... the opposite of a rainbow is a..." *Shadow? A shadow is always black, but can be any size. It's on the ground when you walk, but you can make a shadow bird with your hands. There are only shadows with light, and a shadow can't hurt or feel anything.* "That works!" she whisper-yelled, scribbling down her answer: A shadow

2. *You are sneaking into an enemy camp at night. You have three men on your side and there are ten*

in the camp. Four of the ten men are asleep, half of the awake ones are patrolling the other side of the camp, the last two are at the fire. You send your strongest man into an empty tent. He doesn't come back. An hour later so you send in the other two. After another hour they don't come back either. Why aren't your men coming back?

How was she supposed to know? This whole problem was intensely long, probably filled with tons of useless information. "Why tell me how many men they have?" She whispered to herself. "Ten men, four are asleep, if half of the rest are patrolling, that would be three, so there should be three left at the fire, not two! There's one man left." That didn't answer the question. Was the last man in the tent? "He can't be, it says it's empty, unless…"

She wrote down her answer: **The tent is trapped by the last man.**

It felt like a naive answer, but logicly, it worked. She turned to the next question.

3. *Is Daken Claw a threat to Isarn?*

What was that supposed to mean? Claw was gone, wasn't he? It had been like 9 years since he had tried to kill Vire Malco, and Skye had never seen much of him since. Not like she remembered much of when he was popular. Was he a threat? He'd been a Flame and a Beacon, so he had the experience of a soldier *and* a politician. That had to make him dangerous, right? This was more of an opinion than an actual question.

Skye hesitantly wrote down her answer. I guess so.

4. *What is the best weapon to choose if you are infiltrating an enemy base?*

Nope, she had no clue. The school didn't train them with weapons. They'd only had a few days of weapon identification that year and Skye hadn't been too good at remembering all of the names of each gun.

She wracked her brain for any hint of an idea, but came up empty.

She needed to really think. What basic weapons were there? Blaster, knife, maybe a grenade? A grenade would work, except it was way too loud and once it was used up, she would be defenceless. A blade was good for stealth, but it was small, and she could only fight hand to hand. A blaster was logical, but there were tons of different kinds, and she wasn't sure which one was best. What would happen if she just put down blaster? Was it too vague?

She wasn't positive about her answer, but she couldn't think of anything better, so she wrote it down. **Blaster**

5. *You answer me, but I never ask you questions. What am I?*

Great, another stupid riddle that has nothing to do with becoming a Light. Why were they giving them these questions? Weren't they supposed to be training to be agile, stealthy, intelligent, to have ingenuity, and to be leaders? It was more like training to be an annoying uncle.

She ran the question over in her head, it seemed to be pretty simple, not a lot of variables like the shadow question.

Her commscreen started ringing and Skye's thoughts broke.

"Shoot. Shoot. Shoot." She scrambled to hang up, then stopped dead. *Commscreen.*

That was it. *You can answer a commscreen, but it can't ask you questions,* she realized with a grin. She wrote the answer down.

Skye looked up at the clock. There were two students picking at the lock on the classroom door.

"What are you guys doing?" someone asked.

One of the lock-pickers looked up. "Question 7," he said, then returned to his lock.

"You guys are on 7?" a girl asked. "I'm stuck on 1!"

Skye pressed her eyebrows together. Were they doing things other than writing the test? It made sense now that she thought about it, they were testing more than just intelligence.

She turned back to her test and read the next question.

6. *What is the chemical solution for making a burn-healing elixir?*

Yes! She knew this one off the top of her head. She and her father had made these plenty of times in the lab.

One part red bloom, two parts honey leaf, two parts purified water.

Now for question 7, the one that for some reason involved getting out of your seat.

7. *For this question you must find a partner. You need to unlock the classroom door, you can use any item in this room. You must go one team at a time, if one team is using the door and does not have it open in three minutes, the next team waiting goes. There are security cameras positioned in this room. Failing to follow the rules will end in failure. Do not forget to bring your test and pencil with you.*

Once you are out of the classroom, a teacher will tell you a phrase, that is what you will write as this answer. Make your way to the gym.

Skye had her eyes wide at the task at hand. She glanced at the clock, she still had an hour and forty-five minutes left. She needed a partner. She stood up and looked around the room.

"Is anyone on 7?" she asked.

A mutual amount of "shhhhh" erupted through the room.

The girl who had been talking to Skye earlier raised her hand. "I'm on 6, if you help me I can be on 7."

This wasn't exactly the person Skye wanted as a partner, but she didn't have the time to wait for someone else to finish, so she leaned over the girl's desk.

"The answer is one part red bloom, two parts honey leaf, and two purified water," she whispered.

"You're sure?"

Skye nodded, "My dad and I have made it before."

She nodded and wrote down the answer. "Okay, what do I need to do?"

Skye pointed to the massive list of instructions. "Read that."

After a few seconds she stood up from her chair and she and Skye got in line.

The first team was still there, but no one else had gotten in line, which meant Skye had to wait three minutes before it was her turn.

"My name's Jayla," the girl said, holding up the back of her forearm.

"I'm Skye." She bumped her's against Jayla's in the universal greeting.

"So do you have any ideas for the lock?" Jayla asked, pulling her long, dark hair into a ponytail.

Skye tried to get a view from where she stood, but couldn't see anything but the backs of the two students. "Not yet, if I can see what type the lock is, I'll have a much better idea."

The three minutes were up, and the two students grumbled and walked to the back of the lengthening line.

Skye and Jayla rushed forward. The lock was an old-fashioned padlock, which meant Skye couldn't hack it.

"We need to pick it," Jayla said, rummaging through a drawer in the teacher's desk.

Skye pulled out her commscreen, pulling out her added items, she tried jamming the tipps into the lock hole. None of them worked and she broke most of them.

"Find anything?" Skye asked.

Jayla ran over with a handful of junk. "I found all of this, maybe we can throw something together?"

There was a transmission wire, a screen pen, data chip, and a tube of quick dry glue. "We've got two minutes."

They put the few items on the floor and knelt down. Skye wracked her brain for an idea. Maybe she could pick the lock with the wire? She'd have to strip it down. But that would take too long.

Jayla shoved the screen pen into to hole, it was too big to fit more than the tip. She sighed, "We need to think of something smarter than that, I know."

Skye had her fingers against her forehead in frustration. Her eyes shot open, "I've got it!"

She grabbed the glue and the pen and flipped the lock over on the ring. She started pouring the glue into the keyhole.

"30 seconds," the kid behind them said.

"What are you doing?" Jayla asked.

Before the glue had time to dry, Skye smacked her palm against it to knock out the air pockets. When she was sure the keyhole was filled, she shoved the tip of the screen pen in the wet glue.

"10 seconds," Jayla mumbled.

Skye urged the glue to dry. She glanced at the clock, only 5 more seconds in their turn. She sucked in a breath and twisted the pen. The lock opened.

CHAPTER THREE

Yes!" Jayla cheered, opening the door and running out.

Skye grabbed both of their tests and pencils and followed her.

The teacher was waiting in the hallway. "The key isn't always what it seems," she said, then replaced the lock on the classroom door for the next students.

Skye scribbled the phrase on both of their tests.

"The gym, hurry!" Jayla said, grabbing Skye's wrist and running off.

The hallways were much darker than they usually were, but the two girls found the gym quickly.

Inside were about fifteen pairs of kids, some were leaning over their papers, others were going behind the red curtain that divided the gym.

"Let's see what question 8 is," Skye said, grabbing the papers from her pocket.

8. *Behind the curtain are three doors. Each door has a different obstacle. You and your partner must complete one together. Each door has a one-word clue to what said obstacle will be. You and your partner must be unanimous on which door to take.*

Once decided, you cannot change your mind. At the end of the obstacle there will be a phrase, that is what you will write as the answer to this problem.

They both walked behind the curtain. Three doors were lined up against a wall, each one had a single word written on it. A teacher Skye had never seen was in charge of the doors, opening them for each team that went through.

"Which one do you think?" Skye asked.

Jayla pointed at the first door. "HEAT sounds like a bad idea to me."

Skye nodded. "I agree. That leaves GROUND and WATER. I personally think door two sounds like the best option, we don't want to get our tests wet if we have to swim."

"Alright, I guess we do GROUND then," Jayla said, shrugging.

They told the teacher their choice and were let into the room.

"Oh, sked," Jayla mumbled.

The word "GROUND" apparently meant "MUD". The room was a waist-deep mud pit.

"How do you want to go about this?" Jayla asked.

Skye grimaced. "The only way to do it is to just go straight in." She didn't mind mud, but the idea of swimming in three feet of it didn't sound so fun.

Jayla was already tying her hoodie around her shoulders. Skye started pulling her hair back and tucked both folded tests into her pocket.

She pressed her foot into the sludge, glad she had worn her heavy boots. Her foot eventually reached the bottom and the other foot followed. The mud was up to her hips which made it extremely hard to walk. Jayla helped Skye get her footing and the two started slowly making their way down the 40 foot long tunnel.

"So, since we obviously have time in here, we should get to know each other. We haven't had any time to talk since we started," Jayla said.

"Sure, I guess."

"Okay. What's your family like?"

"I have a mom and dad, and a little brother. My dad is a chemist, and my mom works at a restaurant. My brother is 11, his name's Locke. How about you?"

"My dad works at an electricity plant, I don't have a mom, but I've got two older sisters, so it's kind of the same thing I guess. They're names are Nyra and Nyree, they're twins and three years older than me."

"Did they pass the finals?"

Jayla shook her head, which was hard to see in the dark room. "Neither one of them did, which is part of the reason why I want to so badly. I'm sort of the baby, so beating them at something would be a defining moment, you know?"

After a pause, Skye spoke up. "Are you scared about becoming a Light?"

Jayla thought for a second. "No. I'm actually not scared. I guess a lot of people are, but it's not like we're being thrust into battle. We're getting years of training to protect Isarn. Plus, it's been like almost ten years since anything remotely dangerous happened here. I don't have a reason to be scared."

Skye smiled a little. Jayla made a good point.

After a little while, Jayla looked up. "Hey, I think we're halfway there."

Skye groaned. "My legs are burning like crazy, I hope we won't have to run after this."

"Eh, it's not so bad," Jayla said, grinning in the dark. "I think it's kinda fun."

"So which Guild do you think you'll be in?" Skye asked.

"I'm pretty sure I'm gonna be in Agility, how about you?"

"Probably Intelligence, that's what my dad was."

Jayla nodded. "Yeah, I could see you as Intelligence, are you good at, like, math and stuff?"

She shrugged. "Yeah, I usually fall asleep in math class though."

She nodded approvingly. "Everyone does."

They continued to talk, none of their conversation was particularly interesting, but Skye and Jayla had fun with it and didn't mind the tedious task as much. Skye had lost track of how long they had been in the tunnel by the time they climbed up on the platform at the other end.

"How much more of this are they gonna make us do?" Jayla mumbled, wiping the chunks of mud from her leggings. They were still soaked and stained no matter how hard she scrubbed.

"Hopefully not a lot," Skye said, searching the walls for a message.

"Here it is," Jayla said, pointing to the wall. "*The choices you make always affect the future.*" She waved her hands in the air at the camera in the corner. "Very ominous, guys. Nice work."

Skye laughed and scribbled it down on both tests. "We only have a few more questions."

They opened the door and stepped into the opposite side of the gym.

"What are we supposed to do?"

Skye read the next question.

9. *I am blue in the morning, red at night. Closed in the heat, open in cold. I hide in the shadows, but crave the light. Find me and you will find your answer.*

"Oh! I know this one," Jayla said. "We need to get to the science lab!"

The two girls tried to run, but their legs were sore from the constant strain of walking in the mud, so they settled for an awkward hopping limp. Jayla handled it much better than Skye, but even so, she still couldn't walk right.

"What is it?" Skye asked.

"You'll see when we get there."

Skye looked at Jayla suspiciously, but didn't say anything.

They eventually made their way to the science lab. Jayla immediately raced to the corner. There were artificial habitats filled with animals, plants, and who knew what else.

"Look for a blue flower with three petals, I think the clue is hidden near that," Jayla said.

"What's the flower called?" Skye asked, rummaging through the floating planters.

"It's called a Winter Ripeweed. I had to do a science presentation on them last year. Their petals change color in different seasons, but they thrive most in the cold. Their petals are good for clotting blood quickly."

"Is this it?" Skye gestured to a blue flower.

"Yes! Okay, look for some clue-" Jayla pulled a screendrive from the dirt.

"What is that?"

Jayla placed it in Skye's hand. "Beats me, you're the smart one."

Skye held it up to the light. "We should try plugging it in." She pulled out her commscreen, cleaned out the dirt from the drive, and stuck it in the adapted port.

"Don't you have to plug that into a larger screen?" Jayla asked.

"I upgraded my comm to take all sizes of drives. VACA, what's on this?"

"Processing," the electronic voice buzzed.

"Woah! What the sked is that?" Jayla yelled.

"It's a voice controlled assistant I made for different devices. Her name's VACA."

"Does it have a face? I feel like it needs a face, or a body. No, that would be creepy. How'd you even make that?"

"It was an algorithm I developed with access-"

"Nevermind, forget I asked, that's *way* too much smart people talk for me."

"The drive contains four words," VACA said, flashing the bold letters on the small screen. *Look at the clock.*

Both girls' heads flew to the timer on the wall. They only had 33 minutes left.

"We gotta hurry, this is the last one," Jayla said. "They probably made it super hard." She opened the test to the next question and filled in the answer to the previous one.

34

10. *Make your way to the library. Once you are there, you must retrieve a red key from somewhere in the building. You will be given a volume detector, if your disruptor reaches a high enough sound frequency, you will have a ten minute penalty before being able to try again. There is a limited amount of keys hidden so you must hurry. Once you have your key, unlock a box for a unique code word. Return your test to the room you started in before the timer is up or you will fail.*

"We're going to have to be quiet," Jayla mumbled. "I'm gonna be awful at this."

They ran to the library. Skye's legs burned but she focused only on finishing the test. She was so close.

They opened the door to the library and a teacher clipped a volume detector to their shirts. Apparently this wasn't a team challenge. Skye didn't dare talk, but she made eye contact with Jayla, and she seemed to understand. They both seemed to agree that they should work together.

Jayla motioned to the back of the library, and she and Skye tip-toed their way there.

The library was three stories high, the stark white shelves held almost all of the school's books. The books on the shelves weren't actually real books, they were book-shaped storage holders, when someone wanted to read a book, they could download it on their commscreen by just scanning the ship.

There were probably about forty kids in the library. Some were covered in mud, like Skye and Jayla, others were soaked, and a few kids looked like the tips of their hair was singed, Skye figured they'd gone in the HEAT door. *Idiots.*

Jayla started pulling the books off the shelves and laying them quietly on the floor in a pile.

Skye had an idea. She grabbed her folded test from her pocket and scribbled a message down on the back of the test. She handed it to Jayla.

We can write what we want to say. We need a plan, I can take one side of this shelf, and you can take the other.

Jayle grabbed her test and pencil, flipping it over, she wrote a reply.

Okay, this is a good idea. If I find a key, I'll stay and help you find yours.

I will too if I find one first.

Thanks. It's nice having a friend out here.

They each started on a half of the back shelf, as quietly as they could, stacking the books on the floor. The minutes passed by. The shelf was cleared and no key was found.

We need to look somewhere else, Jayla wrote.

Skye sighed, knowing she was right. She was extremely aggravated that they had wasted ten minutes.

I'm going to check around the chairs and couches, Skye wrote back.

Jayla nodded and went to check the furniture upstairs.

Skye had to use all of her strength to not lay on the couch and fall asleep. She tore out the cushions, searched around on the floor by the chairs, and flipped the edges of the carpets up to check under them. Nothing.

She glanced at the clock hopelessly. They only had twenty minutes left. She was completely drained, her legs were sore, she had a horrendous headache, and she was dirty and tired. She had come into this expecting a simple test on what she had learned that year, instead she'd had to escape a locked room, answer ridiculous riddles, and stomp through a pit of mud.

As quietly as she could, she laid down on the floor, setting her head on the uncomfortable carpet. She was about to close her eyes when she noticed a speck of red amongst the white of the library. A key. It hung from the railing on the highest floor. It wasn't over.

Skye leapt to her feet. She had 15 minutes left. With her sore legs matched with her hasty excitement, she lost her balance and tripped, sending her toppling into a stack of books. The green light on her volume detector turned red. She'd blown it.

CHAPTER FOUR

Skye sat on a bench with her eyes firmly fixed on the key. Her only chance to finish the test was if no one found it. Why was she so clumsy? She had almost guaranteed her passing the final test and graduating, but she'd messed it up. She sat on the bench, alone, waiting for the timer on her volume detector to go off so she could get back to searching.

Maybe this would be a good thing. If she didn't pass the test, she wouldn't have to leave her family. Sure, she'd have to get a common job, but at least she would be home with them. Then why was she so disappointed? She shouldn't care that she probably wouldn't get to become a Light, she hadn't really wanted to from the beginning. But now…maybe the idea had popped into her head that she and Jayla would graduate together. Maybe she'd even hoped they would be in the same Squadron. Now that wasn't going to happen.

Jayla came running down the stairs on the tips of her muddy boots. She was holding a bright red key and had a huge smile on her face. It diminished when she saw Skye sitting alone.

What happened? she wrote when she came over.

I tripped and my volume detector went off, I still have 5 more minutes to wait.

What are we going to do?

You should go. It's not fair for you to not graduate because you're waiting for me.

I'm not leaving! After your timer is done, you'll have 4 minutes left to find a key, it's not over. I can look for another one while you wait.

I found a key. It's hanging off the rail of the third story steps, I just have to get it.

That's great! What should I do until then?

Go.

I said, I'm not leaving.

Fine, at least get your code word and write it down.

Jayla ran off to the boxes on the wall and came back a minute later with her test rolled into a tube.

Skye waited in agony as the time ticked down. Three minutes on her clock, seven on the timer. Two minutes on her clock, six on the timer. One minute on her clock, five on the timer.

So close.

3...

2...

1...

Skye bolted from her seat. Her eyes never left the red key. She was almost there, only one more flight of stairs. She was ten feet from the key. Five. Three. She could almost reach it.

From out of nowhere a hand reached down and swiped the key from the rail.

NOOOOOOOO!

Skye looked up in utter shock and horror.

A boy had the key clenched in his fist. He shrugged and gave her a smirk, then ran down the stairs.

Skye stood there speechless. She had been *so close.*

She looked at the timer, she had four minutes. 240 seconds. 240,000 milliseconds. And it was ticking away. She clenched her fists and scanned the shelves for hints of red. Nothing. She ran through the library and pleaded for sight of a key. Desperation filled her mind.

Three minutes.

She frantically darted her eyes around the room. Nothing but white. Her gaze wandered to the ceiling. *There!* A bright red key hung at the top of the domed roof. Completely out of reach.

Of course she found the impossible one. Maybe it wasn't impossible. She'd come down to the wire earlier with the lock, it had been her quick mind and creativity that had gotten her to this point, she wasn't giving up yet.

The key looked like it was barely hanging onto a hook. She needed to hit it with something. *I can't set off my detector,* she thought. That crossed out throwing her boot. Unless…

Skye darted down the stairs. The clock bore only two minutes.

Jayla jumped up when Skye ran over. Skye scribbled down her instructions and thrust the paper at her friend. She ran across the library before Jayla had finished reading.

Skye watched the top of the balcony as Jayla ran up the stairs and ripped off her boot. Skye was putting all her faith in this throw. She couldn't miss this. Jayla threw her muddy shoe. It hit the key perfectly and both came tumbling down. Skye lunged to catch the bright red key. She caught it.

Skye didn't have time for the boot, so she raced to the locked boxes. She shoved the key into the hole and heard a soft click. The box opened and she scribbled down the word. Skye risked a glance at the clock.

30 seconds.

She needed to get to the classroom. Now.

Jayla came sprinting next to her. The detectors deactivated as they ran out of the library.

The lights in the hall were flashing red as the 30 second countdown blared through the school.

"We're almost there!" Jayla screamed.

20 seconds.

They turned into the last hallway.

10 seconds.

Skye's heartbeat felt like it was ripping her chest apart.

5 seconds.

The classroom!

3 seconds.

2 seconds.

1 second.

The two girls bursted through the door as the timer hit zero.

CHAPTER FIVE

Skye and Jayla took their seats at the back of the class.

"Sked, that was hard!" Jayla said, gasping for breath.

The teacher came in a few minutes later with the rest of the students from the class. They each took their seat from earlier and the screen lit up with the principal's face.

"Congratulations to all who finished the test. We have tested you to an extreme, and only one who excels in all Guilds will have passed the test. We will grade your final answers, and by tomorrow, you will know if you have passed. Until then, you are dismissed for the rest of the day." The screen turned black.

Everyone brought their tests up to the teacher. Some kids were wearing proud smiles, others had ashamed eyes.

"Do you want to hang out?" Skye asked hopefully. "You come over if you want, but you don't have to-"

"Of course! I'd love to. I don't have anything planned, I figured we'd be in school all day. I'll go home and change, and be over at your place in say, half an hour. I gotta go grab my shoe."

Skye gave Jayla her home code number and they said goodbye.

As Skye made her way to her hovercycle, she couldn't help but feel a spark of pride. She had completed the unnaturally hard Finals, *and* made a friend. Frankly, she was more proud of the friend.

As soon as she walked in the door of her house, she collapsed onto the couch.

"That you, Skye?" Dad called from the lab.

"Yeah," she said, forcing herself to get into a sitting position. She settled for laying on her back with one leg propped up.

Her dad came running up the stairs. "How'd it go?"

"Um, I did it?" She got up to look for food in the kitchen.

He followed her in. "So you finished it?"

Skye nodded, pulling a jug of milk. "I did all of the questions, I won't know if I passed until tomorrow." She started drinking straight from the carton.

"That's amazing Skye!" He pulled her in for a hug, splashing them with milk in the process. "I'm so proud of you."

"I had help. We had to do a question where we had to pick a lock, and we needed a partner. Me and this girl Jayla did it together and we actually ended up staying together for the rest of the challenges. I wouldn't have finished the last one without her."

"You should probably go take a shower," he said, glancing at her legs which were completely covered in mud.

Skye finished off the carton and headed upstairs. As soon as she came down from her shower, there was a knock at the door.

"Hi, come on in," she said, leading Jayla into the living room. She was wearing a clean hoodie and black leggings and her hair was still slightly wet from her shower.

She kicked off her boots and set them on the rack. "So, what do you want to do?" she asked.

Skye shrugged. "Do you want to see my lab?"

"You have your own lab? Does it have like chopped off limbs attached to robots and stuff?"

"What! No, where did you even get that idea?"

Jayla shrugged. "I saw it in a movie. It was awesome."

"Well, I don't chop off limbs, I make mechanical devices and algorithms."

"Okay… I still think the limb-robots would be sick, but I do want to see your genius space."

Skye led her down the stairs into the basement. Her dad was hunched over his desk, scribbling down an equation.

"Hey, Dad, this is Jaya, the girl I was telling you about," Skye said.

"It's nice to meet you Mr. Zareb," Jayla said, holding up the back of her forearm.

He put his against it. "Nice to meet you too. Congratulations on the Finals."

"Thanks, Skye was a big help."

"I'm just going to show her my lab," Skye said, motioning for Jayla to follow her.

She said goodbye to Skye's dad, and made her way to the back of the basement.

"Woah, this stuff is all yours?" Jayla asked, her eyes wandering around the small space.

Skye tried to clean up the mess on her large desk. "Um, yeah. Most of the technology I made myself-"

"Wait, is that chair... *floating?*"

Skye nodded as Jayla pulled the white chair from under the desk. "I made it for easier storage, rapid movement, and reaching things. Just don't stick your hand under it. The magnetic field would crush your bones."

"You made this?" Jayla said, sitting on the smooth seat. "Dude, you're smarter than I thought."

She shrugged. "It didn't take being smart, I just added the same negative magnetic pulse hovers have, the floor's already metal, so it wasn't hard to come up with."

Jayla leaned back on the floating chair and kicked her feet up on the section of desk that Skye had cleared. "You know, you might end up being in the Ingenuity Guild. You're smart, but you have a crazy level of creativity. Like filling the lock with glue, I would have never thought of that."

Skye had never thought of being in Ingenuity, she'd always just assumed Intelligence would be hers. But Jayla did make a good point. "Maybe. But it's not like we get to pick."

She spun in the chair. "True. You think you passed?"

"I don't know, some of those riddles were pretty sketchy, I think I did good though."

There was a pause. Skye spoke up, "I wonder if they'll put us in the same Squad."

"Wouldn't that be great! Too bad there isn't a great chance we'll be together–that's saying we both even pass."

There was another silence.

"Do you think you could do it though," Jayla said.

"Do what?"

"Make a limb-wielding robot."

Skye laughed. "If you provide the limbs, I'll be glad to try it."

CHAPTER SIX

Skye wandered into school with the hundreds of other students. They were going to announce who had passed the Finals, and Skye couldn't be any more nervous.

"Skye!"

Her head whipped around in time to see Jayla come running over. Skye was amazed she'd been able to find her in the crowd.

"You nervous yet?" she asked.

Skye sighed. "I'm terrified."

"Same, this is so crazy! I'm so excited, but nervous at the same time."

The speakers started buzzing with the vice principal's voice. "Attention students! Make your way to the auditorium where Principal Maxwell will announce this year's graduates."

The crowd of Sparks started heading to the auditorium, an excited buzz traveled through the air around them.

Skye and Jayla took their seats in the huge room. Once everyone had sat down, the principal came onto the stage.

"This year we have 115 graduates out of 963, which is unfortunately one of the lowest graduation rates in history." The room filled with nervous chatter. "Everyone please, quiet, quiet. To be fair, this is one of the hardest finals we have ever given, so it made sense that it was hard on you. But the Academy of Light expects only Isarn's best students. I will be reading off the names of all of the passing students beginning in alphabetical order."

Great, Skye thought, *Z is going last.*

Jayla gave her a sympathetic smile. Her last name was Payge, which meant she was also pretty far down the list.

Skye hadn't realized the principal had started reading off names.

"*Everett Aire, Silver Akis, Hope Amaw.*" With every name he read, a round of applause would erupt from somewhere in the building.

"I'm so nervous," Jayla said.

Skye held out her hand, and Jayla eagerly grasped it, squeezing Skye's knuckles tight.

"You'd be surprised about how many times I thought I would puke last night," Skye said, causing Jayla to relax and laugh.

The principal kept reading. "*…Eden Debro, Zaithrian Delainey, Galan Devure…*"

Skye would zone in and out as the names were read. She was trying not to worry, but she had been working to this point for her entire life, and if it had all been for nothing... no. She was going to pass. She just kept repeating those words in her brain.

"...*Caitlyn Mailour, Valarie Mayire, Castien Morox, Jethspar Nactix, Luken Noro...*"

As the list came closer to P, Jayla's hand tightened its grip. Skye felt herself getting more tense as the names rolled by.

"...*Klair Pane, Syvis Pare, Verron Pavax...*"

"I can't take this," Jayla pressed her face into her knees.

"...Jayla Payge..."

Her head shot up. "What! I- I did it?"

Skye jumped up from her chair and cheered.

She got down and Jayla was crying tears of joy. She pulled her in for a hug.

"Thank you Skye, I never could have done it without you," she whispered.

Jayla sat down with the biggest smile spread on her face. She was in a daze for a few minutes.

Skye was overjoyed that Jayla had passed, but at the same time she was trying to calm her nerves. They were calling out the W's now.

"...*Gracely Wayve, Vacore Wesley, Analyne Wev...*"

Skye had been trying to keep track of how many names were left, but she had lost count. Jayla had her hand gripping Skye's again.

"...*Caxton Yazz, Brinkley Yev, Keleb Yev*." The principal paused. "And our final graduate is Skye Zareb."

* * *

The students filed out of the auditorium, Skye and Jayla arm in arm.

"We both passed!" Jayla cheered for what must have been the tenth time. Do you think we'll be in the same Squad? I wonder what creature I'll get. I can't wait to find out my Guild!"

Skye and Jayla had probably spent about five minutes freaking out in their seats after Skye's name had been called. They both were unable to process the fact that they had passed.

Skye had been dreaming and dreading passing Spark training for so long, and now knowing she had done it, she wasn't sure if she was more psyched or scared.

Jayla hit her in the arm. "You're already worrying about it, aren't you!"

"I'm not..."

"Yes you are, you're the worst liar I've ever met. Look, you should stop worrying about this, it's an adventure. Adventures are scary, I know, but they're also a chance to have the time of your life."

"I know...It's just-"

"No. Have fun, Skye. Be excited for once in your life."

"You realize you've only known me for like two days, right?"

Jayla waved her hand in the air. "I can tell a lot about a person in two days. I can also tell you've been nervous about this for way too long, and that it's ruining the fact that you passed the Finals. The *Finals*, Skye."

"You're not nervous at all?" Skye asked, crossing her arms.

"Sked yeah I'm nervous! But I'm being a big girl and not letting my nerves ruin my excitement." Jayla kept talking. "So what are you and your family gonna do?" She was practically skipping down the hall.

"I don't know, we'll probably go out to eat or something." That was pretty much what they did whenever Locke's team won a blackball game or when Skye passed a midterm.

"That's fun. Man, I can't wait to rub it in the twins' faces when I get home. They're gonna be so jealous!"

Skye laughed at Jayla's sibling rivalry.

"So, do you think we got a good chance of getting in the same Squad?" Jayla asked.

"Well, there were 115 graduates, five graduates per squad, so that's 23 squads. So we've got a 1 out of 23 shot of being together."

Jayla shrugged and glanced away quickly. "I've had worse odds."

CHAPTER SEVEN

One week later, Skye's family pulled their hovercar into the school parking lot.

Her nerves were on edge, but she kept repeating the words Jayla had said. She needed to stop worrying, she'd done plenty of it for the past week, she was ready. Maybe.

"Go ahead and get with the other kids, we'll be in there in a little bit," Dad said.

"Alright." She ran up the steps and into the building.

The whole school was decorated in white and gold. The usually plain hallways were glowing with rows of sparkling lights. Balloons covered the ceilings and the floor was sprinkled with flower petals.

Skye hurried to the auditorium. If she had thought the halls were pretty, these would be priceless art. The high arched windows were sprinkled with glitter, making the entire room sparkle. Scattered around the room stood five carved crystal statues, one for each creature the Sparks would be chosen by when they became a Light.

Dragons chose brave, hard-working, strategic students. A pegasus chose someone who was bold, ambitious, and charismatic. The thunderbird would choose someone creative, clever, and daring. The griffin chose a strong, smart, sensible person. And lastly, the kelpie would choose someone who had determination and passion.

Skye gazed at the statues in awe, wondering what creature she would be chosen by. Any of them would be amazing to train with, not to mention fly with, but she had her eyes on the griffin. It had the hind legs of a lion, and the wings and head of an eagle, it was by far the coolest one to her.

"Skye! Thank the Eagles I found you!" Jayla came running up.

"Hey Jayla. Is something wrong?"

"What? No, I was just starting to believe I would never find you in this mess. We've got like a billion people in here!"

"I know, it's crazy." A billion was a *bit* of a stretch, but there were hundreds of people.

The auditorium was filled with students, parents, and teachers. An excited aura seemed to vibrate from the walls. Everyone was buzzing around, trying to get into place for the ceremony. The seats where the students had sat in only a week ago, were starting to fill with friends and family.

"I don't know about you, but I hate these ceremony outfits," Jayla said.

All of the students were wearing matching uniforms. They all wore a long sleeved white shirt with a lace trim attached to the sleeves. It was supposed to symbolize them growing wings like the Eagles and flying away to protect Isarn. The girls also wore a knee length white skirt, while the boys were in pants.

"It's not so bad," Skye said, picking at the edge of her skirt

"Whatever, I can take it, but this shirt is itchy!"

Skye laughed. "Is your family coming?"

Jayla nodded. "Yep, my dad and sisters are coming. They were so jealous that I graduated, but they tried to act like they didn't care, it was pretty funny."

"Attention everyone!" The speakers started booming. "We will begin the ceremony in five minutes. Please make your way to your seats."

Skye and Jayla made their way behind the curtain and followed the crowd of students. There was a teacher attempting to get them into lines.

The graduation would go in alphabetical order, which meant Skye would be going last again.

"Hang in there," Jayla said, heading to her spot in the line.

Skye couldn't hear the announcements from behind the curtain, but she knew that the principal would be on the stage now. He would be saying a bunch of stuff about how hard the Finals were, and how proud he was of all of the students. Then he would start calling out names.

As she predicted, the line started moving. The closer she got to the stage, the more she could hear. The principal called Jayla to the front.

"Jayla Bryn Payge, I hereby congratulate you on your success in completing your Spark training. You are now a graduate of Isarn's School of Sparks, and are an official student of The Academy of Light. You will be studying in the Agility Guild for your quick reflexes, flexibility, stamina, and overall athleticism. I again congratulate you."

The crowd erupted into a thunderous applause, and Jayla bowed to the principal, and walked to the other side of the stage.

The line continued to move forward. Finally, Skye stepped onto the stage.

"Skye Sofia Zareb, I hereby congratulate you on your success in completing your Spark training. You are now a graduate of Isarn's School for Sparks, and are an official student of The Academy of Light. You will be studying in the Ingenuity Guild for your creativity, innovation, quick-wittedness, and inventiveness. I again congratulate you."

The crowd broke into applause again, Skye thought she heard Locke screaming a cheer. She bowed in front of the principal and stepped off the stage. As soon as she was behind the curtain, Jayla grabbed her and hugged her. "I knew it! I said you'd be Ingenuity!"

"Can't...breath," Skye wheezed.

"Oops, sorry. But I was right! Congrats, I think they're right on that."

"Girls!" A teacher came up, she didn't look happy. "We need to get situated for the next part of the ceremony!"

Before either of them could reply, she grabbed them by the wrists, and led them to the lines of students.

"We're gonna find out our Squads!" Jayla squealed excitedly.

The curtains opened and the rows of teenagers filed onto the stage. There was more applauding, and the principal came out again, this time with Vire Malco.

"They dragged him out here," Jayla whispered in observation.

"We are honored to have our great Vire attend this momentous graduation ceremony." There was more clapping, and cheering, and the Vire began speaking.

"I am honored to be here, it is quite an enjoyment of mine to be a small part of these bright students' lives."

"No one talks like that," Jayla mumbled.

Skye had to hide her laugh. "You don't like Vire Malco?"

"He's fine, but I think we should have a new one soon, he's been Vire our entire lives."

"Shut up you two!" someone hissed.

"It's not like they're saying anything exciting," Jayla shot back.

Skye tried to pay attention to the principal as he started talking again.

"-and I am very proud of these students. Now, I have a list of all of the new Lights who will be divided into Squadrons. We will be putting together students who either work well together, or by the way they performed in their Finals, we believe will work well together. If your name is called please step forward.

"Light Axenly Frems of the Stealth Guild, Light Jethspar Nactix of the Agility Guild, Light Fawn Linx of the Intelligence Guild, Light Petra Mabring of the Ingenuity Guild, and Light Everett Aire of the Leadership Guild, you are Squadron 990."

There was more cheering as each member of the new Squadron had a Squad number badge pinned onto their shirts by the Vire, and were led out of the auditorium.

"If they're matching us by how well we work together, then we've got a great chance at being together!" Jayla said excitedly.

Skye was thinking the same thing. "I hope we can be together, it would make everything so much easier having you with me." She had hidden her nervousness as well as she could that day, she'd been excited for today, but now that she had time to think about it, she was getting anxious again.

"Stop it!" Jayla whisper-hissed.

"Stop what?"

"Worrying, you're doing it again. You should be waiting to hear your name, if you miss it you're going to look like a doofus in front of the Vire, not to mention most of the City District."

Skye nodded and redirected her attention to the Principal.

"Light Vacore Wesley of the Stealth Guild, Light Ayjay Lindy of the Agility Guild, Light Syvis Pare of the Intelligence Guild, Light Galan Devure of the Ingenuity Guild, and Light Caxton Yazz of the Leadership Guild, you are Squadron 998."

After they were out of the auditorium, the principal continued. "Light Daria Tallon of the Stealth Guild, Light Jayla Payge of the Agility Guild..." Jayla smiled at Skye and ran up to the front.

"Light Luken Noro of the Intelligence Guild, Light Skye Zareb of the Ingenuity Guild..."

Skye smiled broad as she made her way up to the front. She was pretty sure Jayla had screamed in her excitement.

The principal looked at her in concern, but finished his list. "And, uh, Light Zaithrian Delainey of the Leadership Guild, you are Squadron 999."

They walked over to receive their pins from the Vire. Skye had seen him on the cybernet, but meeting him in person was a thrill. She wasn't super into politics, but it was still an honor to meet the Vire of Isarn. He was probably around fifty. He had grey hair combed to the side and kind eyes. The most striking part of his features was his scar. The long pink mark spread from his temple to just below his lip. He had gotten in when Daken Claw had tried to assassinate him at his reelection ceremony nine years ago.

"It's an honor to meet you sir," Skye said as he fastened the pin to the specially designed pocket.

He smiled at her. "It's a pleasure my dear. And an honor as well, I saw your scores, one of the highest in the school. You amazed us all. The Eagles surely fly with you."

Skye thanked him and went off the stage. There was a woman waiting at the door.

"This way, follow me." She led them into the opening room, where dozens of other students stood in clusters of five.

The newly formed Squadron stood awkwardly together for a few seconds, before Jayla squealed in delight and dragged Skye by the wrist to the wall.

"What-" Skye started.

"Look! We're on the wall!" Jayla said.

Skye looked over the framed portraits of the 115 graduates, her picture was at the very end.

"Wow," Jayla said. "We're like, official now."

"What did you think that ceremony was for? Of course we're official! We graduated!"

They stood there for a minute, admiring the wall of portraits, before Skye remembered the other three teens who were apparently her Squadron. She turned around to see that they had followed her and Jayla to the wall.

Skye hadn't really paid any attention to who she had in her Squadron. There were two boys and one girl. The first boy was average height for his age, and had light skin like hers. His dirty blond hair was brushed to the side. Skye also noticed that he had a small black earpiece in each ear, they looked similar to a regular speaker for music, but there was something different about them.

The other boy was about the same height as the first. His skin was a light bronze. He had black hair, loosely spiked in the front and his eyes were a shade of golden brown. He had his hands shoved in his pockets and his back propped up against the wall. The last touch was his crooked smirk. If cocky was a person, he would look like that. Skye thought she recognized him from somewhere, but couldn't put her finger on it.

The girl was slightly taller than Skye. She looked strong, like she worked out or something along those lines. She had flawless, dark skin and her hair was a striking shade of cobalt blue. Skye had never seen anyone who looked as stunning as her. She suddenly felt very boring and plain.

She was about to introduce herself, when Jayla spoke up. "So I guess we're stuck together now. I'm Jayla, I'm in the Agility Guild. We should all get to know each other, so let's each say our name and Guild."

"I'll start," Skye said, deciding to break out of her awkward introverted shell. "My name's Skye, I'm in the Ingenuity Guild."

"I'm Luken," The blond boy said. "I'm in Intelligence."

"I'm Daria," the blue haired girl said. "I'm in Stealth."

"Zaithrian," the other boy said, standing up from his position against the wall. "I'm in the Leadership Guild, apparently."

"Well that's comforting," Jayla mumbled. "So what creature is everyone hoping to get?"

"My parents want me to get a griffin since it's the most respected," Daria said. "But I think I would like a kelpie. It's so amazing how they can control water, I've seen videos of it, it's so pretty."

"I would have *so* much fun with a kelpie," Jayla said in admiration. "Just think of all the cool stuff you could do with it!" Jayla bugged her eyes out. "What if you could make people barf out their own guts!"

"I...don't think that's what you do with a kelpie," Daria said. "I think it's more for flying purposes."

"Oh. That's cool still, but the gut-barfing would be skeding sick!"

"Well, if you think about it," Luken cut in. "Intestines soak up water from the body, so the kelpie could control the water in the gut and force them out a person's mouth."

Daria looked like *she* might throw up.

Jayla bumped the back of her forearm against Luken's. "I think we'll get along just fine, Smart Boy."

Jayla and Luken dove into an in-depth discussion about the probability of the gut-barfing theory succeeding.

Skye swallowed, deciding she should get to know the other members of her Squad, but desperately not wanting to make the first move. She sighed, wishing she was in her lab with VACA and her tools, and walked over to Daria and Zaithrian.

"It's nice to meet you guys," she said, hoping she didn't sound stupid.

Both teens bumped forearms with Skye.

"This is already looking like it's going to be an interesting few years," Zaithrian said, eyeing Jayla and Luken as they talked about guts and horses.

"I feel sorry for whatever creature Jayla ends up getting," Skye laughed.

The two other members of the Squadron came over. Jayla propped her elbow on Skye's shoulder. "You tell them about me yet?"

"No...was I supposed to?"

She flipped her hair. "You should *always* be talking about me. But I meant how we were in the same group during the Finals."

Skye shook her head. "No I didn't, but now they know." She turned to her group. "Were any of you guys together?"

Daria shook her head. "My partner didn't pass his test."

"Neither did mine," Luken said.

"The girl I was with passed, I don't know why we weren't in the same Squadron." Zaithrian shrugged.

Everyone sort of just stood around awkwardly, looking at their feet or at a far off wall, no one really sure what else to do.

Suddenly Skye's head shot up. "You were the boy who took the key from me!" She said, pointing a finger at Zaithrian.

"Oh, um yeah. You noticed that. No hard feelings?" He said, gesturing to her. "I mean, obviously you didn't need it anyway." He gave her a smile, clearly looking for her to accept without hesitation.

"Want me to beat him up for you?" Jayla asked, shooting Zaithrian a glare.

"What? No, no. Do *not* punch him, Jayla. It's fine, it's over. It doesn't matter anyway, we all passed."

"You sure? Cause you sounded *pretty* pissed at him when you told me wha-"

"*Jayla.*"

"Okay, okay, geez, just trying to punch someone on your behalf, no reason to get all worked up." She pointed a finger at Zaithrian. "I'll save it for later."

Daria sighed and mumbled something about getting stuck with *literal* children.

Just in the nick of time, the same woman who had brought them there, came back into the room. Skye hadn't noticed that the rest of the graduates had filled in with their Squads.

"Can I get everyone's attention for a moment please? Thank you. I'm sure you all are very excited to meet your Squadrons, but we have to go back into the auditorium for the last part of the ceremony. Follow me please, and stay with your Squadron!"

The groups filed out of the room in a single file line.

"I'm so sick of this ceremony!" Jayla complained.

"What else do we have to do? I think we just have to go back with our families, right?" Luken asked.

Skye shrugged. "I think so, I don't remember practicing anything else."

As the graduates were led into the auditorium, a large round of applause erupted throughout the crowd. Skye couldn't help but smile. She'd done it. Ten years of learning and training had brought her to this moment, a moment she was sure would play an important role in her life from then on.

The group of teens were brought onto the stage for a final bow. As they rose, the crowd stood on their feet and cheered for the new protectors of Isarn.

"We're so proud of you." Her mom came over and hugged Skye as soon as she stepped off the stage.

Dad came over and kissed her on the top of her head. "That's right we are! My little Rivet isn't so little anymore."

"So do we get to meet your Squad?" Mom asked.

Skye looked around her. "I have no idea where everyone went."

Just then, Jayla came running up. "Hey, Skye. Mr. and Mrs. Zareb, all the parents from our Squad are meeting up over by the kelpie statue to meet each other."

"Thank you Jayla, we'll be right there," Skye's mom said.

She hooked her arm through Skye's. "C'mon, I gotta go find Daria's family, and I don't want to go by myself."

After they had all of the parents and siblings together, the five teens wandered over to the thunderbird statue to talk alone.

Skye marveled at the miraculous creature. Its broad wings spread out in a powerful stance as if it demanded to be feared. The beak was spread like the creature was mid-scream.

Skye broke out of her trance when Jayla started talking.

"I'm *so* excited for tomorrow! I'm nervous, but mostly excited. We're going to meet our Mentors. I hope mine's not strict, although a strict one means I could break the rules, and that's always fun." Jayla stared off into space as she thought of all the ways she could ruin her hypothetical Mentor's life.

"We move in tomorrow," Luken mumbled to himself.

"Oh! And we'll get our creature soon!" Jayla squealed.

The graduates stood in silence, each imagining what creature they would get. Each one fascinated Skye, the thunderbird, griffin, pegasus, dragon, and kelpie.

"I think that will be the best part," Skye said, admiring the statue they stood under.

"I dunno, punching people sounds pretty fun to me," Jayla said, punching and kicking the air.

"This is going to be a *long* few years," Daria mumbled.

CHAPTER EIGHT

That night, Skye sat in her bed restless. She felt so stupid, worrying every single night and day since the Finals, but she couldn't help feeling it again knowing it was her last night in her house. She stood up and decided to get some of her packing done if she wasn't going to sleep.

She picked through her closet, deciding which clothes to take, and which ones to leave in storage. She didn't have a ton of clothes to begin with, but she wasn't going to take everything to her new Mentor's house. Her new house. She didn't like to think of it that way, it wasn't her home. This was her home.

She skimmed through the pile she chose to keep. Mostly t-shirts, hoodies, and cargo pants, but she had a few pairs of leggings, simple dresses, and shorts. She knew they would be wearing uniforms at the Academy the majority of the time.

She threw the pile of clothes into the gigantic box. She took the stash of electronic writing tablets from her desk, the pens, and a few of the desk ornaments, and threw them in the box. Skye fingered one of the small bottle cap shaped devices she had on her desk. She pressed the button, and a holoimage popped up. It was a picture of Locke and Skye after he had made the winning goal of the championship blackball game. He was riding piggyback on her, and both of them had huge smiles on their faces. Locke's mouth was stained from his energy drink and it made the picture even better. She brushed her fingers through the photo. She smiled, remembering the way Locke's team lifted him into the air after the game. And how proud he had been.

She flicked off the image and shoved the photo projector into her pocket. Locke was going to miss her, she was sure it would be emptier without her there to yell at him or him to annoy her.

She packed the rest of her personal items but still didn't find it in herself to sleep. She glanced at her commscreen, it was well past 2 a.m.

She sighed and tucked herself into the bed. She relayed the day's events hoping to find a calming moment. She remembered what Vire Malco had told her. *You amazed us all. The Eagles surely fly with you.*

As she played the scene out in her mind, the seeds of her exhaustion seemed to grow, until finally, she fell asleep with the words ringing in her ear.

* * *

"You almost packed?" Dad asked.

Skye glanced sadly over her bare workshop. "Yeah, I'm done."

He walked up behind her and placed his hand on her shoulder. "You're doing good Rivet, I know it isn't easy."

She nodded and swallowed hard. "I hope my Mentor let's me set up my equipment."

"If not, just keep it in the closet, they never check the closet." He winked at her. Skye figured he spoke from experience.

Skye checked the time on her comm, they had to leave for the Academy of Light soon. She pressed the button on the compact box, shrinking it, and everything inside it to the average box size. She brought it upstairs and loaded it with the other box in the trunk of the hovercar.

After a few more checks, the family piled into the hover. Skye looked out the window longingly as they glided out of the driveway.

The ride was long–about three hours–and Skye spent most of it hunched in the backseat with her music on. But as time rolled on, the city's buildings turned to trees and mountains.

Locke had his face pressed against the window in awe. "Skye, are you seeing this!"

The two of them had spent pretty much all of their lives in the city, the most nature they saw was in the park, which barely counted as wild. Not that this really did either, but that didn't keep the amazement from their faces.

Skye could just make out the tips of what appeared to be towers in the distance. As they came closer, the trees fell away and they came to a swirling entry gate with a large sign overhead. *The Academy of Light.*

The closer they came, the more of the school Skye could see. There were six towers. The center tower was the tallest, reaching much higher than the others. It was clear glass with white wrapping supports that almost looked like a modern ribcage. Windows stretched down most of the length dividing it into floors. Each of the other five towers were built almost the same. These one's weren't as tall as the center, but they still reached higher than most Skye was used to. Their ribcage supports were all different colors. They had to be for the individual Guilds.

"Woah," Locke said. "You're going to *live* here?"

Skye swallowed hard. "I guess."

Dad pulled up the hovercar in the lot with the others. There were about ten people directing parents into the buildings.

Skye and Locke stumbled out and stretched their legs from the long trip. The two of them gazed up at the towers in stunned silence. Mom and Dad came over and Skye and her dad each grabbed a box from the trunk before they all headed into the central tower.

The entry to the tower was a huge trapezoid made of glass and white shiny metal. Skye stepped into the tower and let her eyes wander around the room. It reminded her of a hotel with it's modern-style entry room.

Maybe living here won't be so bad.

Skye and Dad set down the boxes with Locke and Mom, and got in line at the large marble desk. They reached the front and were met with a young woman with a large computer.

"Hello, can I get your name please?" she asked, not looking up from her screen.

"Um, Skye Zareb," Skye said nervously.

She typed some words on her screen, then looked up at them. "Yep, Skye Zareb, floor thirteen, room eight. You can grab your things and head on up, the door opens with your ID chip. Your Mentor is in a meeting right now, so the room's empty, feel free to unpack. Mr. Zareb, I have a few things for you to sign." She handed him a tablet. They thanked her and headed back over to the rest of the family.

"Skye, you go on up to your room. Locke, help her carry up her stuff. We'll be up there in a little bit," Dad said.

Skye and Locke each grabbed a box, and slipped into one of the six elevators. The small wite room was brightly lit, with marble buttons addressing the floor numbers.

"I'm...I'm gonna miss you," Locke said without looking up.

Skye smiled. "I'll miss you, too."

They spent the rest of the elevator ride in silence. Once the door opened up Skye found door eight and pressed her index finger against the panel.

When children in Isarn were born, an ID chip was put in their finger. It held their information, criminal records, and all identification.

The lock clicked, and Skye struggled to open it while holding the box.

The dorm wasn't what Skye had been expecting. The room was more like an apartment, it had a simple living area with a TV screen, two couches, and a low table. There was a kitchen much like the one at her house, only on a smaller scale. The table was smaller than her old one, and it only had two chairs. There were three doors against one wall, Skye saw that one of them was a bathroom. The other two were bedrooms.

"Which one do we put these in?" Locke asked, heaving the box with an exaggerated groan.

"These weigh like two pounds, kid, deal with it." Skye opened the door to a bedroom.

The room was bigger than she thought it would be. It had a large bed, it looked like it had been slept in and not remade. There was a large desk that wound around the corner, a dresser was next to the bed, and a small closet in one wall. There were papers on the desks, and clothes in the closet, men's clothes from what she could tell. This must be her Mentor's room.

"My room is the other one," Skye said.

Her and Locke opened the door and set down the boxes. The room was almost the same as the other one but this one had nothing on the bed except a mattress. There was an empty closet and a huge double desk. The window outlooked the other towers of the campus.

"You want me to help you unpack?" Locke asked, already exploring the room.

There was a knock at the door and Skye and Locke both ran out of the room and found their parents in the hallway outside the room.

"You ready to go, Locke?" Dad asked.

Locke cast a saddened look at his big sister. "I…guess so."

Skye's mom came over and hugged Skye tight. "It's going to be okay," she whispered, stroking Skye's hair.

Both of them had wet eyes as they let go. Dad came over and held her close, he pressed a kiss on the top of her head. "We love you, Skye, we always will."

She squeezed him tight, hoping like a child that it would keep him from leaving. She looked up at her father's tear filled prideful eyes, knowing it was time for her to let go. She pulled back from him and her mom hugged her one last time, whispering in her ear that she loved her. Even Locke hugged her.

Skye put on her bravest face as they walked away, leaving her alone in her new life.

Skye stood in the doorway until her tears stopped. She stared at the elevator her family had just left down, half hoping they would come back up saying they had forgotten something or just to hug her one last time. To tell her they loved her again. But of course, they didn't come.

She gave a shaky sigh, and turned to go back into her room. Just as she was about to close the door, she heard the ding of the elevator. We're they back? She ran back to see her family, but it wasn't them. It was Zaithrian from her squad. She stopped abruptly when she saw him, hoping he hadn't seen her. He did, and stared at her tearstained face and red eyes.

He gave her a small, sad smile of reassurance. He looked like he wanted to say something. Before he could, Skye darted inside and slammed the door shut.

She ran into her room and sat on the bare bed, her emotions threatening to break through their delicate cage. She steadied herself and hastily wiped away her few tears. She wasn't going to cry. She wasn't going to cry. She wasn't going to cry. She was sick of the tears.

She stood up from the bed and wiped her nose on the back of her hand. She dragged the first box into the middle of the room, pressed the button, and the box tripled in size and unlocked. She pulled out the bedding and started making her bed. It was just like she had always done it. The routine brought her comfort.

She loaded her dresser and closet with clothes, little keepsakes, and other things like that. She placed her printer, computer, 3D shaper, and all of the other items from her bedroom desk on the part of her new desk against the wall in the corner area. She recompacted the box and stuck it on the floor of her closet.

The other box held all of her equipment from the basement lab. Glad for the double sized desk, Skye set out her workstation on the other areas of the large desk. She unrolled her wallscreen and hung it above her station. She was disappointed to see that her floor wasn't metal, which meant she couldn't use the floating chair she'd developed. She made a mental note to figure out how to make it work.

After she had finished, she stuck the box with the other, and gazed around her new room. It would take some getting used to but she could see it working out. Her room was still mostly bare walls even after she'd finished unpacking, but it didn't bother her, she liked the simplistic look of things.

Her commscreen buzzed from receiving a message. She pressed answer and a female voice she didn't recognize buzzed through the device.

"Welcome, new students to the Academy of Light. I am Director Cross, the head of this Academy. Be in the Meeting Hall in fifteen minutes with your Squadron for your school briefing."

The recorded message ended and Skye got up from her seat on the bed. She had no idea where the Meeting Hall was, and she only knew where one of her Squad members were.

She threw on her boots and ran out the dorm room into the hall. She was glad to see Jayla, Luken, Daria, and Zaithrian all talking in the hall.

"Skye!" Jayla called. "We were just about to get you when we got these comms."

"It looks like they put our Squad together," Luken said. "I'm in room nine, Zaithrian is in seven, Daria's in six, and Jayla got ten."

"Well," Jayla said. "We have like a few minutes to find a room where we have no idea is, and we have to be there in like ten minutes so..."

"Did anyone get a map?" Daria asked.

Everyone said no, so they settled on winging it.

The five of them piled into the elevator, deciding to start at the first floor and see if they could find some other students.

The elevator ride was an awkward one, no one really knew each other well, besides Jayla and Skye, and it seemed pointless to start a conversation.

Skye didn't want to draw attention to herself, especially from Zaithrian. Skye felt so stupid for crying in front of him. But something about the way he had looked back at her, made her feel like he understood what she was going through. Skye didn't really know him. She knew his name and his Guild, but that was it. She made a mental note to get to know each person in her Squad, her dad had told her they would become like family, she had better know them like family.

The elevator slowed to a stop and the doors opened, revealing the huge opening room again. There were a few teens scattered around, some talking to people who worked there, or with their friends.

"What should we do?" Luken asked.

Zaithrian gazed around the room. "We could ask some of the workers."

They talked to some of the people wearing school suits and were directed to the far left of the lobby where a trapezoid archway led into an addition to the tower.

They thanked the workers and ran inside. It was much like the auditorium back at Skye's old school, but instead of a stage, there was a large podium with a screen behind it. The chairs were divided into groups of five, probably meant for a Squadron to sit in.

There were already a decent amount of students filling the room. Some of them were recognizable to Skye from her old school. Some had come from the other three training schools for Sparks over Isarn. The new Squad took a seat near the center of the room, Skye sitting between Jayla and Luken.

The chatter subdued as a woman walked up to the podium, the screen above her projected a live view so everyone could see her better.

She was probably in her fifties, with shining silver hair and youthful almond shaped eyes. As she started speaking, Skye matched the voice to the one from the comm.

"Welcome new students to the Academy of Light!" There was a round of applause that vibrated through the crowd. "We have 115 new Lights from the City District, 161 new Lights from the Housing District, 109 new Lights from the Produce and Forest District School, and 95 new Lights from the Collective Minority Districts Academy for training Sparks. I am very proud to have these new Squadrons studying to be great warriors and politicians to help our world succeed further." There was more applause, and the Director started again.

"I am sure many of you have questions, and I am here to clear a few things up for you. You will be sent a map of the Academy to your commscreens, as well as a schedule for all of your classes. You will be given school uniforms for your everyday studies. We do studies five days a week. You have learned all you need to know on a scholar's level, here you will learn under your Guild. You will also be chosen by your creature." There was a huge cheer from the students. "You will spend a large portion of time training with said creature by our Trainers who know all there is to know about the creature you are chosen by. You will meet your Mentor tonight, after you have been chosen by your creature, and have had time to train with it. You will not be receiving any missions until your entire Squadron is ready. Any other information will be sent to your commscreens, and my office is on the top floor for anything you wish to ask me personally. As soon as you are dismissed, make your way to the training arena behind the main tower, you will be given instructions on what to do there. Good luck students, may the Eagles fly with you."

"This is so exciting!" Jayla said, practically bouncing as she got up from her seat.

In the corner of her mind Skye's thoughts were still on her family, but they had been pushed there by the excitement of getting her creature.

"A dragon would be amazing," Jayla said. "Oh, but so would a thunderbird. But the pegasus would be so pretty, and the kelpie is beautiful too! And the griffin is so cool. Ugh, I don't know which one I want."

"It's not like we get a choice," Skye pointed out.

Jayla hit the button for the elevator. "True. Which one do you think would pick me?"

"Well kelpies choose some one who's full of passion, and you have plenty of that," Luken pointed out as they stepped into the elevator.

"I'm gonna say Skye gets a thunderbird," Jayla said. "I know I'm right because I've been right about all of her stuff."

"You only guessed what Guild I'd be in!" Skye said.

"And I said they'd put us together, so I'm two for two, and who wants to bet I'll be three for three?"

The group once again came into the main room. They followed the maps they had been sent on their commscreens and found the training arena.

Skye was pretty sure she'd said the word "wow" at least 20 times that day, but she couldn't keep the word from escaping her lips as she entered the training arena.

The oval building wasn't extremely tall, but it was almost a mile wide. There were tons of dome shapes coming from the largest dome. The retractable glass dome covered the center of the building. There were dozens of smaller arenas fit into one side, the other side held the hundreds of creatures.

A man and a woman stood in front of a forming crowd of new students, both looking to be in their early forties.

"I am Cale Ember, this is my wife, Slin, we are the Training Directors of this creature arena," the man said.

"We are glad to have you all as new Lights, but you must do as we say when it comes to these creatures, they are tamed as much as we could without them being under our mastership, you must claim mastership over your creature, that is something only you can do," the woman said.

"We have changing rooms so you can get into your suits, and we'll get started. We have 350 arenas, so some of you'll have to wait. Trainer Slin will show the girls to their changing rooms, and I'll show the boys."

Trainer Slin motioned for the girls to follow her, and she led them into a large changing room with stalls lining the walls.

"There are uniforms in those cubbies, find the one with your name on it and unlock it with your ID chip. After you're dressed, head out and I'll set you up with one of my Arena Hands," she said, heading out of the room and shutting the door.

"Let's hurry so we can be first!" Jayla said, running to the wall of locked boxes

Skye followed more timidly, but still before the other girls. She found her cubby near the very end and grabbed the items and went into a stall.

She wore a long sleeved blue shirt with thin leather upper body armor. She had leather wrist guards fitting over her wrist to almost her elbow. She had black pants and sturdy boots. She'd also braided her auburn hair into a simple side braid like Trainer Slin had done.

Jayla came out a few seconds later wearing almost the same thing, except her undershirt was green. She'd done her hair in a messy ponytail. Soon Daria came out, wearing her blue hair in a bun, and wearing a purple undershirt.

"Okay, we're all here, can we go out there? I'm dying of excitement!" Jayla jumped out of the room.

They had all gotten ready decently fast, so they got to go with the first.

A man came over to Skye and led her to one of the arenas, Jayla gave her a thumbs up as they walked away.

He stopped in front of the closed door of the arena. "My name's Lian, I'm going to be helping you. When you go in there, there will be five gigantic creatures that could kill you if they wanted to." She stared at him with bugged out eyes. He saw her scared expression. "But don't worry, you'll be fine, just don't make 'em mad, especially the dragon…or the thunderbird, or the grif-you know what, just don't get any of them mad. I can't help you tame one, you have to do that on your own. You know they choose you right?"

She nodded.

"That's true, but it won't usually just walk up to you, you have to engage it, show it you. Try to calm it down, get it peaceful. I'll try to tell you what to do in the moment, but this is all you. I'm really only here to make sure you don't get eaten, cooked, electrocuted, drowned, or trampled."

He gave her a smile that was supposed to calm her, but didn't help much.

"You got all that, kid?"

She nodded slowly.

"Great! Just remember not to make them mad." He walked over to a lever. "Okay, you're gonna have to run, I can only keep this thing open for a few seconds so they don't get out. Ready?"

She got into the running position. "Um, yeah, I'm ready."

He pulled the lever, the door opened, and Skye ran.

CHAPTER NINE

Skye was in awe and close to fainting all at the same time. Five legendary creatures stood in front of her.

Some of them were content with standing still. Others, such as the dragon, were trying to fly out of the top of the cage, which was blocked with a glass dome.

Skye wanted to back as far as she could away from the massive beast, but her feet remained stuck to the ground.

"Alright kid, you're doing great, you just gotta go and do it," Lian said from behind the thick walls. There was a small rectangle cut out just large enough for his eyes.

Skye took a steadying breath, this was just another project, she needed to do what she did when she worked on a device. She would analyze the object, engage the problem, and fix it. Simple.

She studied the massive beasts in front of her. The kelpie. It was a beautiful black horse, with a smooth coat that gleamed from the sun. Its mane was made of what looked like seaweed, it hung in front of the horse's face, almost covering one of its big blue eyes. Its tail was made of seaweed as well, it stopped just short of the floor. It seemed to be staring at her.

Skye took a small step to it, mumbling softly. She slowly made her way closer, the kelpie never moved. She was only a few feet from it now, she could reach out and pet it if she wanted. Gently lifting her fingers, she showed the animal her hand, then slowly moved it to stroke its muzzle.

The kelpie closed its eyes and let Skye brush her fingers against its cool nose.

Skye smiled, amazed at herself and this beautiful creature. But there was something inside her that knew the kelpie wasn't for her. She withdrew her hand from the kelpie. It opened its eyes and shook its mane, spreading salty seawater into Skye's face. It winneyed loudly and leapt into the air. It gracefully galloped through the air, water forming under its hooves as it stepped on open air, and disappearing as it withdrew.

Skye looked in wonder as it ran in the air, so graceful and sure, so magnificent. It floated back down to the ground and calmly trotted into one of the cages against the wall. An iron door shut behind it, leaving only four animals with Skye.

She looked back at Lian, she couldn't see much of his face through the hole, but she could tell he was giving her an encouraging grin.

She turned back to the beasts, a smile starting on her lips. She looked over at the remaining creatures. She'd always wanted the griffin, maybe that would be the best one to do next.

The griffin was pacing back and forth about fifteen feet from her. It stood tall, with its strong eagle head, wings, and claws in the front, and the lion's hind legs and tail in the back. It had golden brown lion legs, and a wispy tail, the pads of the back legs made no sound as he walked, but the talons of his eagle legs scratched the stone floor as he paced. Its pure white wings sprouted from the lion portion of his back, majestic and tall. Its golden beak and sharp eyes fit onto its eagle face, which was covered in silky white feathers.

Skye tried taking a small step forward. Suddenly, its head jerked to her, meeting her eyes in a piercing gaze. His head darted into the air, and its wings spread wide. He released a deafening screech as he flapped his wings wildly. His figure rose into the air.

Skye darted backwards. Its wings blocked out the sun. He screeched again and Skye screamed. She jumped to the ground and held her hands against her ears.

Silence.

Skye looked up as it soared back to the ground. It cocked its head curiously, studying her thoroughly. It gave another large screech, then walked calmly into one of the pens. Again, the iron door slammed behind it.

She closed her eyes and took a deep breath, allowing herself a moment to calm her racing heartbeat. Her hands were shaking and sweating. She opened her eyes and wiped the sweat from her forehead. She stood up and started studying the last creatures. She was definitely leaving the dragon for last. The pegasus seemed like the safest option, since if she made the thunderbird angry enough, it could electrocute her.

The pegasus was kneeling down near the back of the arena. It looked peaceful with its wings folded against its body. It opened its large silver eyes and something in its gaze stopped Skye in her tracks. The horse spread her feathery wings wide into the air, the sunlight wound through the gaps leaving a trace of shadows over the ground. The pegasus was like the kelpie in a way, but the kelpie seemed more *mature*. This felt to Skye like a little kid, this pegasus was bursting at the seams with energy.

Skye started walking over to her again. She could almost feel the vibrancy of the creature's mind, she felt the giddy excitement, the joy.

As she neared, the pegasus leapt from her spot on the floor. She gave a playful whinney, and started trotting around the room, her silver-speckled tail flapping playfully behind her. She went right past the dragon and thunderbird like she didn't notice them, or maybe she did and just didn't have it in her to let the larger beasts ruin her fun.

Skye laughed at the way the horse leapt into the air, then dipped down a second later, making her mane fly up wildly.

Skye came to be about two feet away from the beautiful creature, the pegasus stilled, staring at the strange human with interest. Skye stroked the sides of the pegasus's face gently. She slowly made her way to the side of the horse, never lifting her fingers so she always knew that Skye was touching her.

Skye thought of trying to mount the creature, but there was no way she could get up onto its back without help, and she doubted the pegasus would like that, even in her calmed state.

She was about to make her way back to the creature's front, when she had the eerie feeling of being watched. She turned around slowly. Her breath caught in her throat. Hovering over her, was none other than the thunderbird.

CHAPTER TEN

The thunderbird screeched and spread his wings into the air. The gigantic bird had its face only a few feet from her own. It screeched again and its wings whipped down to blow air in Skye's face. She took a small step backwards.

Trying not to focus on how easily this bird could kill her, she tried to remind herself of how she had calmed her nerves for the other three creatures. She felt behind her hoping to find the pegasus but the animal had left.

Calm down Skye. It's simple. Do what you know.

She examined the beast. It had the shape of a giant hawk, but it seemed to have softer features, not just in smoothness, but they seem less jagged than another bird of prey would have–maybe lighter or even more fluffy. She couldn't decide if it was more teal or blue, maybe it was both. His giant feathery wings were now folded against his body. White feathers covered most of its underbelly, tying in with the blues. Skye liked the pointed owl-like ears on its head, they made it look a small bit less terrifying, and a smaller bit more cute. It stood with its head a few feet taller than her and about two times as long as her. It had two legs that had the same tealish blue feathers running almost all the way to his sharp talons.

She looked the animal in the eye, trying to get a feel of what it was like. She could tell it was strong, smart, loyal, the things she would expect, but there was something deep down in the creature's eyes that told her it felt something else. Sorrow. Fear. Hurt.

Skye looked wide eyed at the thunderbird. It seemed like her in a way. She summoned all of her nerves and slowly reached her hand out. The thunderbird cocked its head in curiosity at her outstretched hand. Understanding seemed to cross over its face and it brought its head a few feet lower so she could reach it.

Skye smiled a little, and petted its softer-than-expected head. Its eyes, which had seemed so terrifying only a moment ago, seemed to hold a deep joy.

Suddenly, he knelt low, leaning down his head.

Oh no. She knew what he wanted, the only problem was that it was definitely something she *didn't* want to do. She made her way to the side of the huge bird. As carefully as she could, she slipped her leg over the side of the thunderbird. She didn't want to be on its wings, so she slid up a little so she was sitting just above where the wings started.

The thunderbird screeched and jumped into the air. Skye wildly grasped for something to cling onto. She dug her fingers into the thick blue feathers in front of her. She willed her fingers to keep their hold. She tried not to imagine what would happen if she let go. Slowly, she looked up, realizing that they had reached the top of the dome.

The bird was now soaring in circles just low enough so that Skye wouldn't be pushed up to the glass ceiling.

Even in Skye's evident fear she couldn't help from smiling. It felt good to fly. She let the words sink into her mind. She was *flying*.

She clutched the bird's feathers so tightly it must have hurt him, but if he was in pain, he didn't let Skye know, he just continued to fly.

Skye was certain she had been chosen by her creature, she felt like they were connected, like they were meant to fly together.

"You wanna get down now?" Skye asked, nervously gazing down at the far away ground.

It only cawed in reply, but slowly started a descent. It gingerly landed on the ground, its tails sweeping the floor.

Skye slid off her thundbird's back, and landed shaky-legged on the ground. She grabbed onto its broad blue wing to steady herself and immediately regretted it. She'd probably hurt it. Instead of the thunderbird crying out in pain or swatting her away, it leaned its body against Skye to support her. *Huh*, she thought.

Skye looked around her and saw that the dragon had also gone into the wall cage, leaving just her and her creature.

"Lian, what am I supposed to do?" Skye asked, not taking her eyes off the thunderbird.

"Just wait a minute," he said.

After a few minutes, Lian came into the arena with a leash. "Here, take this." He handed the leash to Skye, staying as far away from the thunderbird as possible. "See if you can get it around its neck, we gotta lead him out of here and into you Squaron's pen."

Skye took the leash and slowly walked up to the bird, whispering softly to it that it would all be okay.

"Bend down for me, okay?" she said softly.

The bird didn't budge.

She softly petted its neck and it lowered it so she could reach better. She slipped the rope around its neck, making sure to keep it loose.

When the thunderbird realized what Skye was doing, it jerked its head into the air, trying to get away from the rope. Before Skye had time to let go of the rope, she was being thrust into the air. She smashed against the floor and everything went black.

CHAPTER ELEVEN

Skye woke up in a daze. Where was she? She couldn't remember what had happened.

"Skye! Guys she's awake!"

Skye recognized the voice as Jayla's. She blinked her eyes rapidly to help her vision clear. When her eyes focused she saw Jayla, Luken, Daria, and Zaithrian all hovering over her.

"What happened?" she asked, holding a hand to the lump on her head.

"Some guy said that you had been thrown by your creature while trying to get it into your pen, somebody brought you to the medical room," Jayla said.

Skye sat up, propping herself up against a pillow. "What are you guys all doing here?"

"The guy came into our Squad's pen with your thunderbird, he told us what had happened, and we ran over to see if you were alright," Zaithrian said.

"We talked to the school medic," Luken said. "He said you have a concussion. They gave you the treatment medication, so you should feel better in a couple hours."

Skye nodded. "Did they say how long it'll be until I can leave?"

"He said you can go back to your room once you woke up, but you have to take it easy for the rest of the day," Daria said.

Skye tried to stand up, but nearly fell over.

"Maybe you should wait a little bit," Jayla suggested, grabbing Skye's arm to steady her.

"No, no I'm fine. I want to go back to my dorm."

Daria grimaced. "I think you should wait, even just a few minutes. You took a hard hit to the head."

"Yeah, you already got knocked out on your first day, you better take it easy if you want to make it through the rest of the year," Zaithrian said with a slight smirk.

Skye shot him an annoyed look, but his expression didn't change.

Skye sat back down on the bed. "Fine, I'll wait."

"Good." Jayla sat in a chair next to the bed and crossed her legs, resting her elbows on her knees. "Because I have a *lot* to tell you."

"Shouldn't you guys be doing... something? I thought you were supposed to start training."

Zaithrian sat in the other chair, propping his boots up on the edge of Skye's medical bed. "Not really. The only other things they have us doing is trying to bond with our creatures, but we'll be doing that a lot, so we can skip it."

Daria let out a small sigh.

Jayla perked up. "I saw your thunderbird, it's beautiful! The one in my arena was red, but I love the way your blue one looks."

"What did you get?" Skye asked.

"I got a pegasus, not the coolest one in my personal opinion."

"Why not? The one with me was nice."

Jayla threw her hands in the air. "How am I supposed to attack people with a sparkly horse?"

Luken cut in. "I don't think we're actually attacking people."

"Shush, Smart Boy, I can have my dreams. Okay, but hear me out, dragon: fire breath. Thunderbird: electricity. Griffin: deadly claws and beak. Kelpie: can literally make a pool of water and drown someone. Pegasus: flaps wings." She stood up. "I'm just saying, if I'm in a life or death situation, I don't see how this thing's gonna help me."

"Well you kind of need to trust your creature completely, so you might be in deep water there," Zaithrian said.

"And why don't you tell Skye what you got, Zaith," Jayla said, pouty.

"Zaith? I had higher hopes for a nickname from you, after all, you gave Luken 'Smart Boy'."

"What would you rather me call you? Captain Sassy?"

He seemed to be weighing the options over in his head. "I'll take Zaith for now, but Captain Sassy seems like something I could live with."

"Are you two going to keep fighting or can I go back to my dorm?" Skye asked.

"Oh we're not nearly finished," Jayla assured. "But I've wasted enough of my time bantering with a childish imp."

"Okay…" Zaithrian said, giving a confused glance to the other three members of their Squadron. "But I got a dragon, Skye."

"Really?" Skye asked, amazed that someone would willingly go up to the monstrous beast.

He nodded.

A few minutes later, the doctor came in, gave Skye some instructions, and said she was ready to leave.

Skye could walk on her own by then, but Jayla insisted on holding her arm to keep her steady just in case.

By the time they were back into the main tower, the sky was turning dusty red from the setting sun. A few stars were just starting to show in the haze of clouds. Both moons shone in their usual bright shades, illuminating the sky around them.

"Do you need me to help you get into your room?" Jayla asked when they reached their floor.

"No, I'm fine, thanks."

Jayla said goodnight and went into her dorm. Skye said goodnight to everyone else, and went into the room. Instead of it being empty like she expected, there was a man seated at the kitchen table.

He looked up from the five screens he had set out in front of him. "Skye Zareb?"

"Um, yeah?"

"I'm your Mentor." He motioned for her to sit at the table.

Skye eagerly sat down, weary from the long day.

He looked back down at his screens without adding to that.

Skye studied him. He was young, probably no older than 25. He had dark, short hair that was so sloppy Skye wasn't sure if it was intentional or not. His nose and eyes were sharp, giving him a hard expression, but his rumpled clothes and shaggy appearance seemed to dull his hardness.

Skye drummed her fingers on the table. "So..."

"Huh?" he said, not looking from his screens where he appeared to be typing something. "If you need food there's stuff in the productor-"

"No, I meant...I don't know...aren't you going to tell me your name or something?" Skye asked.

"What? Oh, yeah sorry, I've been really busy lately." He bumped the back of his forearm against Skye's. "I'm Revin Donte, nice to meet you."

"It's nice to meet you too Mentor Rev-"

He shook his head. "No, please, you don't need to call me that. Revin is fine."

"Sure."

"You get all unpacked?"

"Yeah, I finished when I got here."

"Good, good." He was already typing on his screen again.

Skye sat awkwardly for a few minutes.

Revin didn't look up. "So what's the story with your face?"

"Huh?"

"Kid, you got a bruise the size of a dragon egg on your forehead, looks like you were bleeding around the eye, you've got a nasty cut in your sleeve, you've got some story."

"Oh." She hadn't actually seen herself after her accident, she probably looked awful. "I, uh... fell."

"Off what? The Vire's tower? Kid, you gotta give me more than that."

Skye sighed. "I was being chosen by my creature and I got flung across the arena- you're not even listening, are you?"

His head jerked up. "No, I swear, I was..."

"Then what did I just say?"

"Okay, well... fine, I wasn't listening. But you oughta give me some slack kid, I've got a super important report to work up."

Skye decided to abandon the story. "What, are you like a student or something?"

101

"I'm way past my Light days. I'm a Beacon now. I'm on the Vire's Council, which makes me extremely busy."

Skye leaned to see what was on the screens and Revin flicked them off.

"And it means my work is extremely confidential. I think you understand."

Skye nodded, feeling a slight burn on her cheeks.

"Good. Um, I'm not exactly sure what I'm supposed to do. You want something to eat? I can make you something, unless you know how to cook, I'm not too great myself."

"I'm not really hungry, I'll eat later."

"Um… okay." He looked like he had no idea what he was doing. He grabbed a crumpled electosheet from the counter. "Uh, okay. I have to do these things I guess. I didn't pay very good attention in my Mentor classes if you know what I mean." He quickly looked over the extremely thin tablet-like screen. "Okay, I need to establish some base rules with my student," he mumbled to himself. "Alright kid, I'm going to level with you, my Mentor was skeding awful, super strict, tough, basically without a soul, you know what I mean. I don't want to be like that, so I'm not gonna be like that I guess. Um, okay… rules. Be back in the dorm by say 11? Does that sound reasonable, I have no idea."

"That sounds fine," Skye said.

"Okay good. Um, you can have your Squad come over and all that stuff, I'm not going to really make rules on that. I don't care what time you want to go to bed, but don't keep me up all night if you're not going to sleep. Uh, try to get your assignments done on time, don't leave your stuff all over the place, if your room is messy I don't really care. I can't really think of anything else, I'll just assume you won't destroy anything, or get into trouble, you seem like a decent kid, I think you know all that."

"Yeah," Skye said, not really sure how else to answer.

He glanced at the clock. "Um, so you have a couple hours for whatever, I have some work to do, if you're hungry there's food around here."

"Okay, I'm gonna take a shower, I'll eat later," Skye said.

Revin had been right about her having a huge bruise on her head, the purple mark looked awful. After an excessively long shower, Skye slipped into a pair of sweatpants and a comfy t-shirt, and came out to see that Revin was still working at the table.

Skye decided to leave him alone, she'd have some getting to know each other time later. She grabbed a bowl of cereal, and went into her room. She slid into the chair her room had come with, remembering she still needed to adjust her floating chair. She flicked on her screen and VACA's voice filled the room.

"Is this the new place? Not as nice as I hoped, but I guess it's better than that dingy old basement."

Skye took a spoonful of cereal and shoved it into her mouth. "Laboratory, VACA. You'll get used to it eventually, I guess we'll both have to."

"Oh, stop being so dramatic Skye, you'll live."

Skye smiled. "Check my messages, will you?" She started typing on her computer.

"You have two messages," VACA said. "Your parents asked how your first day was and said they miss you already."

Skye nearly choked on her cereal, an immense amount of emotion bubbled up inside her. With the craziness of the day, she'd barely had time to think about her family, but now she felt an oncoming flow of tears threatening to break loose. She blinked them back, she'd told herself she wouldn't cry.

Skye typed a reply, telling her parents she had been chosen by a thunderbird, leaving out the part where she'd gotten a concussion, and told them about her Mentor.

"What's the other message?"

"The device isn't registered under my contacts list," VACA said.

"Well throw it up on the screen." Skye said in confusion.

Hey Skye, this is Zaith, our Squad is meeting in Luken's dorm at 7, we totally get it if you don't want to come tonight after your concussion, but we're just going to all talk for a while.

Skye glanced at her clock, it was a few minutes past seven, she could go.

"Do you know who the message is from?" VACA asked.

"Yeah it's from a boy in my Squad, you can add him to my contact list."

"What name should I use?"

Skye thought a minute. "Captain Sassy." She smiled as she went out. "Power off when you're done."

She debated getting changed into regular clothes, but decided that the thought of getting out of her comfy sweatpants sounded worse than being judged for wearing them.

"I'm going over next door, my Squad is meeting up," Skye said.

"Yeah, go ahead," her Mentor called.

Skye dashed out into the hallway and knocked on Luken's door. A woman answered it, Skye figured it was Luken's Mentor.

"Um hi, I'm Skye, I'm in Luken's Squadron, I got a comm saying we were meeting up-"

"Yes, come in. Everyone is in his room, first door on the right."

"Thank you." She came inside and knocked on Luken's bedroom door.

Jayla answered. "Skye!" She dragged her inside and shut the door.

Luken's room was laid out the same way as Skye's; desks, bed, closet. Everyone was seated around the room, either on the bed, the floor, or the desk.

"Hey everybody, sorry I'm late, I just got the message."

Jayla dragged her over to the bed and made her sit down with Daria then plopped down between them both.

"Are you feeling better?" Zaithrian asked.

"Yeah, my headache is mostly gone."

Skye was glad to see she wasn't the only one not wearing nice clothes, everyone was wearing either pajamas or sweatpants.

"We just got started," Jayla said. "We were all talking about getting chosen by our creature."

"I was telling them about mine," Daria said. "You didn't miss much." She turned her attention to everyone. "I was just drawn to the kelpie as soon as I went in, and I just started petting it and it used its water to bring me up onto its back. Did you guys see it fly? It's so beautiful. The way it stayed in the air by forming water droplets under its hooves."

"I saw the one in my arena do it, it was amazing," Skye said.

"You're so lucky you got a kelpie," Jayla said. "You could totally win in a water war!"

"I know. But I'm not going to abuse her power, I don't think that's right."

Jayla stood up on the bed. "Are you kidding? If I had a horse that could control water, I'd use it all the time!"

"If you had a horse that could control water, we'd probably all lose our minds," Zaithrian mumbled.

"And our guts," Luken added.

"Anyway, all I was saying was that the kelpie was amazing," Daria said. "After I flew with it for a few minutes, someone helped me bring it into our Squad's pens."

"So you only interacted with one?" Skye asked.

"Yeah, you didn't?"

"No. The thunderbird was the fourth one I tried. I felt connected to each one a little bit I guess, but the thunderbird was such a strong connection, I just knew."

"I went straight up to the dragon," Jayla said.

"I'm pretty sure we all knew that was going to happen," Zaithrian told her.

Jayla ignored him. "It didn't really feel right though, and even when I was mad, I just knew it wasn't right. Then the pegasus came over, you can probably guess the rest."

Everyone looked to Luken. He shrugged and ducked his head a little. "I got a griffin." He didn't elaborate.

"Well my dragon sure trusts me," Zaithrian scoffed. "I walked up to it, and it tried to cook me."

"Seriously!" Jayla squealed. "I wish I could've seen that. I can already picture Zaith running for his life and screaming like a little girl as a dragon chases him around the room!" She rolled back on the bed laughing.

"I'm sure that's not how it went," Skye insisted.

Zaithrian rubbed the back of his neck. "Well..."

Jayla snorted, wiping her eyes. "This is priceless."

"Maybe we should change the topic to something more important," Daria said.

"Yeah, I think Jayla's about to pass out," Luken pointed out.

"Who here got an awful Mentor?" Jayla asked, finally finished with her laughing.

"Eh, mine's not so bad," Luken said. "But I've only known her a couple of hours."

"At least you didn't get mine," Jayla said. "She's one of those, 'oh yes I'm ever so delighted to make your acquaintance, I'm sure you are a delightful young lady' people."

"Well mine doesn't seem too bad, I don't think he has any idea what he's doing though," Skye said. "He's working as a Beacon while being my Mentor,

I don't know why he is even mentoring, he seems really busy already."

"Is he strict?" Jayla asked. "Cuz mine sure is."

"Not at all."

"Lucky!" Jayla yelled.

"I don't think mine likes me very much," Zaithrian said.

"I wonder why," Jayla mumbled.

"What kind of missions do you think we'll be doing?" Luken asked.

Skye had been wondering the same thing. The thought of something actually life threatening made her sick to her stomach, but what else could they possibly be doing?

"I don't know," she admitted. "But I hope we can do it as a team."

There was a long pause, no one wanted to think what kinds of things they could be doing.

"Hey, we still don't know each other too well, why don't we ask each other questions or   something?" Jayla suggestd.

"First question," Daria said. "Where do you see yourself in ten years?"

"Okay, wow tough question right off the bat," Jayla said. "I'd say some doughnut shop somewhere, probably eating a chocolate dipped, one with little rainbow sprink-"

"Yeah, I don't think that's what she meant," Skye said.

"I wanted to be a Flame as a little kid, but I guess everyone did. I think I'd still like to do that," Zaithrian said. "But, hey, staying alive is my biggest goal."

"Maybe Skye's should be too," Luken said, causing everyone to laugh.

"I don't think you people understand what a serious question is," Daria said with a sigh.

"Sked yeah we don't!" Jayla said, pumping her fist into the air.

"Alright, I have a question," Luken said. "What is your favorite thing to do?"

Skye perked up at the question. "I love inventing. Mechanics, engineering, all of it."

"And she's real good at it too," Jayla put in. "She showed me her lab back at her old house, she built a floating chair. And this crazy voice thing, it's so freaky."

"It's a voice activated control algorithm," Skye corrected.

"Really?" Luken asked. "You designed an algorithm? Aren't those extremely complex?"

Skye nodded. "Yeah. Do you want me to show you? I have it on my commscreen."

"You uploaded an algorithm to a commscreen? I thought the base chips couldn't handle something that developed?"

"I replaced the base chip with a customized one I made modeled off of one in my laptop. Skye turned on her commscreen, VACA's electronic voice started buzzing.

"Voice Activated Control Algorithm loading… Skye, what have we got now?"

"Hold. The. Eagles. It talks?" Luken said in astonishment.

"Who's that?" VACA asked.

"VACA, meet my Squad." She held the camera out so VACA could see the whole room.

"How is that possible?" Zaithrian asked.

"Electrical mechanics is my strong suit, I've been doing stuff like this for as long as I can remember. One day I was lonely, so I decided to make myself a companion, after a *ton* of experimenting and updating, VACA happened. She has access to the entire cybernetwork, and learns, so she is always figuring out how to solve problems."

More astonishment buzzed around the room.

"I've done a small bit of this kind of work before," Luken said. "I'd love to work with you sometime, though now I work on more of scientific experimentation, I still love to invent." He took out the black earpiece he wore every time Skye had seen him. "I made this when I was younger, it's a hearing device."

"Wait, can you not hear?" Jayla asked.

"Yeah, I had an accident when I was younger, and it caused permanent damage to my ears. I developed this device to substitute as a transmission for the damaged cochlea, it senses sound waves and sends them directly to my hearing nerve."

"Have you shown this to the medical division? They could use something like that." Skye asked.

"I've thought about it, but it's not perfected yet, and my parents don't think it's a good idea to get publicity while I'm so young. Plus, I doubt they would take me seriously, I mean, I'm a kid."

Skye nodded. "That doesn't make it any less of an important device, I think it's amazing that you could develop something like that."

"Hey, if you two are done nerding out, I have to get going, my Mentor is gonna freak if I'm not back soon," Jayla said, getting up from the bed.

"I should probably get going too," Daria said.

After they had left, Skye realized she probably shouldn't be the last one there. "Well, thanks for having me over, Luken."

"Sure, maybe we'll do it again tomorrow."

"Yeah, see you guys later."

She made her way back to her dorm, when she opened the door, Revin was still in the same spot he had been in the whole time.

"Do you ever stop working?" She asked.

"Don't think so," he said.

"Well, uh goodnight then," she said awkwardly, heading into her room.

Tucking herself into bed, she couldn't help feeling a small pinch of homesickness. She missed her mom fussing over her cuts, she'd probably freak if she found out Skye had been thrown by a thunderbird. She missed Locke, he made everything more fun, even if he was annoying. She missed being able to talk to him, he was smarter than she gave him credit for. She missed her dad most of all, he was always the one to ask her how her day went, he always came to say goodnight to her.

She gripped the blankets closer to her chest, glad for something to cling onto. She wasn't going to cry. She needed to move on, she would still miss her family, but she shouldn't just focus on what she had lost. She had new friends, real friends, not just some wires and programming, but people who cared about her. She had a Mentor who would show her how to excel in her Guild, she had a new home with a bright future.

CHAPTER TWELVE

VACA, alarm off." Skye groaned as she rolled out of bed, tripping on her blankets.

"Good morning Skye, you have one new message."

Skye slid into her chair at the desk. "Show it on the screen."

The message was from her dad, wishing her a good day.

After a little while of going through the cybernet, Skye decided to start getting ready. She saw that Revin was up as well, Skye was glad to see that he was not on a tablet of any kind.

"Morning, kid," he said, sipping his mug of kopi.

"Good morning," she replied, pouring herself a cup of the warm drink from the pot on the stove.

"So for today's lesson, I think we'll be practicing some of the methods I used to use when I trained as a Light."

"What were those?" Skye asked, taking a seat at the table.

"I used to have my sister develop codes and put them on bombs," he said, sipping his kopi as if it was perfectly normal.

"Bombs?" Skye gaped. "What kind of stuff are you training me for?"

"Anything. That's what I'm supposed to do, teach you to be ready for anything."

Skye swallowed. "Are you sure I need to be ready for *bombs*?"

"I don't know," he said sharply. "I just don't want you to go in blind. You never realize how much you don't know until it's down to the wire and you can't do what you need to." He stood up from the table. "We can start off smaller, but I want you to be prepared. One hour." He walked off into his room, slamming the door a little louder than needed.

Skye shuddered slightly. She finished her cup of kopi, then ate a quick breakfast before getting dressed. She had found that the dresser in her room held a few school uniforms. The long sleeve shirt was a light shade of gray, the pants were a darker shade of the same color made of thick material with loads of pockets lining the legs. She had a red arm band that fit tightly around her bicep. Each Guild had a different color, Ingenuity was red, and Jayla had said Agility was blue, but she wasn't sure about the others. She fastened on the pin the Vire had given her at the graduation ceremony. It was a golden badge shape with her Squad's number on it. She also wore a pair of black boots and tied her hair up into a ponytail.

Revin was waiting when she came out from her room. He had a similar uniform to Skye. His was completely black and his armband was gold–the color of Mentors–and it had a red stripe to signify that he was training an Ingenuity. He was slightly less sloppy from last night. He had shaved the stubble off of his face and his hair looked like he had at least *tried*, but he still had deep bags under his eyes from a sleepless night.

"You ready?" he asked.

Skye nodded.

"You gotta get going for the opening session, you should know where my training room is, they probably sent it to your commscreen."

"Al-alright," she said shakily.

"Come on kid, you'll be fine." He patted her on the back. "The first day's always crazy, but you'll figure it out, we're ingenuitive, that's what we're best at."

Skye nodded. "Okay."

"Now hurry up, you're going to be late!" He practically shoved her out the door.

After she had left, Revin looked at the empty space where she had just stood. He gave a drawn out sigh. "I really have no idea what I'm doing."

* * *

Skye's Squadron found a row of seats in the large room they had gone to the day before. Lights milled around while waiting for Director Cross to take the stage and give the week's announcements.

"I can't wait to start training!" Jayla said, practically bouncing in her seat.

"I think it's going to be interesting," Skye said, stressing the last word.

"Ha, you worried?"

"You could say that."

"Well, I think it'll be fun."

Director Cross soon came to the podium. "Good morning Lights, I have a few things to adress for today. We are expecting our new students to excel here, but we have to give them grace for their first days, like other students showed you. Squadrons 773, 888, 892, and 716, you will be doing your reconnaissance missions this week, your Squad Leaders have the details for your missions. That's all I have for this week, you may go."

"Do you know where you're going?" Jayla asked.

"I'm pretty sure it's listed on my schedule," Skye said, powering on her commscreen as they walked out of the room.

"See you guys at lunch," Zaithrian said, heading to the Leadership tower. Daria and Jayla followed him out the door to their towers.

Luken's tower was right next to Skye's so they walked together. The towers were each spaced along the edge of the school ground. The Intelligence and Ingenuity towers were on the left side of the main tower, the Agility and Stealth were on the right. The Leadership tower was behind the main tower.

Luken and Skye walked through the campus. The crowds of students were rushing in clusters to get to their lessons on time.

Skye was more than beyond nervous about her first lesson, she had no idea what to expect. Revin didn't exactly seem like the best teacher if she was being honest with herself, but maybe he would know more than he seemed. But that felt like a long shot.

"I think we could design something pretty cool," Luken said, breaking Skye out of her thoughts.

"Um, like what?"

"Well, I've been thinking of things that might prove a challenge when we go on our missions. Like communication. We obviously won't be able to talk to each other while we're in the air, and we can't type on our comms if we need to hold onto our creatures, so maybe a radio-like device would be something to try."

"I never thought of that. It seems like something that could be useful, we can try developing something."

"Great, we can try working on it later today. I'll see you at lunch!" He raced off to the green tower they had just reached.

Skye walked a little farther until she made it to the Ingenuity tower. She stepped inside and her jaw dropped at the entry room. A workshop area the size of her entire house was in one corner. There was a library, art studio, and who knew what else. Skye yearned to explore the room, but she had to get to lessons with Revin.

She gave a quick glance around the room for the elevator. Nothing.

She felt a tap on her shoulder and turned around to see who had touched her.

A girl with a red armband pointed to the far wall. "You new? The stairs are over there. Lessons are up there."

"Oh, uh thank you," Skye said shyly.

The girl nodded and left to go into the library.

Skye went over to the stairs and let out a mental groan. This tower was huge. She started climbing, already imagining doing it every day.

Skye checked her commscreen and saw that Revin's training room was on floor 17. *Seriously*, she thought, making her way up. She was definitely going to be late.

She tried to keep herself from sprinting, she didn't want to be a sweating mess when she made it to her Mentor's room. After a long, tiring trek, Skye made it to her floor and found the door with 'Mentor Revin Donte' written on it. She pressed her finger to the pad and the door slid open.

The room was bigger than she had expected, it had large windows that let in plenty of light. There was a seat and desk placed in the middle of the room, probably for her, and another larger desk a few feet away. There were vials of liquids and beekers full of chemicals on one wall. It looked like there was a full chemistry set. There were bins in the back of the room but Skye couldn't tell what was in them.

"You're late," Revin said from his seat at his desk.

"I know, sorry it won-"

"Kid, I'm messing with you," he said with a laugh. "I was never on time, I don't blame you. Are you all set for today's lesson?"

"Uh, yeah I think." She sat down at her desk.

"Good, 'cause I'm not," he said in all seriousness.

Skye furrowed her brow. "Like, emotionally not ready?"

"No, no, I'm not ready, literally. I didn't finish preparing your lesson this morning. So just... give me a second."

"Um, okay." Skye drummed her fingers on her desk as Revin typed something onto his computer, then scribbled something on an electosheet.

After a few minutes, he stood up from his desk. "Okay, so you know there really isn't much I can do to help you become more ingenuitive, that's something you're naturally good at. That's why this is the hardest Guild to train, you can get more intelligent by learning things, you can become more agile by doing physical training, but you can't do much to help someone be better at being creative and inventive, but I want to teach you to have good intuition, to know how to use your cleverness, to make good calls. I want you to really excel in what you're just naturally great at." He slapped a sheet and a jumble of wires on her desk. "Figure this out." He sat back down at his desk, turning on his computer and doing what seemed like Beacon work.

Skye glanced down at the pile of parts on her desk. It looked like it was a commscreen. Or *had* been a commscreen at least. The small device was in pieces, wires jutted from the back of the black base, the screen was split into four pieces, and the microchip was definitely not functioning.

She read the sheet. *This commscreen was damaged. You must have it functioning before we break for lunch. There are a few parts in the back of the room, but I can't guarantee everything will be there, so you must make some of*

your own. Hurry, there will be severe
consequences for failure.

Skye sucked in a breath, taking another look at the practically destroyed commscreen, then back at Revin. He was at his computer, but now he had put earpieces in to drown out Skye.

She fingered the screen, examining it from all angles. She had no hope in fixing it in the few hours before lunch. *One step at a time,* she reminded herself.

With a steadying breath, she started removing the wires. She needed to repair the split ends. After the painstaking task of retwisting the miniscule wires back together, she flipped the commscreen over and started replacing them in their correct spaces. The screen would prove a challenge, the cracked mess would be nearly impossible to fix without the right materials. She raced to the back of the room where Revin's note had said there would be parts. She noticed a few parts she could definitely use for other repairs, but no screen to replace the demolished one.

She muttered under her breath and grabbed a few more pieces she would need and ran back to her desk. She pressed all of the pieces of the screen together, glad there weren't any missing. An idea suddenly popped in her head. She rushed over to where the vials and chemicals were displayed against the wall. She quickly scanned the row of labeled bottles and found the three she was looking for. She grabbed a pair of gloves and goggles before taking a few drops of the red beaker and putting them into a new vial. She was really hoping she remembered the formula correctly. She stirred the mixture until it started bubbling slightly, then poured the new chemical into a spray bottle. She carried it over to her table and sprayed it over the cracked screen. She pressed the detached pieces together until it was as close to her own commscreen as possible. She set it to the side and peeled off her gloves. She used the magnifying feature on her goggles to get a better look at the microchip she held. It wasn't cracked, that was something she was glad for, but it looked like a few of the power outlets had been damaged.

After returning from another parts run, she used the microwelder she had found, and started her delicate repair on the structure of the chip. After half an hour of precise cutting and welding, she was sure she had repaired the chip.

She rubbed her pounding head and checked the time. She had a little less than an hour left. Revin was still at the same spot he had been since she started. Skye was starting to believe he never stopped working.

She turned back to her project. The screen she had set aside was now finished its chemical reaction to her mixture. The screen which had been in ruin, was now perfectly merged together, the only scar it bore was a slight hairline crack running over every part where she had connected the completely detached parts. She couldn't help but smile knowing she had taken her knowledge of chemistry and used it to help her in being a Light. Her dad would be proud. She slipped the microchip back into the base and snapped the screen into place. Now for the moment of truth. She bit her lip, begging her work to succeed. She pressed the button. The screen lit up. She had fixed it.

She beamed at her work as she checked all of the different features to make sure they were working properly. They were. She checked the time, she had 45 minutes left until lunch.

"Huh," she said to herself, partially amazed at herself for getting such an exacting task done so quickly.

She stood up and placed the commscreen on Revin's desk. He looked up in surprise, taking out an earpiece.

"You finished?"

She nodded.

He turned it on, doing all of the same checks Skye had done. He checked the time and looked up from the device to Skye. "I knew you could do it, I just expected you to take a little longer."

"Um… thanks."

There was a pause.

"What exactly were those consequences you warned me about?" Skye had to ask.

"Huh? Oh yeah, it was that if you didn't finish I would have to buy a new commscreen."

"What? Was that *your* commscreen?"

"Yeah, I dropped it in the parking lot on my way over. And then it got crushed in the magnetic field from a hovercar. But I figured you'd be able to fix it."

Skye just stared at him blankly.

"So, I don't really have anything else for you to do right now. I've been busy with Beacon work, so I guess just do whatever until lunch break."

"What exactly do you do as a Beacon?" Skye asked, propping herself up on the edge of Revin's desk.

"Different things," he said, shrugging. "Sometimes I simply file and write out reports, but I've got a much bigger project right now."

"What is it?"

"If I told you, I'd have to kill you."

Skye swallowed.

Revin laughed. "Don't stress about it kid, it's just some boring work, I'll straighten out the mess soon."

Skye wandered back to her desk, wondering what kind of crazy scandal Revin could possibly be caught up in.

CHAPTER THIRTEEN

Skye grabbed a tray from the rack and joined the cafeteria line. When she reached the front, the lunch lady slopped a ladleful of… something onto her plate. She took her tray and scanned the room for someone from her Squadron. In a room where everyone wore the exact same clothes, it was a hopeless task to look for a face. Out of the corner of her eye, Skye noticed a head of bright-blue hair. She made her way to the back of the cafeteria where Daria sat with Luken.

Skye slid into a seat at the table. "Hey guys."

"Oh hey Skye, have you seen Jayla or Zaith? We haven't found them yet," Luken asked, taking a spoonful of pudding.

"No I haven't," Skye said.

Just then, a loud voice boomed over the chatter of the cafeteria. "SKYE ZAREB STAND UP ON YOUR CHAIR!"

Everyone stopped talking. Skye slowly stood on her chair, her face was a mix of embarrassment and confusion.

Then she saw it. Jayla was making her way through the crowd with Zaithrian at her heels.

"Oh my gosh," Skye mumbled, getting down from her chair as Jayla sat triumphantly at the table.

"Really?" Skye asked.

Jayla shrugged, casually taking a bite of her lunch. "What? Me and Zaith couldn't find you guys, so I screamed. And it worked."

"Why did you have to make it me, though?" Skye asked.

"That's what best friends are for aren't they?"

Skye sighed. "So how did your training go?"

"I literally stretched the *entire* time! She didn't even let me do anything fun. They have the most amazing equipment in my tower," Jayla said.

"Well, me and my Mentor just went through some more strategies," Zaithrian said.

"Aren't you in the Leadership Guild?"

"How do you think I learn to be a better leader?" Zaithrian said, sassing Jayla's sarcasm. "And I have to learn much more than just Leadership. They're training me to be a soldier."

Skye swallowed hard at the word, she hated to think of herself, all of them, as soldiers. They were just kids. Kids close to being adults, but still. She knew the academy just put a fancy word over it, but Zaithrian was right, they were training to be soldiers.

"I can't wait to train with my pegasus," Jayla said.

"I thought you weren't happy about the pegasus," Luken said.

"Well, I would still rather a dragon, but that doesn't mean I can't be excited about what I got."

"Are we having creature training after lunch?" Daria asked.

"Yeah, I think we'll be training as a Squad tomorrow," Luken said.

"Are we going to name our creature?" Jayla asked, staring off into space and most likely coming up with a name for her flying horse.

Skye shrugged. "I don't know, but I would assume we would, we can't really just yell at it by its species."

They all finished their lunch, and by the time the bell sounded, the group was well on their way to the training arena.

A few students were already there talking with Trainer Slin. Trainer Cale came over to their Squadron.

"Alright, you guys go get changed, then I'll show you to your Squadron's pen." He walked away to talk to the next group.

The girls and boys split to go into their changing rooms. Skye found the cubby with her name on it, and found the outfit she'd worn the day before. This one was clean and didn't have the rip in the arm like her other one. Jayla and Daria also found theirs and the three of them got dressed and went out to the boys.

Trainer Slin came over to their group. "What's your Squad's number?"

"999," Zaithrian told her.

She typed something on her tablet, the motion for them to follow her. She led them through the extravagantly large building, until she turned to a door in a long hallway.

"There's an Arena Hand in there to help you get started, but, but this is mostly you guys. You have to get personal with your creatures, that's the only way to establish trust."

Everyone nodded and Trainer Slin pressed her finger to a metal pad.

"Good luck kids," she said, walking away as the door started opening.

The room Skye stepped into was much like the arena she had been chosen in. It had the same tall domed ceiling and walls. The floor here was soft sand instead of the stone floor she'd had in her room yesterday. In one of the curved walls, were five cages built into the white metal. One of those held her thunderbird. Skye swallowed hard.

"Hello everyone, I'm Venna, I'll be your Arena Hand for this year," the woman said. She was tall and athletic looking, with a long blonde braid trailing along her back.

Everyone said hi, then Venna walked over to the pens. "There's no best way to do this for the first time, so I'm going to open the cages all at once and you can each try to lure your creature to a more open space in here." She placed her hand on a lever. "Are you ready?"

Everyone lined up side by side, readying themselves for the chaos that was about to occur.

"We're ready," Zaithrian said.

Venna nodded and flipped the lever. As the heavy doors rose, Skye could make out the feet of each beast. Her thunderbird was on the far right. She slowly made her way closer as the door opened wider, her senses drowning out the other voices and screeches. With a final click, the door stopped going up, revealing her thunderbird completely free.

CHAPTER FOURTEEN

Skye stared into its eyes. Cold, icey, hard. The thunderbird didn't move. She took a step forward. Another. And another. She didn't take her gaze from the lock of her creature's eyes. She reached her hand up, almost close enough to pet its face. She gingerly lifted her fingertips to brush the thunderbird's blue feathers. With no idea how, she managed to somehow coax it out of its pen and to the edge of the arena.

Venna came walking up towards her and the thunderbird. "Good job. The first thing you want to teach your creature is to come with you, you seem to have mastered that quickly."

Skye ran her fingers over the bird's sharp beak. "What am I supposed to do?"

"That's up to you. You need to establish trust with him, it is a him by the way. Get him to trust you in whatever way you think will work."

She nodded, having absolutely no idea how she was supposed to do that. "Does he have a name?" Skye asked.

"All creatures have a name, you can learn it if you listen." Venna walked over to Jayla.

She couldn't help but sneak a peek at Jayla's pegasus. It was beautiful, but she figured every winged horse was. The tips of its wings were black, they slowly faded into the pure white of the pegasus. The only other dark color was a small star of black fur on its forehead, Skye found it marvelous that the shape was so perfect.

Skye turned back to her own creature before she got any more distracted.

"Hey, boy," she mumbled softy, stroking his feathers. "My name's Skye."

His fuzzy triangular ears perked up at the word.

"Sky? You like that?" she whispered. "You love the sky don't you?"

He seemed to nod almost, which didn't seem as strange as Skye thought it would be. She didn't feel weird talking to a thunderbird, she somehow *knew* it understood her.

"You miss the sky don't you? I can feel it in you. I know you want to be free, I know you want to fly, you want freedom."

He gave a small chirp, something so miniscule it seemed not fit for such a large beast.

"What's your name, boy?" She moved in closer, letting her whole hand make its way down the thunderbird's neck.

She felt a pull in her heart, it was a longing feeling, she recognized it. She wanted to fly. She wanted to jump on her creature's back and burst through the ceiling into the open air. She wanted to touch the clouds as she flew through the clear sky. She wanted to soar in the midnight air, not caring about her troubles, not feeling pain, not being afraid. She wanted to be free. But she wanted to be free with him.

Skye looked back into his eyes. "Your name is Kade isn't it?" How did she suddenly know? But as soon as the word had left her lips, she knew it was right.

The bird nodded, a subtle movement that made more than enough sense to Skye. "I will fly with you. I don't know when, but I know I'll help you be free, we'll both be free in the clouds someday."

Kade lowered his neck. Skye knew what he wanted. She wanted it too. She slipped a leg over his neck and scooted down so she was resting above his wings. She had to clutch onto him with her legs and arms when he stood up straight again.

"Woah."

Skye looked behind her to see that Zaithrian and his huge black dragon. But his attention wasn't on his dragon. It was on *her.*

Great, now he's looking at me, she thought. There was some reason she was so much more nervous about flying in the dome now.

She swallowed hard and turned to her thunderbird. "Come on, Kade," she whispered. "Let's fly."

He spread his wings and launched into the air. The sensation of flying had Skye trembling with excitement and fear. But mostly fear. She clutched Kade's feathers as tightly as she could. Why the *sked* had she done this?

As she was about to tell Kade to land, a picture played in Skye's mind. It was of Locke. She imagined how amazed he would be to see Skye flying a thunderbird. She pictured her mom and dad watching her, a look of worry and pride on both of their faces. And oddly enough, the way Zaithrian had whispered "woah" as he stared at her, made Skye want to stay flying. She took courage from the three thoughts, and very slowly, she let her eyes open. She loosened her death grip on Kade's neck, she trusted him to not let her fall.

As they circled near the top of the dome, Skye felt a large smile spread across her face. Tightening her grip with her legs, Skye carefully let go of the bird's feathers completely. She closed her eyes peacefully and spread her arms wide. She let the forming wind push her hair back behind her in auburn waves. The cool air kissed her face. It was just like back at home when she rode her hoverbike. Only 100 times cooler.

Kade cawed happily and Skye couldn't help but laugh.

After a few more circles in the air, Skye replaced her grip on Kade's feathers. "Alright, boy, let's go back down."

Kade hesitated, but cawed and dived back down to the ground.

"Slow down a little, boy," Skye told him nervously.

He didn't slow.

"Kade slow down," Skye tried again.

He continued to dive.

The ground was coming closer.

"KADE!"

The ground was only a few yards away.

Skye screamed and braced for impact. At the last second, Kade pulled up and landed gracefully. If only Skye could say the same. The drastic change in speed sent her tumbling off of the thunderbird's back and into the sand.

Zaithrian ran over and helped her up. "You okay?" he asked, scanning her over.

Skye's cheeks burned in embarrassment. "Yeah, I'm fine."

"What the sked was that!?" Jayla yelled, running over.

"I fell," Skye said.

Jayla started talking a mile a minute. "Well duh, everyone knows that. But you were flying! Like really flying! And you didn't even have your saddle or anything. That was amazing! Oh my gosh that was so cool. Wasn't that awesome Zaith?"

"It was extremely cool," he agreed.

Skye pushed the hair from her face. "Um... thanks, I guess I kinda messed it up by falling off."

"Nah," Zaithrian assured her. "That was the best part."

Venna ran over followed by Luken and Daria. "Are you alright?" Venna asked.

"Yeah, I'm fine," she assured her.

"I've never seen anyone bond so quickly after being chosen. That's remarkable how quickly he let you ride him," Venna said.

"Really?" Skye asked.

"It usually takes over a week of training before a creature lets their rider actually fly with them."

"Well we all knew Skye was going to be the 'super amazing and skilled one'," Jayla said. "Or at least *I* knew it."

"So are there saddles for riding?" Skye asked, looking nervously over at Kade.

"Yes, I have a saddle for each of you, although I never expected to get them out this early. I'll get your thunderbird saddle, but I think we should wait until next time to practice flying though."

"Can I pet him?" Jayla asked as soon as Venna was gone.

"What?" Skye asked.

"Can I pet your thunderbird? He's so pretty and he looks kinda fluffy and cute."

"Um... I guess so, I don't think he'll hurt you."

Jayla made her way over to Kade with a noticeable lack of carefulness.

Skye went with her to calm down the massive bird. He was still slightly riled up from his flight.

"Hey boy," Skye said, holding out her hand.

Jayla copied her movements and matched her slow pace.

"This is my friend Jayla," Skye said.

Kade cocked his head curiously at Jayla, his fluffy ears twitching curiously.

"Hi," Jayla said, holding out her hand a little more.

Kade cawed, then brought his head lower so Jayla could reach.

Jayla smiled and patted his head and scratched behind his fluffy ears. Kade closed his eyes happily.

"Did you find out his name yet?" Jayla asked. "Venna said we'd figure it out, and you seem like the one to get it."

Skye nodded. "His name is Kade. Venna was right, I just sorta *knew*. Have you figured your pegasus's name yet?"

Jayla continued to stroke the feathers on the large bird's face. "Not yet, but I think I'm close. If that makes any sense. I think I'll know soon."

"So what do you think of yours?" Skye asked, joining Jayla in petting Kade.

"He's good, I think I'll like him a lot. I can't wait to ride him though."

Jayla stayed for a few more minutes before heading back to her pegasus. Soon after that, Venna came in with a large, oddly shaped saddle.

"I don't think it's too good an idea to try it on him right now, but you can get a guess on how it'll work." Venna pointed out all the different parts and how she would get it on.

"Is that safe?" Skye asked, glancing with concern at the very open saddle.

Venna nodded. "It's perfectly safe. We try to keep them lighter and more open for the thunderbird's wide flight movements."

It made sense... but it still didn't look completely safe to Skye.

An idea popped into her head. She tucked it in the pocket of her mind, promising herself to look at it later.

"Until next time, just start connecting with him, get his full trust and get to know him a little," Venna said as she walked over to someone else.

Skye spent the next hour just petting Kade or talking to him. She climbed onto his back and focused on getting him to stay on the ground while she was riding.

"Good boy," she whispered. "Let's just walk."

After a considerable amount of time, Skye figured out how to get him to walk on command. He only went a few steps, but still, it was progress. And it was more progress than anyone else had made, not that she thought of it as a competition.

As far as she knew, Jayla had tried getting on her pegasus and had been bucked off multiple times, but that might have been because she was literally jumping onto him. Zaithrian had told her he had made a little progress, but she didn't exactly know what he meant by that, as far as she knew he hadn't tried getting on his dragon. Daria was doing well with her kelpie, Skye had taken some time to watch them work, it was amazing. Kelpies used their minds to control water, and they used it in the most beautiful ways. She wasn't completely sure about Luken though. She'd seen him run out of the arena a few times, but she didn't know why. She actually hadn't seen him very much at all during training.

Venna didn't actually help any of them much, Skye was pretty sure she'd actually left for at least an hour, but she figured that the Arena Hands weren't supposed to bond with a creature that wasn't theirs.

After having done training for a few hours, a loud bell rang through the arena building.

"Alright, that's it for today," Venna said. "Now let's see if you can get them in the pens."

Skye led Kade to the wall of pens. He followed her coaxing hand without revolting, or at least he had been. When Skye got close enough to the cages, he realized what she was trying to do and screeched wildly, launching into the air.

Skye scrambled away from him, fear rising high into her body. Her heart pounded as wildly as Kade's broad wings. Flashbacks from being thrown from him only the day before flooded her mind.

Daria lept from her kelpie's back and pulled Skye away from the beast. Skye backed against the wall.

Kade's eyes met Skye's fear-filled ones. He stopped screeching, he stopped flapping, he landed back down on the ground.

Skye watched as he slowly came closer to her, he seemed so gentle all of the sudden, like he knew somehow that he had scared her.

Jayla and Zaithrian had also huddled around her, each one ready to protect her if the bird striked. But Skye knew he wouldn't. Kade wouldn't hurt her, he had never tried to hurt her.

She pulled away from the group. Holding her hand out to calm her thunderbird, she inched her way closer. *He won't hurt me*, she realized. She turned her pace to a regular walk, knowing she didn't have to be afraid of Kade. He wouldn't hurt her. She reached to pet his face. He didn't pull away from her, but instead welcomed her hand and moved closer to her.

"I know you don't want to be caged again, but it has to be this way. It isn't fair, I know, but I'll be back. When I come back we'll fly again, we can fly as long as you like, but you need to go in the cage for a little while. I'm sorry, but it has to be that way. I'll be back the day after tomorrow, and then we'll fly. I promise."

Kade seemed to nod, Skye could almost feel words form in her heart. *I will wait for you.*

Then the bird straightened, and walked into his cage.

Skye almost cried watching him walk away, but she held it in, she would fly again soon.

CHAPTER FIFTEEN

Skye twirled a screen pen between her fingers, looking over her sketch before sliding the screen to Luken. He stared at it for a few minutes, made a few adjustments, and passed it back to Skye and the cycle continued.

Squad 999 was meeting again, this time in Skye's room. She and Luken were at work on the earpiece design Luken had mentioned earlier. So far they were about nowhere. The two of them were hunched over Skye's desk. All they had was a model from Luken's hearing aid device, but they had nothing new.

Jayla was telling everyone her idea to get rich on the cybernet by filming all of their crashes during training and turning it into a epic fail video. She was still the only one in favor.

"Has anyone learned their creature's name yet?" Luken asked after passing the screen back to Skye.

Daria spoke up. "My kelpie's name is Laveni." She paused to think for a few seconds. "It's odd how I could just tell, its like I had known all along and it just-"

"Clicked," Skye interrupted. "Like it made sense all along and you wondered how you never realized it before."

Daria nodded. "That's exactly right."

"Well, I sure haven't!" Jayla exclaimed. She was doing handstands in the center of the room, her dark hair piled on the floor under her. "I think he hates me. I can't even get on the skeding thing's back."

"Maybe if you tried being gentle," Skye suggested.

Jayla snorted and flipped over onto her feet. "Have you *met* me? That's not going to work."

Skye shrugged and turned back to her work.

"I think I'll know soon," Zaithrian said. "What about you Luken?"

He only shrugged quietly and looked back down at his work.

"What do you think we'll be doing for Squad training?" Daria asked.

"My Mentor said that we're being trained by one of our Mentors for each lesson, I guess that way we learn other stuff besides just our Guild," Zaithrian said.

"Do you know who's mentoring us tomorrow?" Jayla asked.

"No, I have no idea," he admitted.

"Well I sure hope it isn't mine," Jayla said.

The three who were not working started a conversation and Skye and Luken continued on their project.

Skye scribbled down some ideas on the electrosheet. Luken paused to look at her new discovery.

"I'll be right back!" he said excitedly.

"Where are you going?" Skye asked. But he was already gone.

"There's no way I'm letting Smart Boy do secret stuff alone!" Jayla yelled as she followed him out the door.

"I have literally no idea what is wrong with her," Skye said.

"I'm pretty sure no one does," Zaithrian said, coming over to the desk. He sat on the chair Luken had been using. He bent over Luken's sheet and examined the tech terms written on Skye's sketch.

"You can understand this?" he asked, holding the sheet up in front of Skye.

"Yeah. It's really not that complicated." Skye realized how cocky that sounded. "But I've been doing this for years so I've gotten good at it." Oh look, she made it worse. "I mean- well- I just- yeah I can read it."

Zaithrian laughed. "Well it sure makes no sense to me."

Jayla and Luken came bursting back into the room, both carrying handfuls of parts. They dropped them on the desk.

"What's this? Skye asked, picking at the metal and wires.

Zaithrian got up and Luken took his seat back. "I had some spare parts I brought in case my hearing aids got broken. We're going to need them for the design, you saw the sketch?"

Skye nodded but took another look at the drawing. The design should work in theory.

"You brought the parts we need?" she asked.

"I don't think I have everything, but we'll have to work with what we have since I don't know where to get more," Luken said.

Skye thought of the parts bin back in Revin's Mentor room. "I might have an idea on where to get more parts, but we'll see. Until then we have to work with this. I also have a few parts from my workstation back at home, but I doubt I have the right wires, the ones we need are looking to be AG2s, I'm pretty sure I don't have one that small."

The two of them dove into a deluge of science and mechanics that the other three couldn't dream of understanding.

"Do they realize we won't be doing recon missions for months?" Jayla whispered.

"Maybe we should tell them," Daria suggested.

"Probably," Zaithrian said. "But they're in their own world of gears and wires, and I'm pretty sure there's nothing we can do to get them out."

CHAPTER SIXTEEN

Her second day of her Ingenuity training, and Skye was already late. She and Luken had stayed up *way* later than they should have and they had barely gotten any progress on their earpiece devices.

After a long trek up the stairs, Skye burst into the room where Revin was seated at his desk.

"I'm sorry I'm late, I was-" Skye started.

Revin held up a hand to stop her. "Don't make excuses. Admit you were wrong and learn to fix the problem."

Skye nodded and took her seat at the smaller desk.

"So kid," he started. "I've told you before that I had an awful Mentor, and I think in a way I want to be better and renew him in a sense."

Skye nodded and he continued.

"So instead of a typical lesson, I figured it would be a good idea for me to understand *you*. If I can get to know you I can better understand how to teach you. Plus we're going to be stuck together for a few years so we might as well get to know each other a little better."

"Um... okay," Skye said.

He propped his feet up on the desk. "Let's hear about you."

Skye tried to loosen up. "Well, I lived in the City District, my house was pretty close to the park on 31st and Brinker. So I went to the park a lot. I have a little brother named Locke, he's 11 and he is great at blackball, he's on a pretty good team. My dad is a chemist, he's developed a few really cool medicines. He only works from home, that way he has more time to spend with my brother and I. My mom works at a restaurant, she never really was around much before I moved out though, but she's really understanding and whenever I would freak on her she always stayed calm and-" Why was she telling him all of this? She didn't want him to know about all of that. Did she?

"It's okay, keep going. Tell me about what you like to do."

Skye wanted to stop talking and hide in a cave with her tools and VACA and never speak to anyone again. But... she also kinda wanted to tell her Mentor about her life. Revin listened like he actually cared, and that made her want to tell him everything.

"I like to program and work with wires and technology. I had a lab back at my old house. I built all sorts of things, but my best one is VACA, she's a voice controlled algorithm and she controls all of my tech."

Revin perked up. "Really?"

Skye felt like smiling. "Yeah, I could show you if you want, but I guess that's not really training or anything."

"Oh training can wait, I want to see this thing."

Skye pulled out her commscreen and opened VACA's file. The crisp voice filled the silent room.

"Hey Skye- woah wait who is *that*?" VACA asked.

"VACA, this is my Mentor, Revin. Revin, this is VACA."

"Woah," Revin whispered. "You made this all by yourself?"

Skye nooded.

They spent hours going through VACA's skills and everything she could do. Skye found it funny how Revin was constantly gaping at her work. After Skye finished Revin leaned back against his desk.

He ran a hand through his hair. "Kid, I don't understand you. Not one bit. Algorithms this developed are at the tip of impossible, and for a sixteen year old kid-"

"She finished me when she was fourteen," VACA informed him.

He stared at Skye. "Seriously?"

She nodded again. She liked praise, but it was so awful and awkward and it was impossible to stay humble without acting like she didn't care.

"I'm impressed, kid. Sked, I'm more than impressed, I'm flat out blown away! How? How did you know how to do this?"

She thought for a moment. "I didn't. I figured it out as I went along. I learned what worked and what didn't by trying it out, if I failed I tried again. And I failed a lot. But I guess I got it right a lot too. I guess I was being ingenuitive."

"You're a good kid, Skye. A little odd, but I guess all the best ones are."

The bell chimed through the building, signaling that lunch break was starting.

Skye slipped the commscreen back into her pocket and looked to Revin for approval that she could leave.

He sat at his desk with his elbows supporting his cupped hands where his chin rested. He wore a blank stare on his face.

"Hey Revin can I go?" Skye asked.

He didn't look up. "You deserve a Mentor better than me," he mumbled so quietly Skye couldn't make out his words.

"What?"

He ran a hand over his face. "Uh, nevermind. Yeah Skye you can go to lunch. You- I'll see you tonight."

Skye looked back as she headed out the door.

* * *

In the cafeteria, Skye's mind was busy on what she had heard Revin say. Or what she hadn't heard him say anyway.

She didn't see anyone from her Squadron in the crowd of Lights so she took a seat at the nearest empty table. She was pretty sure she knew what was coming.

After a few minutes of peaceful eating Skye heard the unmistakable sound of her best friend.

"SKYE ZAREB WHERE YOU AT?!"

Skye sighed and stood up on her chair as she figured she'd have to do for the rest of her life. Jayla came running over, soon followed by Luken, Daria, and a smirking Zaithrian.

"I can sure get used to this," Zaith said, sliding into the seat next to Skye.

Jayla took the seat on the opposite side of her. "Well screaming Skye's name is the most effective way to find her in this crowd."

"You realize you can comm me right?" Skye said, holding her commscreen in front of Jayla's face.

"Okay, fine, the commscreen is more *effective*, but the screaming is so much more *fun.*"

Skye sighed. Arguing with Jayla was hopeless.

"So I figured out who's Mentoring us today," Luken said, taking a seat on the other side of the table.

"Yours?" Skye asked.

He nodded. "Mentor Chloe is pretty good. She's smart and isn't too harsh. I think you'll all like her."

"Did you get any information on what we're doing?" Daria asked.

"No, she wouldn't tell me anything, but I think it has something to do with Varlem," Luken said.

"Varlem? Why are we learning about that?" Jayla asked.

"Well I guess we'll be crossing the border between the islands sometimes," Skye said.

Skye already knew a decent amount about Varlem, The nation was an island across the ocean from Isarn, she had never been there, but people said it was very different from Isarn.

"Well, anyway she had a bunch of books on it. *Real* books, not the downloads or anything. Like paper and ink. Isn't that crazy?" Luken asked.

"I wish we used real books still," Skye said.

"I guess they aren't as efficient anymore," Luken said. "But sometimes I miss a good old fashioned book."

They all ate their lunch and finished their conversations as the bell rang.

"Are we doing this in the Intelligence tower?" Jayla asked.

Luken nodded and they all started their way to the green tower. The stair climb was much longer and much more tedious since Luken's training room was on the 49th floor.

"Why don't they put an elevator in here?" Jayla whined.

"I don't know, maybe they want to wear us out before we get there to make us worse at everything," Zaithrian said.

That made everyone laugh, even if they were all exhausted by the time they reached the floor.

Luken opened the door and they all stepped into the room. It was much like Skye's, she figured they would be. The only difference was that instead of chemistry sets, puzzles, and spare parts, Luken's room held real books, 3D models of the insides of different creatures, and charts with mathematical equations. There were five small desks in the center of the room, Skye figured they had been brought in for Squadron training.

"Hello everyone, you can all have a seat," Luken's Mentor said. She was tall with dark skin and black hair in dozens of tiny braids. She had a soft voice and warm eyes, she seemed nice enough.

They all sat at a desk and Mentor Chloe set a large book in front of each of them. Skye read the title of the thick red book: *The Language of Varlem and How To Speak It.*

"Wait are we learning an entire language?" Jayla asked, gaping at the huge book.

"Yes, you are, and it is much easier than you would think, Varlemesse is quite similar to the language we speak here, I'm sure you'll pick it up quickly," Mentor Chloe said.

Skye knew bits and pieces of the language, but she didn't speak it fluently, she always figured it was a useless act.

"The books you have are filled with the language. There are lessons planned out inside and tips on how to practice them. I want you to do at least three lessons in between lessons with me," Mentor Chloe said.

"Why don't we just use our commscreens, I'm sure there are learning apps on the cybernet," Jayla said.

"Because there is no better way to learn than learning with a book and a pencil."

She showed them what to do and how to do it, then returned to her seat where she was reading–to no one's surprise–a physical book. Skye had to admire her for it.

The lesson was boring, even Luken looked tired, but Skye finished her workpage and had learned most of the letters and how to say "Hi, it's nice to meet you" in Varlemesse, though it seemed pretty pointless.

By the end of the three hour period, Skye had a headache and a massive craving for a nap.

The Squadron decided not to meet up that day since they were all tired and Skye started back to the main tower. Revin wasn't home when Skye made it back to their dorm. She figured he probably had more Beacon work or something like that.

She tumbled into her room, a million thoughts buzzing in her head. She wasn't sure what to do for the rest of the day, she could do her homework, but the thought of that made her head hurt. She plopped into her desk chair and spun to face her room. A memory dug its way back into her head and she leapt from the chair. She rummaged through the bins of parts she had brought until she had found the folded white chair that was supposed to float. She examined the chair, then the floor under it, and set to work. She lost track of time as she worked, she never seemed to pay attention to things like that when she had her tools. She worked for a while until she heard a knock on her door.

Her head shot up. "Come in."

Revin stepped into her room, he was back to his sloppy state with his messy hair and rumpled clothes. He looked tired.

"Hey kid." He held up a white plastic bag. "Brought you dinner."

Skye spun from her work. "Thanks, I didn't eat yet."

"You've been in here for a while." He placed the bag on her desk.

156

Skye looked out the window and saw that both moons were high in the pitch black sky. "Oh. I guess I lost track of time."

"Eh, it happens to everyone. What you working on now?" He leaned over her shoulder to get a better look at her project.

Skye pulled the fast food from the bag and started eating. "It's a chair I made back at my old house. It has the same negative magnetic pulse a hover has, but the floor here isn't metal like the one in my old lab, so I'm trying to tweak it to work on this floor."

He rubbed his chin. "Have you tried a magnetic conductor strip?"

Skye twirled a screenpen in her fingers. "I thought of it, but I don't have any."

"I'll be right back," Revin said, heading out the door.

Skye raised her eyebrows in surprise but before she could question him, he was gone. She turned back to her dinner while she waited. About ten minutes later, Revin came back with a bin of parts.

"There should be one in here." He threw the bin on her desk with a clang.

The two of them started digging through the bin of parts until, eventually, Revin found one.

Skye and her Mentor spent hours working on the hovering chair, connecting, sealing, detaching, and anything else that would make the chair work.

Finally, Skye flicked a small switch and the chair hovered perfectly.

"Would you like to do the honors?" Revin asked, motioning for Skye to sit on the floating white chair.

"I would," she responded, starting to sit down.

Just as she was about to sit, Revin wrenched the chair from under her and Skye fell on the floor with a thud. Revin burst into laughter and took the seat for himself, propping his feet on the desk.

Skye sat on the floor where she had fallen. This was exactly the kind of trick Locke would have pulled on her back at home. She laughed and reached to turn off the chair. Revin held her back with one hand and she was left trying to struggle.

She sat back on the floor, accepting her defeat. Revin laughed as he sat down next to her, he had a spark in his eye Skye never noticed before.

In that moment Revin felt exactly like a big brother to Skye. He was here to teach her how to become a Light, but he might also be there to teach her how to become an adult and show her how to grow. He was smart, but he also was funny and kind and was just fun to mess around with.

Skye wasn't sure what would come out of this whole mess, but she sure hoped Revin would end up being her sort-of-big-brother by the end of it. Because in that moment, Skye was sure that was exactly what she needed.

CHAPTER SEVENTEEN

S̲kye, guess what!" Jayla yelled from the other side of the creature training arena.

Skye was in the middle of scrubbing Kade's talons. Definitely *not* her favorite part of owning a thunderbird.

She stood up and smoothed the stray pieces of hair from her ponytail with the back of her hand. "What is it?"

Jayla came running over with her pegasus trotting behind her. "I figured out his name!" She beamed and the winged horse seemed to almost do the same. The two of them looked so mischievous together, even if one was sort of a horse.

"Really?" Skye asked, giving Jayla a hug. Zaithrian had learned that his dragon's name was Ryo a few days before, and they still hadn't learned about Luken's griffin.

"Yeah! It's like you said, I just knew. It clicked when I was running with him, it just makes so much sen-"

"Are you going to tell me this name?" Skye asked.

"Oh! Yeah, sorry. Skye Zareb, meet my pegasus, Zeno." She gestured proudly at the horse.

Zeno seemed to recognize the girl's prideful look, so he held his head high as if he was being awarded.

Skye laughed. "That's great Jayla."

Jayla leaned on the pegasus smugly. "Yep, me and Z-Boy are gonna be having some serious fun around here!"

"I'M NOT DOING ANYTHING WITH YOU!" Zaithrian called from the other side of the arena.

"NOT YOU!" She yelled back. She looked over at Skye with an eye roll. Skye could only laugh.

"So what's up with Kade?" Jayla asked, walking over to run her fingers through his soft feathers.

"Other than him being a real pain, nothing," Skye said.

"That bad, huh." She turned to speak to Kade. "You're in deep bud, you got *Skye* mad."

"I'm not mad, I just can't seem to get anywhere with him."

"Hmm, tough. Have you tried trust exercises? You know, the ones where you jump from 30 feet in the air and wait for him to catch you."

"No way! Why would I even think of doing that!"

Jayla shrugged. "Just a suggestion. I'd take him flying around if I were you, he really seems to like that."

"He does," Skye agreed. "I guess I should take him up. Has Venna come back yet?" She scanned the room for their Arena Hand.

Jayla scoffed. "Uh, nope. She keeps ditching us. Not like I care though, now there's no one to make sure I don't try any backflips off of Zeno or something."

Skye was used to Venna leaving them alone, it seemed crazy that the school just let them hang out with fire-breathing and lightning-shooting creatures without supervision. But she guessed that was part of their training.

Jayla walked back to her area and Skye started strapping on the saddle the way Venna had shown her.

She jumped up onto the saddle and stroked Kade's neck until he calmed down. She still hadn't gotten used to the thin straps keeping her from falling to her death.

"You ready to fly, boy?"

Kade spread his wings wide in response and leapt into the air. Skye still hadn't gotten used to her thunderbird's enthusiasm when it came to flying.

"It's nice up here, isn't it?" Skye asked, mostly to herself but also to Kade.

She gazed up through the clear dome above her head, she knew it was going to be an adventure when she got out there.

"Skye look!"

She looked over to see that Jayla was soaring in the air on her pegasus's back only a few yards from her.

The dome was large enough for probably three of them to be flying at once, but that didn't make Skye feel less crowded. She had a mini panic spike every time Jayla came a little closer.

"Isn't it cool?" Jayla asked. She had to scream for Skye to hear. Luken was right about needing communication devices.

"Yeah!" Skye yelled back. She decided to head down so that Jayla could have the whole sky to herself, and she was also worried Kade would freak out if Zeno got any closer.

When Skye landed, she took off the saddle and let her thunderbird eat a bucket of fragworms; disgusting slugs that wiggled and looked like sludge. Skye felt like puking every time he ate them.

Skye decided that she would go over to see how Zaithrian was doing with his dragon. She had a small fear of the massive black winged creature, but figured Zaithrian had it under control. And she *really* couldn't stand the smell of those fragworms.

Skye walked over to where Zaithrian and his dragon trained.

"Hey Skye," he said when she approached. He was slouched up against the back of Ryo's neck. He looked like he had almost started falling asleep.

"Um, hi. What are you doing?"

He slid off the dragon's scaly back. "Just doing some... bonding. She's a pretty chill dragon, she likes it when I-"

"Take a nap on her?" Skye asked.

"Oh yeah, she loves it." He yawned and leaned against Ryo's wing, Skye was amazed that he could just *do that*, like he wasn't scared of the dragon at all.

"So what's up with you?" he asked.

She shrugged. "Nothing, it's feeding time and I needed to get away from Kade's lunch, they still have their eyes and everything."

"You seem to be doing better than all of us with this training. It's kind of amazing."

Skye shrunk at his compliment. "Yeah, I guess. It hasn't been that good though, he's hard to work with. All he wants to do is fly."

"Do you like flying?"

Skye shrugged. "I like it, though Kade makes it pretty interesting by trying to do twirls in the air and stuff like that."

He seemed to be thinking about his words carefully. "Do you want to fly with me?"

"Like-like on your dragon with you?" Skye asked.

He nodded. "If you want to..."

Skye pictured herself flying on the back of a dragon, soaring through the air with Zaithrian. Then

163

she pictured herself falling off the dragon and plummeting to her death. Why was she so scared? She had just as high a chance falling off of Kade as she did Ryo, maybe even higher. But for some reason flying on the back of a dragon just seemed so much scarier.

"Umm, thank you, but maybe some other time would be better…"

"Yeah, yeah, of course. I probably should go do… some more training then, I'm really busy with that and- you know." Zaithrian smiled, but Skye could tell he didn't really mean it.

"Yeah, thanks anyway though," Skye said awkwardly.

Skye felt awful as she walked back over to her thunderbird. She hated making people feel like that. She sat down next to Kade as he munched happily on his wriggling worms.

"I'm so bad at this," she told him miserably.

He cawed his agreement and continued to eat.

"I'm glad we're in agreement," she mumbled, looking up at the top of the dome where Zaithrian and his dragon were flying.

She sighed. "You have no idea how lucky you are, Kade."

He cocked his head curiously at Skye, a worm half-dangling out of his beak.

She scrunched her nose at the smell and gave a small laugh. Thunderbirds were odd creatures, odd, lovable creatures.

CHAPTER EIGHTEEN

This training exercise is simple," Mentor Lonan called over the chatter of students. "Each of the four Squadrons will be given a flag to hide somewhere in their portion of the arena. The objective is to collect as many flags as possible and return them to your base while also protecting your own flag. Your guns are loaded with paint capsules with your team's color on them. If you get hit three times, by any and all teams added up, you're out. Last team standing or first team with all four flags wins. Do you all understand?"

Skye swallowed and nodded along with the other students. It was a Squadron training day, and Zaithrian's Mentor was teaching them. The Leadership Guild wasn't one that they were learning to master, that was Zaith's job, the other four of them were learning to follow his orders.

They were in a big circular arena with three other Squadrons. Obstacles filled the room, giving them a ton of stuff to climb on and hide behind. Jayla was the most excited of everyone. After over three weeks she still hadn't dulled to the physical toll training every day took.

"This is going to be so much fun!" She jumped up and down next to Skye as one of the other Leadership Mentors started talking.

"We will be closing the barriers so no cheating is allowed. You have ten minutes to develop your strategies and hide your flags."

Then the sound of machines buzzed and closed the walls of the arena, leaving four equal quarters. Zaithrian burst into action.

"Okay everyone, listen up. We need to hide our flag at a high point, that way we can keep a better watch of what's going on and it's harder to reach." He took a quick look around the room and pointed at the perch near the back of the room. "There. Daria, have you gotten any practice with sniping?"

"A little bit."

"Okay, you'll be in the tower with the flag. Take out anyone you see coming up. Luken, I want you on the ground in defence. You'll be an easy target, but your job is to take out anyone that makes it past Dar. Jayla, you're on offence, you're our fastest one here, so I want you to sprint after the flag as much as possible. I'll join you on offence. And Skye." He looked over at her with a hint of a smirk. "You're the decoy."

* * *

Skye stood against one of the obstacles, gripping her paint gun with sweating hands. The flashing red lights blinked with a countdown.

10.

9.

8.

The barriers started to rise.

7.

6.

5.

She could see the other sides of the arena coming into view.

4.

3.

2.

1.

The red flashing lights dimmed and a siren announced the start of the game.

"Here we go," Luken mumbled next to her.

Skye started making her way against the edge of the circle. They were going for the red team's flag first. Skye had an interesting job. She was playing both offence and defence. She would stay in the middle, taking out intruders, and–if she got the chance–attacking. She wasn't looking forward to that part. Or really any part for that matter. She wasn't a fan of getting shot at.

She kept close to the wall, curving with the circle as she went. She still hadn't seen anyone yet but she could hear the sound of guns firing their paint. She had to hope that wasn't her team.

Footsteps thundered around where she walked. Skye froze. She gripped her gun tight and didn't breathe. The running continued. They were coming this way. Skye ducked behind a wall and dropped to her knees. A boy from the yellow team scampered past on his way to her team's flag. Skye shakily raised her gun. She could take him out. He already had a green splash of paint on his helmet, she just needed two shots on him.

She aimed and let out a breath. Then she pulled the trigger. Skye jolted from the gun's kick. The blue paint capsule exploded on the wall next to the boy. His head darted to Skye and he ran. Before she could think, her hand flew up to shoot again. Five shots rang from her gun before Skye got a hold on herself.

The yellow team's mentor let out a yell. "Conn Blakely of the yellow team is out!"

Skye blinked. She'd taken someone out? The *first* person?

"Alright, alright," Zaithrian's voice came into the headset in her helmet. "Nice job guys. Daria, what's your status?"

"No one's made it over yet," Daria said. "So far I think they're going for the other flags."

"Good. Stay alert. I'm with Jayla on the right side, going up to red. Neither of us have been shot. Skye? Luken?"

"I'm good," Luken said. "Daria's right, no one's come yet."

"Move up a little bit more Luken," Zaith commanded.

"Skye what's your position?"

"I'm coming up on the left side like you said. I've only seen one person, the kid who got out."

The sound of gunshots rang around the arena and two more students were announced out–both from the red team.

"Change the plan," Zaithrian said quickly. "Go for yellow."

"Why?" Jayla blurted. "We're almost at red."

"Everyone's going to go for red now that they're down two, we go to yellow who's got to have only one defence. Hurry."

Jayla groaned but complied.

Skye quickened her step and crossed into the yellow team's section. Her gun stayed gripped tightly in her hands.

"I'm in yellow," Skye said, eyes darting across the arena covered in blocades. "Where are you guys?"

"We're almost there," Jayla said.

Something smashed into Skye's back. She whipped around and saw a girl from yellow holding her gun, getting ready to shoot again. Skye darted away from her. Her feet pounded against the arena floor and she dove behind a blockade. She pulled the gun up, ready to shoot. Ready for someone to come and take her out right there.

"I got hit," Skye said into her helmet.

"Where are you Skye?" Zaithrian said.

Skye looked up. "I- I'm by the wall with the giant 4 on it. There's a big black rectangle. I'm right by that."

"On our way," Jayla said.

Skye spotted movement. Then heard a gunshot.

"Sked!" Jayla screamed.

"Retreat!" Zaithrian yelled.

Another ring of shots and Skye bolted.

Mentor Lonan's voice echoed out. "Jayla Payge of the blue team is out."

"Oh no," Daria mumbled. "I see three targets coming this way."

"Luken, get them," Zaithrian said. "Skye, fall back."

Skye started to turn when a flash of yellow fabric caught her eye. The flag. "Wait there's a flag! Right here."

"No, Skye, fall back," Zaithrian said.

"But it's right there! I can grab it in a few seconds."

"Skye, no, fall back."

She stared at the flag. It was completely unguarded. She shook her head at Zaithrian's words. She could grab it and run back to their base. She gripped her gun and ran towards it.

"I said fall back!" Zaithrian yelled.

Shots pelted her from all sides just as she was about to reach the flag.

"Skye Zareb of the blue team is out."

CHAPTER NINETEEN

Jayla ripped the helmet off her head and chucked it on the ground. "Come on we were doing so good!"

Skye ducked her head and set her helmet on the shelf. After she'd been shot down, Zaithrian had been caught in the open. Luken and Daria were overrun and the green team pulled out as last surviving.

Zaithrian pulled off his helmet and glared at Skye. "When I give you orders, you follow them. Understand?"

She didn't meet his eyes and nodded. "Sorry," she mumbled.

His brows pushed together. "There's no 'sorry' here!" he barked. "If this had been a real situation, you'd have been dead. You get that?"

Skye swallowed and nodded, her throat burning with tears.

She looked to Jayla–anyone really–for back up, but they all looked away.

Luken kicked the floor. "We're in for a lecture now."

At that moment, Mentor Lonan charged into the room. "That was the worst performance I've ever seen!" he said, not even a touch of kindness in his voice. "I don't even know what to say to the five of you."

"So how about you don't then," Jayla snapped. "We know we screwed up! You don't have to make it worse."

He stood in front of Jayla and glared down at her. "You most definitely need me to 'make it worse'. You need me to tell you *exactly* what you did wrong, or you'll never learn."

Jayla didn't back down. "No. We know what we did wrong. And right now, we're all mad, tired, and none of us want to get yelled at about how much we sucked today. So, no, we don't need you to tell us exactly what we did wrong. You need to let us go home so we can think about it ourselves."

Mentor Lonan's jaw tightened. Everyone froze. Jayla didn't cower.

"You are all free to go. We'll discuss today at our next squadron training."

Everyone except Jayla gaped. She only smirked.

Mentor Lonan nodded at them and left the room.

Skye pulled off her armor and set it on the shelves with her helmet. Her gray school uniform was sweaty from being underneath her thick armor. She could feel the bruises forming from the paint capsules. Even with the thick armor they had hurt a ton.

No one said anything as they grabbed their stuff and left. No one wanted to talk about the fact that they had done miserably.

Zaithrian didn't even meet Skye's gaze. He was still angry apparently. Skye felt awful. She'd been the reason they'd lost.

Jayla at least gave her a quick nod before grabbing her backpack and heading out. Luken and Daria didn't say anything, but at least made eye contact with Skye. Zaithrian only brushed past her.

Skye's body ached, but it didn't compare to the burning guilt in the pit of her stomach. She grabbed her bag and walked out, her shoulders sagging.

CHAPTER TWENTY

"Can I talk to you for a second?"

Skye stopped at Zaithrian's words. "Um, yeah."

Jayla, Luken, and Daria all left to go to their morning classes.

Zaithrian motioned his hand to walk and they started making their way to Skye's tower.

He was quiet for a bit, before clearing his throat and looking down at his feet. "I'm really sorry about how I acted yesterday. And it was terrible of me to yell at you for something like that. Sometimes I- I forget that it's not real. I get carried away. And- I'm just really, really sorry."

"I should have listened to your orders. You had a reason to be mad. It's fine-"

"No, no it's not fine." He stopped walking and grabbed her arm. "Look, I don't want you to say it's fine. It's not. And I know that. I want- I don't know. I want you to be mad at me or something."

"You want me to be mad at you?" Skye asked with a little laugh.

"No- I don't know, I don't just want you to forgive me and that be the end of it. Do you want me to do something for you? You wanna slap me in the face? Please just- don't let me off the hook."

Skye started walking again, Zaithrian trailed after her. "It's fine. Really," she said.

Zaithrian didn't say anything until they reached the base of Skye's red tower.

He stopped in front of the door and shoved his hands in his pockets. "Try to think of something, okay? Please?"

Skye saw that there was no changing his mind. "Alright." She nodded. "I'll try."

He gave the tiniest of smiles and nodded at her. "Thanks."

"You're going to be late now," Skye said, looking at the time on her commscreen.

He shrugged. "I'm already gonna hear it from Mentor Lonan, might as well add to the deal."

"It's not fair he's only taking it out on you," she said.

He shrugged again, not giving her a smart comeback this time. "I guess I'll see you at lunch then. Don't forget to think of something."

"Don't let him go too hard on you," she said, turning to go.

He smiled a little. "I'll be fine.

CHAPTER TWENTY-ONE

Skye opened the door to her classroom and the water in her boots squished under her step. The rain was pelting down hard since it was in the middle of a season change, and Skye tried not to drip all over the floor. It was pretty hopeless.

"Here, kid," Revin said, throwing a towel across the room. It hit her in the face and he tried to hide his grin. She dried off as best as she could before sitting down at her desk. That's when she noticed the second desk next to her.

"What's that for?" Skye asked.

Revin threw his feet up on his desk. "Do you know what the most common job for an Ingenuity graduate is?"

Skye shook her head even though she knew it was a rhetorical question.

He leaned back in his chair. "For an Ingenuity graduate the most common job is weapon design and production. One of the most admirable traits an Ingenuity grad has is our ability to create, and the Flames are always looking for new weapons. That's why today you're going to be designing and building one."

Skye sucked in a breath. She knew close to nothing about weapons, and now she had to make one?

"Don't worry kid, I've called in an expert. Or at least someone who knows more about it than you. Same thing." Revin dismissed the thought with a shake of his head.

"Who?"

Just then, a knock came on the door and Daria poked her head in the room. "You wanted to see me, Mentor Revin?"

"How long is it gonna be before you kids stop calling me Mentor?" He sighed and waved his hand. "Yeah, come on in Dar, have a seat. I was just explaining it to Skye."

Daria cast Skye a questioning glance and slid into the desk next to her.

Skye didn't know why she became more nervous as Daria sat down next to her. Out of the four other Lights, Skye knew Daria the least. There wasn't a particular reason for it other than she was awful at making friends if they didn't start up the conversation. And like Skye, Daria didn't seem like a fan of that.

"I've brought Dar in today because the two of you will be working on constructing a weapon. Daria has been training with weapons for the past two months, and Skye's been inventing, so it seemed like a good idea to put you two together and

179

see what you could make. Mentor Baylyne agreed that you girls would be able to do well here. Whether you need just today or all week, you'll be working together on developing a new weapon that could be used in any kind of combat. There's parts in the back and I've brought in some guns you might want to examine or take apart. This'll also help you work on your teamwork and you'll get more comfortable working together. I've got some work to do, so uh go ahead."

Revin put earbuds in and started ignoring the two of them.

Skye was used to him doing it by now. He had more of a hands off approach to teaching. It had actually worked pretty well so far.

"How do you want to go about this?" Daria asked. "You have a lot more experience in this kind of work than I do."

"Oh, um, okay." Skye stood up from the desk. "I guess the first step would be to design it. That way I-we can actually start putting it together."

Skye grabbed the laptop from her backpack and powered on the computers and turned on the screen that covered the back wall of the classroom. "VACA, connect my laptop to Revin's classroom screen."

Skye grabbed a screenpen and handed one to Daria. "We can start with a sketch. Do you have any ideas for what kind we want to do? I really don't know much about this kind of stuff."

"I think the easiest weapon would be a gun," Daria said. "Not too much to it and best for overall combat."

Skye nodded. "Okay, that seems good." She wrote out blaster in scratchy handwriting on the screen.

"Either blaster or bullets. Blasters are quieter and you don't run out of bullets, but guns with bullets cause more damage internally."

Skye fought off a wave of nausea. She knew it was part of being a Light, but the idea of it made her sick. She hated the idea that she'd be making a weapon. And she hated the fact that Daria seemed perfectly fine with it. But…it was for peace, wasn't it? That was the whole reason she was there in the first place. To help maintain peace. Or that's what people were telling her anyway. She didn't like the thought that she would ever be fighting for another reason, but the more she trained at the Academy, the more she got the feeling that her training wasn't just for keeping peace.

"I- I guess blaster," she mumbled, writing it on the screen. "I'll need to see how the lasers are formed in the gun if I'm going to duplicate it."

Daria nodded slowly. "Okay…I guess we'll need to decide how we want the blaster to look. I think we should go for a smaller one, something you could hold with one hand." she shrugged. "But that's just what I prefer because if it's more compact and easier to keep on you at all times."

"Alright. I guess you can start drawing up a design?"

Daria turned her attention to sketching something. Skye went to the back of the room and grabbed one of the blasters and started to take it apart so she could figure out the mechanics.

"So is this how Ingenuity training normally goes for you?" Daria asked.

Skye didn't look up–a habit she'd fallen into years ago. "Pretty much. Revin is a pretty relaxed Mentor. He usually just works while I do my lessons. There isn't much he can do to teach me to be more Ingenuitive."

"Yeah, I guess that makes sense. I kind of wish Mentor Baylyne was more relaxed, she's not terrible though." She sighed. "My parents are pretty serious about my training. They both graduated Lights and Flames so they have pretty high expectations for me."

Skye noticed how her voice dipped quieter when she talked about that. Her own parents had always been so relaxed about her schooling, she'd never thought what it would be like if they'd put pressure on her.

"What about you?" Skye asked, deciding it was a good idea to change the subject. "How's Stealth training been?"

"I've had a lot of fun. Mostly I've been training with target practice. But Mentor Baylyne said that soon I'll move on to espionage and infiltration, which seems like a lot of fun."

"That sounds cool," Skye said, getting distracted by her work again.

She'd started to take it apart to see how the gun created the lasers inside of it. The mechanics were actually pretty cool. She was confident she could replicate the components to fit in the body of another gun. She didn't really get the point of designing the gun to be different, if it shot the laser, it should be the same as every other blaster, right?

"How do you thin-"

Skye was interrupted by a beeping noise coming from Revin's desk.

Her head shot up to see what was making the noise. "What's that?" Skye asked.

Revin didn't answer, his eyes glued to his commscreen.

"What's wrong?" Skye asked, seeing the worry etched across Revin's face.

"I have to go," he said, grabbing his coat from the wall.

"What?" Skye asked, standing up from her seat. "What do you mean you have to go?"

Revin pulled the hood over his head. "There's-there's an emergency in the Sanctuary District. I need to go."

"The Sanctuary District?" Daria asked.

"Why? What's going on?" Skye asked.

The Sanctuary District was where creatures were bred for Lights and Flames. Nothing ever happened there, especially nothing Revin would have to deal with.

Revin opened the door, his eyes still watching his commscreen. "Finish up with your thing. I have to go."

"Revin!" Skye yelled as he headed out the door.

She ran to the door and into the hallway. "What's going on Revin!" she yelled.

He only ran down the stairs. "Go back to the classroom kid, I have to go."

"Wh- Revin, what's going on?"

But he was already gone.

"Skye."

Skye turned back to the classroom where Daria stood, leaned over her commscreen.

"Skye you need to see this."

Her breath caught in her throat when she saw the screen.

The live news broadcast showed the domes of the Sanctuary District up in flames. One picture was displayed in the corner of the screen. Skye recognized the man instantly. The hard teal eyes and smirking face could only belong to one criminal. Daken Claw.

CHAPTER TWENTY-TWO

Jayla caught Skye's arm in the cafeteria. "Did you see what happened?" she asked, panic flooding her eyes.

"Yeah- Revin left- he went to go help," Skye's face burned with panic. "He went to the fire, he's going to go help. Jayla he's going to get-"

"He'll be fine, Skye," Jayla said, trying to reassure her. Skye's brain didn't believe her words.

The students were all talking in the cafeteria at once. No one knew what to do. Nothing like this had happened in over *nine years.*

"Where are the others?" Jayla asked, straining to see in the crowd of students.

"I uh- I think Daria went looking for the boys," Skye said.

"There's Luken!" Jayla said, grabbing Skye's arm and pulling her across the room.

They found Daria, Luken, and Zaithrian huddled in the corner, all watching on Zaith's comm.

"Skye!" Zaithrian yelled. "Guys, come here!"

Jayla and Skye huddled around the small screen. Flame Squadrons had arrived and were starting to put out the fires.

"Everyone's saying it's Claw," Zaithrian said, his voice hard. "They don't have any definite proof yet, but they all are blaming him."

"There were a few people that said they saw him," Luken said, eyes glued to the screen.

The screen shifted to a reporter in the newsroom. "We have new footage supplied from a sanctuary worker." The screen shifted again to a bad quality recording of a group of riders on kelpies. The camera zoomed in on the rider in the front. Even in the grainy video, Skye could tell it was Daken.

"That confirms it," Daria mumbled.

"That makes no sense," Zaith said. "Claw left- he was gone for years-"

"Attention Lights!" The voice of Director Cross boomed through the speakers in the cafeteria. "We ask that all of you make your way back to your individual dorms. We don't have full details on what is happening, but we require civil actions and obedience for the safety of everyone. You will be contacted by the school board once more information comes in."

The crowd of students started running to the exits. Skye's squadron didn't move.

"We should stick together," Zaithrian said.

187

"But they said to-"

"I couldn't care less about whatever the sked they're telling us to do," Zaithrian snapped. "We stick together. I'm leader of this Squadron, and I'm giving my orders."

* * *

"Dude, are those doughnuts?!"

"You know, we're kind of witnessing a monumental attack on the government right now, and you're talking about doughnuts."

"Shut up, Smart boy."

"Can you stop stealing my food?" Zaithrian said. "Jayla, do you understand that this is kind of a huge deal and that there's a chance we could get attacked by the same people who just destroyed the entire dragon enclosure in the Sanctuary District?"

"If I'm going to die, I want to have my doughnut."

Zaith rolled his eyes and brought everyone into the living room where the screen was playing the news. No one knew what to do. It was hectic. And Skye was doing her best not to have a panic attack.

The walls of Zaithrian's dorm felt too close. The talking was too loud. The fear was too real. It was *all* too much.

She shut her eyes and focused on steadying her breaths.

A hand slipped into hers and squeezed it reassuringly. "It's gonna be okay."

Skye squeezed Jayla's hand so hard it must have hurt her. But Jayla didn't falter. She let Skye hold onto her, and Skye was beyond grateful for that.

"Why would he attack the enclosure?" Luken asked.

Among way too many other things, Skye had been thinking about that too. It made no sense. Daken Claw was not much more violent than the symbol of a few riots over years after he'd attacked the Vire. It didn't make sense that he'd actually *do* something. He was wanted all over Isarn for years, and his face had hardly made the news since he had attacked the Vire at the inauguration. Was he finally doing something?

The hours passed. The news was just repetitive nonsense. The reporters tried to act like they knew what was going on, but it was obvious they didn't. The Flames eventually put out the fires, and things sort of calmed down.

"Breaking news, there is live footage coming in from one of the Flame Squadrons-"

The camera shifted again to a sky view coming from a Flame's camera.

"Sweet kingdom of the Eagles," Jayla mumbled.

The pack of kelpies was surrounding–in the air–a flock of dragons.

"He didn't kill the dragons," Daria said, breathless.

Skye didn't blink. "He stole them."

A blast of water shot at the camera and the video turned to static.

CHAPTER TWENTY-THREE

Skye woke up leaning against the arm of the couch. It took her a minute to realize why she was in Zaithrian's dorm, but at once it all came flooding back. The attack. Daken. Revin.

She threw off the blanket and got up from the couch. That sent Daria—who was sleeping on the other side of the couch—right awake.

The wallscreen was still on the news. The volume was so low she could hardly hear it. Luken and Zaithrian were sitting on the floor, talking quietly. Jayla was folded up in the armchair, asleep, but her face was strained like she was having a nightmare.

Daria yawned and sat up, blinking to clear her vision.

"Has anything changed?" Skye asked, hugging her arms around herself.

Zaithrian ran a hand through his hair. "Not much. They're investigating how Daken got through, but they haven't found anything. I think they still have some Beacons and Flames stationed there."

Skye sat down on the couch again. "Did Daken get away?"

Luken nodded.

"How?" Daria asked, sitting up. "He was flying with a giant mob of dragons. How did they lose that?"

Luken handed her his commscreen. "That."

Skye leaned over to watch. It was a recording of the news, it looked like another Flame camera. It was following Daken's parade of dragons as they flew. Then they vanished. Just like that. Gone.

Daria's face twisted in confusion and a hint of fear. "How-"

"No one knows," Luken said, shaking his head in confusion. "I can't stop watching it- I can't figure it out. It has to be some sort of device, but there's no way to just make a herd of dragons vanish–and in the air." He shook his head again and stared off into space, deep in thought.

"Whatever it is," Zaithrian said. "It's going to be an issue."

"Has the school said anything yet?" Daria asked.

"I haven't gotten anything."

Jayla screamed and shot up from her sleeping position.

Everyone whipped their heads to see what happened.

Jayla was holding her head in her hands, curled up in a ball. She was whispering to herself hysterically.

"What's wrong?" Skye asked.

"Are you okay?" Luken asked, standing up.

Jayla sat up and wiped the hair from her face. "I-I'm fine- I just had a dream." She shook her head and was breathing heavily. "I'm fine. I- I'm gonna go back to my dorm."

She got up and ran from the house before anyone could react.

"Wait Jayla," Skye jumped from her seat and followed her out the door. "Jayla what happened?"

Jayla turned around in the hallway. "Nothing- it was just a stupid dream- I'm fine."

Skye paused. "Are- are you sure?"

She nodded quickly. "I'm fine."

"If you want to talk about it-"

"I don't."

Skye stopped. Jayla never acted like this.

She must have noticed Skye's confusion because she hugged her arms around herself and looked down. "It's just...It's scary."

"Yeah, the whole thing with Claw- I'm afraid too."

Jayla had the look on her face that almost said that wasn't what she had meant. But she said nothing. "I'll see you at lunch I guess," she said, giving Skye a small smile to prove she was okay, then went inside her dorm.

* * *

Skye still hadn't heard anything from Revin, but the school had sent out a message saying they would be returning to their typical lessons that morning, so everyone had gone back to their dorms to get ready. She wasn't really sure what to do but she finished getting ready in her school uniform.

As Skye was heading out of her room, her commscreen started ringing. Revin. She quickly answered it.

"Revin?" she asked, holding it up to her ear.

"Hey kid." His voice was tired and raspier than normal.

"Oh my gosh, Revin what happened? I watched it on the news- did you go, oh please tell me you didn't actually go-"

"Calm down, Skye," his voice was calm and collected. "I'm fine. I just went down as a representative for the Board. I wasn't in any danger."

Skye tried to get her heart to stop beating so fast. "But-"

"Really Skye, I'm fine. I just helped the Flames with some of the clean up and stuff like that, none of it was dangerous. I promise. I'm on my way home now."

"You are?"

"In a plane flying back to the Palace District. If they let me leave when I get there, I'll be home this afternoon."

Skye swallowed and nodded. "When you get home…are you going to tell me what's going on?"

Revin sighed. "I don't know. Everything's so hectic right now… I can't say much, not like we know much anyway, but I'll tell you what I can. Okay?"

Skye nodded. "Alright."

"They letting you guys go to lessons?"

"Yeah, we're being called to the Meeting Hall for a briefing. I think they said we'll be doing our regular lessons too."

"Oops," Revin mumbled. "Uh, sorry about that. I definitely won't be back in time. You're good to take the day off from lessons."

Skye paused. "Are you sure you're okay?"

Revin let out a small laugh. "Yeah kid, I'm good. You okay?"

Skye hesitated before answering. "I have a lot of questions."

He sighed. "Me too kid, me too."

CHAPTER TWENTY-FOUR

Oh my gosh Revin I thought you said you were fine-"

"It's not that bad!" He protested, collapsing on the couch. "Just a few stitches, no big deal."

Skye sat down next to him and examined the row of stitches curving on his temple to his eyebrow. She clutched her hands together. "I thought you said you weren't in any danger–you *told* me you weren't in any danger."

Revin kicked off his shoes and laid his head back. "I wasn't. The cleanup got a little messy and there was a lot of metal. I fell and cut my face, but I'm fine. Really."

Skye sighed and stood up. "Do you want dinner? It's pretty late, I can make you something if you want."

He shook his head. "Thanks kid, but I don't think I can stomach food right now." He gave her a small reassuring smile, but it only made her worry more.

"Was it as awful as it looked on TV?" she asked quietly, sitting on the other couch and pulling her knees to her chest.

Revin closed his eyes and ran a hand through his hair. "It was horrible. I haven't seen this kind of destruction since…" He sighed and went to rub a hand over his face, but stopped short before he could touch the stitches. "Death count of 76 trainers and 148 injured. Creature loss of 93% of the dragons ready to be Mastered." Revin cursed and smashed his clenched fist into the arm of the couch. "No one even saw him coming. He was in and out so quickly…and he just disappeared." Revin shook his head and stood up. "I can't tell you much kid, but-"

"Go to bed, Revin," Skye said. "You look terrible. You can tell me tomorrow."

He sighed with a nod and walked into his room without another word.

Skye was practically dying of curiosity, but seeing Revin come home safe had eased her worry for the most part.

She wanted answers, but she also almost didn't want to know what had really gone down. Isarn had threats, and she knew that. There was always someone who didn't like how things were done. But this? This was *so* much worse than any rebellious action she'd seen in her life. Were things really changing? She'd only been at the Academy for a little over two months, but she'd really started to like it. And if something was happening…

Skye shook her head and took steadying breaths. Anxiety crept through her like a parasite, threatening to take over. She couldn't let that happen.

She stood from the couch and pulled on her shoes. A walk around the campus might be just what she needed. She walked out into the hallway and found Zaith leaned against his door on his commscreen.

He looked up when he saw her. "Can't sleep?"

She hesitated. "...it's like 6 o'clock?"

He pressed his lips. "Right..." He cleared his throat. "Where you headed? I could give you an escort." he gave her an exaggerated bow.

She laughed a little and shook her head. "Just going to take a walk...I need to clear my head."

He nodded solemnly. "I know how you feel. Guess I'll leave you alone then, I have a feeling I'd make a pretty sorry serenity partner." He gave her a small smile and saluted.

He hesitated only a second before heading inside his dorm.

Skye put her hands in her pockets and took a ride down the elevator to the ground level. Not a ton of people were around. The Academy had a campus curfew at 10, but even now a lot of people weren't out around. That probably had something to do with the Claw attack.

Oh look, there she was thinking about it again.

She groaned and stepped out into the campus. With summer coming up, the air was a nice cool temperature and the sky was still bright with sunlight. Though it was fading, the light gave off bright golden steaks of sun that danced across the stone campus ground. Skye took in a deep breath and instantly felt so much better. It was so calming out here. While her stomach still had that thick feeling of worry, it did seem less than it had been.

Revin was okay. Her friends were unharmed. She was safe. And yet the fear didn't stop gnawing at her.

CHAPTER TWENTY-FIVE

Skye led Kade to her edge of the dome so she could feed him. She'd started making progress with him again. Not much. But at least he listened to her now. Most of the time. He was getting more and more used to letting *her* take control when it came to flying. Soon, they'd fly outside the dome, but there was a lot of training left before that. They *all* had to be ready, and while she had started to make small amounts of progress, no one could really agree. Daria was doing okay, but she always ended up soaking wet after every training day. Jayla was actually doing pretty well, Zeno seemed like the perfect creature for her, but the pegasus's wing had been hurt while Jayla had been flying him, and the only training she could do for two weeks was walking. Zaithrian and his dragon had gotten along well at first, but when it came to Zaith learning how to let the creature take the lead...he did pretty miserably. And he was *way* too stubborn to ask anyone for help. And then there was Luken. She couldn't figure him out. He seemed to be almost...afraid of his griffin. She couldn't really blame him, she'd been terrified of Kade, but even after over two months here…he still wasn't comfortable with the creature.

She glanced over at where Luken was working. He was next to the griffin, slowly stroking its feathers. He seemed okay.

She threw the bucket of fragworms on the ground in front of Kade. "Stay," she instructed, crossing the dome over to Luken.

"How's it going with him?" Skye asked, walking up next to Luken.

Luken turned around. "Oh. Uh, not too badly. Today he's okay. What's up?"

Skye hadn't actually thought this far ahead before she'd walked over. "I just came to see how you were doing. Have you found out his name yet?"

Luken sighed. "I don't know. I can't seem to get anywhere with him. And it's not his fault–it's mine I'm sure." He shook his head. "Venna said I need to learn to trust him…but I have no clue how I'm supposed to do that."

Skye studied the griffin carefully. His pure white feathers were bright, and with the sun coming through the dome, his golden fur shone. The griffin was a noble creature, highly respected for its likeness to the Eagles. Some said that griffins actually came from the legendary creatures, Skye had never been sure if the tales were true, but standing so close to the griffin, it was hard to think it wasn't one of the majestic Eagles' own.

She turned back to Luken. "Is there any way I can help?"

He sighed with a shake of his head. "Not really, but thanks. I just-" he looked up at the griffin and shook like a chill had gone through him. Luken tensed. "I just don't see how I can be comfortable around him. He's just such a powerful creature. It would take him almost no effort to-" He stopped himself short and took a step away from the griffin.

Fear. It was clear on Luken's face. So that was what made it so hard to work with his griffin. He was afraid of him.

"You good, Smart Boy?" Jayla said, walking over to them.

He seemed to snap back to normal. "Yeah...yeah I'm fine."

Jayla looked over at Skye to ask what was going on, but Skye gave her a hardly noticeable look that said she would tell her later.

"I should probably make sure Kade is okay," Skye said, giving them both a small wave and heading back to her area.

She started cleaning up the fragworm mess and thought of how to help Luken. There really wasn't much she could do. *He* had to be the one to train his griffin. She couldn't do that for him.

Skye looked over at where Luken and Jayla were talking. Luken was fine now. He was laughing. He was normal. The griffin had even

202

moved a little closer, and Luken seemed unbothered. Jayla gestured to the griffin and Luken looked up at it. Skye couldn't see his face too well from across the arena, but she could tell he was scared. Jayla reached for his hand and lifted it up to the griffin's face. She let go as he ran his fingers across its smooth beak. Then he looked down at Jayla and smiled. He said something Skye couldn't hear.

Skye tried to hide her grin. This was going to be interesting.

CHAPTER TWENTY-SIX

The weeks started to form into a routine. Skye would train with Revin, her Squad, and Kade. Her thunderbird training had slowly started to become easier and easier. Kade was getting used to letting Skye take the lead, and he seemed so much more comfortable with it. Her whole Squad had gotten better with their creatures—especially Luken. Jayla had been helping him for a few weeks, and since then he'd gotten much better with his griffin. And he'd found out his name was Phenton. Rumor was that they'd get to go on their first recon flight soon.

Eventually Skye realized she had been at the Academy of Light for over four months. The time had seemed to go by so quickly. And with nothing more about Daken Claw, she'd begun to forget he'd even attacked a few weeks ago.

Skye awoke one morning to the unmistakable smell of bacon and powder cakes. Skye rolled out of bed groggily, her nose leading her into the kitchen. There stood Revin with an apron at the stove frying and flipping at the same time.

"Morning, kid," Revin said.

"What's with the breakfast?" Skye asked. Revin rarely even ate breakfast, let alone make it for them both.

"I thought you could use a little surprise today," Revin said, flipping the small red cakes on the pan.

"Any particular reason?" Skye asked, taking a pair of tongs and turning over the burning meat in the sizzling pan.

"Well, I heard from a *very* reliable source that today is the first day you and your Squadron are taking your creatures out of the arena for flight practice."

Skye's stomach did a flip of nervousness and excitement. She'd been waiting for this for weeks, and dreading it for even longer. So many things could go wrong.

"So I figured that you would be a nervous wreck until then, being super worried and anxious and very you-like, so I decided you needed a special breakfast." Revin flipped the cakes onto two plates, and she placed a few strips of cooked bacon onto each and they both sat down at the table.

The cakes were some of the best Skye had ever eaten, fluffy and sweet with just the right amount of sour fruit. The bacon was only slightly burnt, but the greasy meat melted in her mouth.

"Thanks," she said.

"Eh, no problem kid, you deserve it."

Skye loved days like this. Days where she sat in her pajamas and ate a slightly unhealthy breakfast and the sunlight that filtered into the windows caught the dust in the air making the room feel cozy. Days like this made Skye feel like she was back at home with her family and enjoying her mom's homemade breakfast every weekend morning.

"So, you nervous?"

Skye nodded. "Yeah, but I guess I'm a little excited too."

"That's good. You never want to be too nervous that you forget to have fun. You'll do good. From what I've seen in your reports, you and that thunderbird have a tight bond."

Skye paused. "What creature did you have when you were a Light?"

Revin stopped chewing for a minute as he must have been replaying his time as a teenager. "I had a dragon."

"What happens to a creature when a Light graduates?" Skye asked.

"A few things can happen. If the Light becomes a Flame, their creature goes with them, if they choose to become a Beacon, or if they move on, their creature can be used for breeding, or they'll let it loose in the wild. I'm not sure what happened to mine."

Skye felt a major shift in his mood, and decided to change the subject. "Are you able to tell me what we're doing for my lesson today?"

"I thought we could skip our lesson for today, maybe do something else until your creature training. It's still kind of a lesson in a way, but I think you'll have more fun than a regular one."

"What is it?"

"Ah, now *that's* a surprise. When you finish up, go get ready, we'll leave in an hour."

Skye got dressed into her school uniform and boots and an hour later she and Revin were heading out of their dorm.

"Where are we going?" Skye asked.

"Not far," he replied, holding open the door and leading Skye into the open campus of the school. "Follow me."

Skye stayed a few steps behind Revin as he started walking to the edge of the patterned stone ground.

"Are those *dumpsters*?" Skye asked as they came up to three large metal containers.

"Sure are. The Academy has them emptied once a week, two of them hold real trash, but the third-" He gestured to a blue container slightly taller than him. "It's full of, well, I'll let you see for yourself."

He gave Skye a boost so she could see over a rail. "Woah." The dumpster was filled with parts. Wires, scrap metal, busted chips, and everything else Skye could imagine. It was like a paradise.

"How did you know this was here?" Skye asked, stepping down from Revin's folded hands.

"When I was a Light, my sister and I would sneak parts from here and build all sorts of crazy machines. I figured you'd want to see it for yourself, I can tell your stash is getting low."

"Are you allowed to do it?"

Revin shrugged. "No one stopped us from doing it. The old cleaners knew we did but they never told the Director about us. Plus, they just dump out all this stuff into the trash plant."

"Where does it all come from?"

"The school mostly, whenever something breaks they just dump it in here and buy a new one. You wanna take some of it? We can work on something and that can count for your lesson today."

Skye wasn't sure. It felt wrong taking this stuff, even if it was just trash. But there was something she *really* wanted to make, and she didn't have any of the parts for it.

"If you're sure we won't get in trouble…"

"I'm positive, kid. Plus, when have I ever gotten us into trouble?"

Skye was about to mention that he had almost gotten them both kicked out of the school by lighting part of their classroom on fire during a chemistry lesson, but he cut her off.

"Forget I asked. Anyway, I brought a box so we can get some of the parts you're gonna need for that idea you already have."

He grabbed a small shrinking box about the size of his fist and set it on the ground. After expanding it, he pulled out another expanding box that was about the size of the one Skye had used to bring her stuff to the school. He expanded the large one and it became a 3 by 3 foot box.

"Double boxing, people don't use it enough," Revin said, opening the largest box and hoisting Skye up to the dumpster. "Grab whatever you need." He launched Skye over the edge with a heave.

She nearly landed on her face into the sharp metal heap. She shot Revin a look. He just grinned and jumped up to grab the rail and hoisted himself into the bin.

"What we looking for?" Revin asked.

Skye's mind was whirring. She drew out a list on her commscreen and handed it to Revin. He looked puzzled but started digging in the piles for what Skye needed. Once Skye thought she had everything she needed, she and Revin piled it into the large box, shrunk it, and stuck the much smaller box into another one so that it was small enough for Revin to hold in his hand.

"Do you want to do this in the classroom?" Revin asked.

"Can we actually do it back in my room?" Skye asked. She much preferred the idea of working in the comfort of her own room.

"Fine by me."

Once they were back inside, Revin placed the bin of parts on Skye's desk and scooched his chair up next to her floating one.

"What are we making?" he asked excitedly.

"This." Skye showed him the sketch she had just finished drawing up.

He looked it over thoroughly and nodded. "What do you need me to do?"

Skye gave him instructions and set to work on her own portion of the project.

They worked quickly and efficiently. Skye had to be conscious of the clock, she had to make it to lunch and to her flight lesson. It amazed her how fast she and Revin worked. He seemed to know exactly what to do and rarely asked Skye for another job to do after finishing his. He just moved right on to the next thing that needed to be done.

"You have 15 minutes until lunch," Revin said, glancing at the clock above Skye's door.

Skye looked over their work carefully. "What do you think?"

Revin rubbed his chin as he studied it. "It's a great concept, I think it could work. I'm just worried you might not be able to truly test it before you fly with it.

Skye brushed a hand over the specially designed saddle for her thunderbird. "I have faith it'll work." But would it? The saddle was supposed to go around the thunderbird's chest and lock into place under his torso instead of the ones the academy used that wrapped around his neck and beak. The one Skye had been developing was supposed to be more secure, since she'd always felt the one the school had given her was too open at the sides for comfort. She'd been secretly taking measurements for the new saddle.

"Well, let's hope Skye Zareb is as smart as she says she is, or it could end badly for her," Revin said, taking another glance at the saddle.

CHAPTER TWENTY-SEVEN

Skye had just finished getting her food when she found Jayla starting to join the line. Skye ran over next to her.

"Hey," Jayla said. "Are you nervous yet? You know what, forget I asked, I already know you are. I'm really excited. Zeno is going to have so much fun!"

Jayla filled her tray and glanced around the huge room. "Who should I call this time? I can't do you, unfortunately."

Skye shrugged, then instantly grinned. "Do Zaith."

"Oh, yes! Great idea." Jayla cleared her throat. "YO CAPTAIN SASSY STAND UP!"

Skye saw Zaithrian stand up on a table near the back of the building, she was pretty sure she saw him roll his eyes. The two of them practically danced their way through the crowded rows of tables, Skye could hardly hold in her laughter. It came even harder to subdue when they came up to Zaithrian.

"Really?" he asked, jumping down from the bench.

Jayla shrugged with a grin as she took her seat. "Hey, me and Skye were together so the most logical solution was you."

Zaithrian pointed his fork at Skye. "It was your idea."

"Hey, nice switch up," Luken said, taking a seat at their table. "Never has Captain Sassy sounded better."

"You guys really need to grow up," Daria said, though she looked like she was trying not to smile.

"Ha, that'll *never* happen," Jayla said.

The group shared their usual conversation of how the beginning sessions had gone, finished lunch, then started making their way to the arena.

They all got changed in the locker rooms and were brought to their arena where Venna was waiting for them.

"You kids ready?"

Everyone gave a subtle nod and proceded to get their creatures from their pens.

"As you know, I can't go on this flight with you, but I expect each of you to act as if I were there. Remember the instructions we've been going over, keep your creatures steady, and most importantly, don't lose your tracker." She handed each of them a small clip for their shirts, and started helping them with saddling their creatures.

Skye wondered if she should ask Venna if she was allowed to use her own saddle, or if she should just put it on Kade and hope she didn't notice.

"Do you need help with your saddle, Skye?" Venna asked, walking over.

Skye shook her head. "N-no I can do it." She gave the Arena Hand her most reassuring smile as she walked away.

Skye brought Kade over to the edge of the arena and opened up the compact box behind him. Once she had the saddle back to its regular size, she started fitting it onto her thunderbird. Her saddle had the same back piece as the arena's and a front handle for her to hold. It clipped together at Kade's underbelly and loosely around his lower neck, keeping everything secure. It had an extra group of side pieces which kept her fitted closer in.

Kade didn't seem bothered by the new saddle, and eagerly leapt into the air as soon as Skye was on his back. They flew around the arena a few times.

"Turn on your trackers everyone!" Venna shouted.

Skye pushed the button on the small device clipped onto the front of her shirt and the red light started blinking.

Everyone gave a thumbs up and Venna pulled the lever, opening up the dome. Kade instantly shot out of the arena and into the open air. Skye clutched onto her handle for dear life as her thunderbird swirled through the air.

Kade danced through the clouds, letting the tips of his wings slice through the delicate mass. He cawed happily, joy easily flowing through him into Skye. She beamed at Kade and his excitement. She let her smile grow wider at the realization that she was *flying*. Really flying. Not just taking laps around a dome, no, she was flying in the air with the clouds and the sun and the wind.

"You love it up here, don't you boy?"

Kade cawed in response.

"Keep us steady," Skye told him, whipping the commscreen from her leg pocket. She flicked on her group's audio connection–a connected call between her, Jayla, Luken, Daria and Zaithrian that allowed them all to communicate until she and Luken finished the real devices–and slipped it into the pocket of her upper arm.

"Skye checking in," she said.

"Luken checking in," came the next voice.

"Jayla checking in."

"Daria checking in."

"Zaith checking in."

"Woah, it's awesome up here," Jayla announced.

"Kade loves it," Skye said.

"So does Ryo," Zaithrian said. "I think they all missed this."

"How long do we have out here?" Daria asked.

"We have to be back in 60 minutes," Luken told everyone. "If we're not back by then, they'll send out the scouts."

"And we'll probably get in trouble," Zaithrian pointed out.

"Unless we're late because we fell off into the ocean," Jayla said with a little too much enthusiasm.

"Where is everyone?" Luken asked. "I can't see anybody."

"I'm too high up to tell where I am," Skye said, gazing down at the endless span of open air.

"I think I see someone," Zaithrian said.

Skye noticed a small black speck off in the distance. "I think I see you Zaith," she said, deciding to bring Kade closer.

"Yeah it's you," he said, coming closer.

When Skye was close enough that she could see Zaithrian easily on the back of his dragon, she stopped coming closer, she didn't want Kade to get riled up.

They were close enough so they could see each other but still had about ten feet between the tips of Ryo and Kade's wings. They glided forward, neither of them breaking off. The voices of the other Lights seemed to fade away as Skye glided through the air. The only thing that occupied her thoughts was the feeling of the wind whipping in her face. It was a little cold, but it felt good, it felt refreshing.

216

She allowed her eyes to close and let her shoulders loosen, she let the sun warm her.

Suddenly, she heard a screech and the rapid jerk to the side. Skye's eyes shot open as she lost her grip on the saddle and started sliding off.

"Kade!" she screamed.

But the bird didn't hear her, he was too busy chasing after Zaithrian and his dragon.

Skye was slipping faster off the saddle. Her hands found nothing to cling to. Then she started falling. And falling. And falling.

Skye screamed as she flailed through the open air. Her limbs tingled with numbness. Her heartbeat was thundering as she fell faster. Nausea flooded through her. She started to feel lighter, tired, she felt like passing out. Just as she was about to slip out of consciousness, she felt a cold slap of water and arms grip her tightly. Then she passed out cold.

CHAPTER TWENTY-EIGHT

Skye? Skye can you hear me?"

A cold splash of water doused her face and she shot up. "What happened?"

"Skye! Oh my gosh, are you okay?"

"Of course she's not okay! Did you see what just happened to her?!"

"WhereamI?" she asked, her words mixing together.

"Do you remember what happened?" Skye realized Zaithrian was talking.

She blinked a few times to help clear her vision. She was somewhere in a field of some sort, and her entire Squad all stood surrounding her. "I- I think I fell," she said unsurely.

Zaithrian nodded, he was checking her pulse and was leaned over her soaked figure. "You fell off of Kade, I don't know why but he got super freaked out and started attacking Ryo. He bucked you off."

"I saw you falling," Daria started. "And I got Laveni to make a water bubble to slow your fall, Zaith flew down and grabbed you."

Skye sat up. "Thank you," she said, it seemed pretty pitiful considering they had just saved her life, but she couldn't think clearly enough to make up something more compelling.

"I guess that's why I'm wet."

"That and the fact that Dar just splashed you in the face *again*," Jayla pointed to the empty bottle in Daria's hands.

"It was to wake her up," she assured her.

After everyone had checked on Skye and made sure she was okay, Skye was feeling a lot better and was standing up.

"Where's Kade now?" she asked.

"He's just over there with the other creatures," Jayla said, pointing to a cluster of trees. "Zaith said that when Kade saw that you were falling, he stopped chasing Ryo and he was trying to catch you. Daria had to break your fall with water so you wouldn't die if you crashed into him. But Zaith caught you instead."

"Where are we?" Skye felt dumb for asking so many questions.

"We landed as soon as we caught you, we're in some field or something, I'm not really sure, but we have coordinates back to the school so we aren't lost."

"What time is it? Don't we have to be back at the school by a certain time?"

"You were only out for a few minutes," Jayla assured her. "We still have a little while to get back so we can wait for you to get your strength back."

After about ten minutes, Skye said that she was strong enough to fly back, a few people protested, but Skye reminded them that they had to be back soon. They agreed to leave as long as Daria stayed close to Skye.

"Kade," Skye said, walking up to her thunderbird.

The blue bird's head whipped around and he let a caw of joy burst from his beak. He ran up to her and Skye ran her fingers through his feathers.

"What happened out there, boy?" she asked. She had decided she wouldn't be mad at Kade for knocking her off, he must have had a good reason for freaking out.

He cawed softly, as if he were apologizing, he seemed to really care.

Words seemed to form in Skye's heart: *I protect you.*

Skye wondered if she had imagined him saying this. She realized that Kade had probably been trying to protect her from Ryo. "You don't need to protect me from that dragon. That's Zaithrian, he's a friend, he and his dragon won't hurt me."

He cawed again and knelt lower so Skye could climb on. She felt a little nervous given her most recent experience, but regardless she climbed on. She inspected the saddle, wondering if it had been most of the reason she had fallen off. She pulled at the tech sheets she had used to cover everything, the material was fine but she noticed a few places the supporting cables had loosened up slightly. She twisted them back together with her fingers as tightly as she could, it wasn't bad as long as she didn't do *that* again.

She tightened the strings on her wrist guards and gripped the handle on her saddle firmly. The rest of her Squad jumped onto their creatures and Skye gave Kade a sharp whistle and he launched into the air.

Zaithrian sent coordinates to everyone's comms and they all made their way back to the school.

"So do we tell everyone about Skye's epic plunge?" Jayla asked through their comms.

"I would prefer we don't tell people," Skye admitted, slightly embarrassed.

"Maybe we should though?" Daria said.

"What benefit does that give?" Luken asked. "If she's not really hurt does it matter?"

"It does matter if she almost died!" Zaithrian said.

"But I know what the problem is now, Kade was trying to protect me from Ryo, plus the bolts on the support cables from my saddle weren't properly tightened. I can fix that and make Kade understand that Ryo isn't trying to hurt me," Skye told him.

A banter flowed through the group. Skye didn't see the point of telling the arena workers she had fallen if everything was fine, but Zaithrian and

Daria both said that she should let the school know what had happened. Luken and Jayla agreed with Skye that it shouldn't matter if she told everyone or not.

"If it was me that fell then I think I should get to decide if we tell the Arena Hands," Skye said. "I don't even see what the big deal is, I'm fine."

"Says the girl who fell a hundred feet from the sky," Zaithrian said.

Skye wished she could glare at him, though she did know deep down that he and Daria were trying to keep her safe. "How about this, I fix my saddle and train Kade to like Ryo and I guess all of the other creatures, and if something like that ever happens again–to any of us–we can tell the Arena Hands and get more help. Sound good?"

Everyone agreed. Zaithrian mumbled something about hoping it wouldn't happen again, Skye had to agree with him there.

CHAPTER TWENTY-NINE

Skye plopped onto the couch in her dorm, completely exhausted. Almost dying sure takes a lot out of you. "I'm home!" she called.

Skye expected to hear Revin call back, but after a few minutes she was still sitting alone in the house. She stood and went into the kitchen, it was odd for her Mentor to not be home. "Revin?" she called. No answer.

Skye found an electosheet taped to the table with Revin's scratchy handwriting scribbled across it.

Something came up with work, I had to go to the Palace District to help. I don't know when I'll be back, there's food in the producer and if you need anything go to Mentor Chloe. I should be back soon but I can't be sure. -Revin

Skye read the note over three times. It was unusual for Revin to have to actually go to the Council to do Beacon work, whatever he was doing had to be a big deal. Last time he had actually had to leave was…Daken.

Skye shuddered and hugged her arms around her chest. Was he back? She had started to believe that he was satisfied with the dragons he'd taken and was leaving it at that.

Maybe Revin had to go for other business? It was possible. But her own thoughts were hardly convincing.

If she kept thinking about it, she would never get her brain to stop. She made herself dinner and sat down at her desk to work as she ate. She quickly finished her homework, it was mostly from her Squad training since Revin barely ever gave her homework, and brought up a 3D image of the saddle up on her screen.

"VACA, highlight all damaged areas."

A few of the rods on the image turned red. Skye brought out the real saddle and started making the repairs. After a few hours of work, Revin still wasn't home. Skye decided to just go to bed and hope he would be back in the morning.

Skye woke up the next day and found that Revin still wasn't back. She wasn't sure what she was supposed to do. They only had meetings in the Meeting Hall on the first day of the new school week, and she didn't have her Mentor to do her lesson with, so what was she supposed to do?

She figured she might as well get ready, so she showered and changed into her Light uniform. She did the homework for the day and finished it about an hour before lunch would start.

Skye turned on VACA just to fill the creepy emptiness of the house, and dug through her parts bins, trying to come up with something to work on.

"Do we have any unfinished projects?" Skye asked.

"You never finished the earpiece comms," VACA told her.

Skye was pretty sure the prototypes were still in Luken's dorm, and he would be with his Mentor doing his training.

"Anything else?" she asked.

VACA dove through all of Skye's past notes and reminders. She came up with quite a few half done projects from a year or two ago, but Skye had left most of those back at home, and the rest didn't seem important anymore. By the time she had to leave for lunch, Skye had nothing to work with and no ideas.

"Power off," she said, sliding on her boots and heading to lunch.

CHAPTER THIRTY

By the time Skye had finished lunch and her Squadron training, Revin still wasn't back. She was getting more and more anxious that something was seriously wrong. And the house felt too empty. VACA was nice and all, but she needed a real person. Revin worked a lot, but he had gotten a lot better about taking time for Skye. It felt weird not having him around for an entire day.

Her comm buzzed just as she was about to sit down. She opened her messages and read the text from Luken, wanting to know if she could come and help him with the earpieces.

They had decided to start working on them a lot more since they'd be going on more recons soon. Everyone agreed not having to hold their commscreens would make flying a lot easier.

She typed a quick reply and got ready. She had started wearing shorts again since the weather had begun warming up. She always changed into cooler clothes when she got home since the uniforms were sweat monsters. She filled her backpack with a few parts she assumed she would end up needing and headed out the door. She didn't bother putting on shoes, none of them did when they visited each other's dorms.

Mentor Chloe let her inside. Skye said a quick 'hi' and walked into Luken's room.

"Hey," he said, not looking up.

"Hey. What did you get so far?" Skye took her hovering chair from her backpack, it was so compact and light that she always brought it when she worked. She set it on the opposite side of the desk from Luken and sat down.

He handed her one of the black devices. "I think I've hit a small breakthrough, I figured out how to connect a tracking signal without disrupting the frequency we have for communication."

Skye observed his progress and nodded. "I should be almost done with the final communication tweeks, then we can test them out. I have a feeling we'll be adding more to them when we're done though."

"Probably," Luken agreed with a laugh. "Us inventors are never satisfied with anything doing just what it's supposed to."

After they had each worked on their own task for a few minutes, Luken spoke up. "I heard Mentor Revin left."

Skye swallowed. "Yeah, he had some Beacon thing going on and had to head over to the Palace District to help."

"Has he ever done that? Leave, I mean."

"Only time he left overnight was when Claw attacked. It has me worried something serious is going on."

Luken was quiet for a few minutes. "Don't you think it's weird that Mentor Revin would take on a Light while he was a Beacon? That seems like a lot of work to juggle all at once."

Skye had thought about it a lot, but had never come up with anything that made sense. She had never bothered Revin about it. "I'm not really sure, it does seem weird."

The conversation died off and they worked in comfortable silence. That's what Skye liked about working with Luken. He never tried to make unnecessary talk or anything. He enjoyed getting to focus as much as she did.

After about an hour, Luken held up one of the small black pieces and examined it. "The tracker is installed, you almost done with the comm installing?"

Skye nodded and quickly finished the communication on her earpiece and the two of them switched so that they could put their part in it.

The second time around went much quicker since they both knew what they were doing and how to do it. Within half an hour they had two earpieces with trackers and verbal communication. Luken had also been previously working on adding his hearing needs to his personal earpiece.

"I guess this is the moment of truth," Luken said, taking out his hearing devices and slipping his new earpiece into place, he had added something so that the signal transferred to both of his ears so he would only have to wear one.

"Can you hear me?" Skye asked to check Luken's regular hearing.

"Yep, at least that works fine. Let's test the mic and comm system. How about you go into the living room and see if we can communicate with them."

Skye walked out into the other room and put in her black earpiece. "Testing testing, Luken can you hear me?"

There was a quick burst of static but it cleared out quickly. "I can hear you Skye. How's it feel to basically be a genius?"

Skye had to smile at their accomplishment. There were plenty of commscreens and small headsets, but nothing to the extent they had made. "It feels pretty great, although I wouldn't say we're *geniuses*."

"Well, turn that little disk on the side and tell me then."

Skye brushed her finger over the disk and her commscreen buzzed in her pocket. She looked down and saw a satellite map of the overhead of the school with a red dot labeled 'Skye' in her position, and a green dot labeled 'Genius' almost right next to the red one. She zoomed in on the map and Luken's dot got slightly farther away until she could find the exact location of him. The tracker was working great.

"Okay, I'm not a genius, but you sure are," Skye said.

Luken laughed. "I'm pretty sure it takes two really smart people to make a genius, but thanks. I'm hoping to find a way to make a projector screen so you don't need your comm to see the tracker, but that's a big project."

Skye agreed and returned back into Luken's room and they both started tinkering with the projector screen idea and how to make it work.

They went through brainstorming and Skye tried to keep her mind on topic, but she was still bubbling with excitement from their achievement that she couldn't focus. And she guessed Luken was too because at one point they both looked up at the exact same time and burst into laughter.

"I still can't believe we did that!" Luken said, high fiving Skye.

"We got an amazing start done, we can add so much to these." Skye held up the small black device. "I already have so many ideas."

"I think we're really onto something big," Luken said. He took out his earpiece and put in his old hearing devices. "I would like to eventually just use the new one, that way I can have everything and still hear."

Skye paused. "How did it happen?" She wasn't sure if that was a rude question to ask, but she had been wanting to know since Luken had told her he lost his hearing.

Luken waited a minute before he spoke. "I was around ten, and we went to visit my sister for her birthday. She had graduated her Spark training the year before and was living at the Academy. Well, she was showing me her griffin and I got excited and ran up to it. I guess I scared it, because it screeched really loudly and I was right up next to it. The noise permanently damaged my cochlea, it's a part of my inner ear that senses sound and sends signals to my brain, without it, I can't hear."

Skye went silent, she had no idea what to say. Was that why Luken had been having such a hard time training with Phenton? It made sense now, he must have some sort of PTSD and that was what made training with his own griffin so hard. "I'm... sorry," she finally said.

He shrugged and turned back to his work, though Skye noticed his head sagged a little more than it had been before. She wished she hadn't brought it up.

After a few minutes of awkward silence, there was a knock at the door.

"Come in," Luken said.

Mentor Chloe came in with two plates of steaming dinner. "I figured you two must be hungry."

Skye looked out the window and saw that it had turned dark and the stars were just peeking out. She knew she should probably go back to her dorm, but the thought of eating dinner by herself made her only want to stay more. *And* it would be rude to leave when Mentor Chloe had made her dinner.

Skye said thank you and took the plate of steaming meat and pasta and placed it next to her so she could work as she ate.

"So what's been going on in here?" Luken's Mentor asked.

Luken handed her one of the small black devices they had been working on for so many hours and explained the basics to her.

She looked it over and placed it back down on the desk. "I'll never understand how you can do any of this."

The two of them continued to test new additions and fix the older ones until the sky was pitch black and Skye and Luken were practically falling asleep.

"We don't have school tomorrow so we can keep working then," Skye said, standing up and packing her items back into her backpack. She stuck her personal earpiece in her ear, said goodnight to Luken, and headed back across the hall.

When Skye opened the door, she saw a new note on the table and a half-finished cup of kopi, the steam still pouring from the top. Skye read the note.

Hey kid, I'm guessing you're at one of your Squad's dorms. I got to come back for a little bit but I have to get back to the Palace District soon. I can't really tell you anything, but there's something big going on and I don't know the next time I'll be back. If I'm not back by Monday, then just do some more inventing for your lesson. Sorry about all this, it's just too important to ignore.

-Revin

Skye examined the note, then the cup of steaming liquid, she had probably just missed Revin by a few minutes. She sighed in disappointment.

On the way to her room, Skye thought she heard the sound of a voice from Revin's room. Her ears perked up, was Revin still here?

She ran back to his room and knocked on the door. "Revin?" she asked.

The low voice continued to speak, Skye didn't think it sounded like Revin. She cracked the door open and saw that Revin's screen was still on. He must have forgotten to turn it off before he left.

Skye walked over to the screen as it repeated to the beginning of the video. A breath hitched in her throat when she saw the face on the screen. The spiked dark blond hair, the hard-angled face, the scars, and the penetrating teal eyes registered immediately in her brain. Daken Claw.

The video started replaying and Skye rushed to turn up the volume.

"Good morning Malco," Daken said, laughing a little at his own words. "You enjoying your change in the news? I couldn't *stand* your repetitive reports of nothing." His laughing expression turned serious. "You know what I want, Malco. And you know I have the guts to do what it takes. I've shown that much already."

The screen flashed to show footage from a few weeks before of the attack on the dragon enclosure. The fires and damage made Skye shudder as she remembered it.

Daken gave a sigh as the camera flashed back at him. "I've waited years for this to finally start, and I'm becoming more powerful by the *day*. You can tell your Beacons that if they had really wanted to avoid a war, they shouldn't have cast their only chance out the window." He paused. "I'm coming. Isarn deserves a chance to thrive, and that can only happen with me seated on the throne. The war's only begun Malco, and you can tell your Board that I'm ready for round two." His cold smirk flashed across his face as he whipped a knife from his sleeve and threw it at the camera.

Skye leapt away from the screen with a little scream.

The screen turned black for a few seconds and started replaying again. Skye quickly flicked it off and covered her mouth with her hands. This had to be what was such a big deal with the Beacons. How had the school not heard about this? She was on the cybernet a little every day, she should have heard about this, it should be all over the news. Unless…the public didn't know.

Skye grabbed her commscreen. "VACA, has there been any news on Daken Claw?"

"What? No. Nothing since the last attack. Why?"

"Nevermind." Skye flicked off her comm before VACA could keep talking. Things must be pretty complicated. She wanted to Comm Revin and make sure he was okay, and find out what Claw was talking about, but she guessed by now that she was definitely *not* supposed to have seen that, and Revin would be furious if she told him she'd watched it. And she couldn't tell her Squadron about the video, she didn't want them in trouble either.

Skye's head spun with decisions, confusion, and fear. Daken was so much more dangerous than everyone had thought. To them, he was a former politician gone crazy who destroyed government property one time, but now… he was a terrorist.

Skye shook her head and tightened her wrapped arms around her waist. She needed sleep. It was late and she had to help Luken tomorrow. But as she crawled into bed she couldn't help but think of the cruel smirk and hard teal eyes.

After a few attempts that ended in failure, Skye decided that sleep was overrated. She grabbed a snack from the kitchen and sat down at her desk. She sat there alone in a dark empty room, fear and uncertainty crawling through her.

She turned on her computer and scrolled around hoping to distract herself. It wasn't working. She spun in her chair and looked out the window, wishing now more than ever that she was home with her family.

Skye remembered the holoprojector she had brought with her. She quickly found it and clicked the button. The familiar photo of her and her little brother made her smile a small bit. She set it on her desk and flipped through all the photos on the drive. There were some of her and Dad, some with her mom, and some with Locke. Some of them were of her in the lab and playing around with different computers. The last photo on the drive was of Skye and her dad working in the lab together for the first time. Skye must have been around six or seven with her front teeth missing and a pair of safety glasses that barely fit. She held a wrench that was way too heavy for her, but she was smiling from ear to ear.

Skye smiled as she looked at the photo, letting her fingers graze through the thin blue-tinted air. A sharp pang of homesickness washed over her. She grabbed her commscreen and dialed her dad's number. She had barely commed her family since she had moved, she messaged them a few times a week, but she missed her dad's voice. She pressed call and immediately realized that it was 3 o'clock in the morning and that her dad would be asleep. She was about to hang up when she heard her dad's voice.

"Hello?"

"Hey Dad, sorry for waking you up."

"Oh, don't worry Rivet I was already up, working in the lab. What are you doing up? Is something wrong?"

Skye debated telling him about the video and about Daken, but she knew deep down that she couldn't. "No, I'm fine, I just couldn't sleep."

"So how's everything around there going?"

"Pretty well. My Mentor had to go up to the Palace District for some Beacon work, so he's been gone for a few days. One of my Squad members and I finished the earpieces that I was telling you about, we attached the tracker and the comming..." Skye told her dad about everything. She told him about Kade and her first out of dome flight, even

237

the part about her passing out and falling off. She told him about all of her training and about how her lessons were going. She told him all she knew about each of her Squad members and about Revin and how much he felt like a brother to her. She told him how much she missed them all and that she couldn't wait to get back in the lab with him.

Her dad listened patiently. When Skye finished he told her about his progress with his work and all about his new serums and experiments. By the time their conversation ended, the sun was just starting to come up.

"Thanks, Dad," said Skye.

"Thank *you,* Rivet. I've missed you so much. I'm so proud of you. Now go get some sleep, you seem to need it badly."

"I love you."

"Love you, too."

When he hung up, Skye felt so much better. She hadn't told her dad about the video, but even without it she felt less restless, less scared.

Skye decided that she wasn't going to get any sleep, it was already 6 in the morning and she doubted she'd be able to fall asleep. She settled for a cup of hot kopi and an excessively long shower. She got dressed in a pair of shorts and a t-shirt–the school didn't make them wear uniforms on weekends–and made a quick breakfast.

Just as Skye was clearing her dishes, she heard a knock at the door. She let Jayla in–still dressed in her pajamas still and talking a mile a minute.

"Hey Skye, I heard your Mentor left for a few days, do you-" Jayla stopped talking and stared at Skye for a solid 20 seconds.

Skye squirmed under her gaze.

"Something's wrong," Jayla said.

"N-nothing's wrong."

"Yes, there is. You obviously didn't sleep, and I think it has something to do with Mentor Revin or his work. And it's been bothering you since, I don't know, late last night."

"How-"

"I'm good, Zareb, very good." Jayla smirked and went into the kitchen to raid Skye's food supply. She poured herself a bowl of cereal and sat down at the counter. "So what's wrong?"

Skye sat down across from her. "Jayla... I don't think I can say... *I* wasn't even supposed to know."

Jayla set down her spoon. "It's probably a really big deal then, and if it is, you should tell your Squad, we're supposed to do that for each other."

"I know-"

"Great. Then spill it."

"Jayla, I don't want you to get in trouble, and this is so much bigger than you think."

"I'm not afraid of getting 'in trouble' I'm good at getting out of that sort of thing. And if it's as big as you say it is, then I sure as sked better know because you can't carry something that big on your own shoulders. I'm your best friend, I'm supposed to help you with these things."

Skye played the variables over in her head. She had told herself she wouldn't tell anyone about the video threat, but now that she looked it over... it *did* make more sense to tell her Squadron. But *only* her Squadron.

"Okay. I'll tell you, but we all need to be there, the whole Squad."

"Alright! We can all meet up here." She quickly messaged the rest of their Squad, and within a few minutes everyone was piled in Revin's room.

"Why are we in your Mentor's room?" Luken asked, trying to fix his bedhead.

"I need to show you something that's on his computer," Skye said.

"Ooh sounds like someone's turning into a rebel," Zaithrian laughed as Skye turned on the screen.

The video was easy to find, Skye turned on the volume and pressed play. The five teens crowded around to see.

No one spoke as the video played through, no one knew what to say. Even after it had ended, not one of them had anything to say for a decent time. When someone finally said something, it was Daria

"So he wants revenge then?" she asked.

"I would guess that since he just threatened the Vire and pretty much all of Isarn," Jayla said.

"He didn't actually threaten Isarn," Luken said. "He said he wants to help Isarn, just not through the Vire."

"I don't care who he's threatening," Zaithrian snapped. "He's a murderer, and he needs to be taken down."

"How the sked are we supposed to do that?" Jayla said.

Everyone looked at Zaithrian. But he was looking at Skye. "What do you think?"

"Wait. You're asking me?"

"You have the most connection to a Beacon on the Board, you seem like the one for the job," Zaithrian said.

"What job?"

"We're obviously going to do something about this," Jayla said.

"Are you saying you want to fight him?"

Jayla was about to say yes, but Luken clapped his hand over her mouth. "No, we are definitely not. But I'm sure there's something we can do- EW!" Luken jerked his hand from Jayla's mouth and started wiping it on his pants. "Did you seriously just lick me?"

"Yes I did, that should teach you not to shut me up."

"I don't think anyone could *ever* do that," Zaithrian said.

"Guys cut it out," Daria said. "What are you saying exactly?"

"What *I'm* saying," said Luken. "Is that Skye's friend is disgusting."

Jayla shot him a look.

"What we're saying is that we're going to do something about this instead of sitting around ignoring the fact that Isarn is now in jeopardy," Zaithrian said.

"Have you asked Mentor Revin about it?" Daria asked.

Skye shook her head. "I haven't talked to him since he left the other day. Plus, I doubt he'd tell me anything."

"True. Adults are annoying like that," Jayla complained.

Luken rubbed his chin. "I'm not sure what we could accomplish if we were going to make a real difference with this issue, this seems like something we really can't have an impact on."

"Well we have to do *something*. I'm not going to just sit here as this guy threatens my home," Zaithrian said, crossing his arms.

After some silence filled with thinking, Jayla spoke up. "Is Daken Claw really his name?"

Luken gave her a puzzled look. "Why wouldn't it be?"

"Because it seems *super* stereotypical that this guy is evil and has literally the most evil sounding name in history."

"You want me to check for you?" Skye asked.

"Yeah I really want to know now, that *can't* be real," she said.

Skye quickly searched 'is Daken Claw's real name Daken Claw?' and clicked on the first article.

"It says here that Daken is his real first name, but he changed his last name before he graduated Spark level to Claw, which was his mother's last name."

"Well what was his real name then?" Jayla asked. "It's probably something super embarrassing!"

"I don't see how this is helping the issue here," Daria said.

"Oh come on, this is helping me plenty."

Skye sighed and typed in the question. It was much harder to find her answer, it wasn't listed on the first ten sites she checked. Eventually she found one.

"Uhhhhh... he changed his name at a young age blah blah blah... okay, says he changed his name from his father's to his mother's before he graduated and has been known as Claw ever since. His parents divorced when he was very young... blah blah blah... found it! His mother's name was Valure Claw and his father is-" Skye's eyes grew wide and she shot up from the chair.

"What? What's wrong Skye?" Jayla asked, gripping Skye's arm to steady her.

"No, that has to be wrong," Skye mumbled.

"What? What does it say?"

Zaithrian ran up to the computer and read the name. "It says Dr. Carsten Zareb."

Skye swallowed hard. "My dad."

CHAPTER THIRTY-ONE

Skye's head was spinning. That had to be wrong. It was. It *had* to be. Her dad couldn't- No.

"It's okay Skye," Jayla said, making Skye sit down on the bed.

"That can't be right. There... there has to be another Carsten Zareb. I can't have another brother- I *don't* have another brother."

"He's only your half-brother, if he's related to you at all," Luken said, already looking on the computer for conformation.

Skye couldn't wrap her head around it. Her dad couldn't have had another child and never told her about it. Could he? She did the math in her head, Daken was about ten years older than her. It was possible.

None of this was making any sense. Her father had lied to her. Her brother was Daken Claw. She was related to a terrorist. It had to be fake. Her dad wouldn't keep something like that from her.

"Skye, I checked the name link... It's true," Luken said, giving her his most reassuring look.

There it was. The nail in her coffin. Skye burst from her seat and ran out the door.

She darted from her dorm, ignoring her friends' calls. She sprinted through the building. She forced herself to keep running. It helped her not to think. She bumped into students and Mentors, but she didn't bother apologizing.

She collapsed behind a tree near the edge of the campus, her racing heart was pounding and her breaths seemed too shallow.

This was making no sense at all. How could she have another brother? Why had her dad never told her he had been married? Why hadn't he told her he had another child? And that that child was kind of the biggest rebel in all of Isarn.

She placed her head between her knees. Why couldn't this be like a math problem? A logical question that has a logical answer. Why did everything have to be so messed up?

Why did this have to happen to her? Just when she was starting to feel normal, when she had made friends, had a great Mentor, and- just why? That was the only question that she really kept asking herself.

"I thought I'd find you here."

Skye looked up. It was Jayla.

She wiped her nose. "I'm sor-"

"No."

"No?"

Jayla sat down next to her. "No. Don't apologize for anything. Not for freaking out, for running away, don't. Your reaction was completely normal. If anyone should be sorry it's me."

"It's not your fault. I don't think any of this is really anyone's fault... maybe my dad's but..."

"If I didn't make you look that up-"

"As much as I wish it did, not knowing something doesn't change that fact that it happened. I still have a terrorist brother, even if I never found out or not."

Jayla gripped Skye's hand. "I know you're not okay, but can I help? Is there anything I can do? I'll listen if that's all you want."

Skye sighed. "That would be nice Jayla." Skye told Jayla whatever she felt. She asked her questions that she knew she would never be able to answer. Jayla proved to be the best listener Skye had ever met.

"I just... I don't know why it had to be my dad. My dad is everything to me, I loved him, I still do... I think I do. Ugh, I don't know."

Jayla sat quiet for a few minutes. "Are you going to talk with him?"

Skye bit her lip. She *should* talk to her dad... but even though she knew the truth, hearing her dad say those words would really make them final. Was she ready for that? And besides, she would need to do that in person, not over a commscreen. And besides the fact that her mentor was out of town, she didn't feel the same burning ache for home she had felt last night.

"You know what? Don't. Not yet at least. Let it sit for a little while. Let's do something fun. Let's have a sleepover. Me, you and Dar, and we won't even mention the you know what. We can just have fun and maybe stay up all night being stupid. What do you say?"

Skye smiled, the last of her tears spilling over. "Thank you Jayla, you're really the best friend anyone could ever ask for."

Jayla hugged her. "I'll always be here for you Skye, always."

CHAPTER THIRTY-TWO

Do I really even need to pack anything?" Skye asked. "We live two seconds from each other."

Jayla and Daria both sat on her bed. It had been a hectic day, Skye's friends had all agreed that Skye should wait to talk to her dad. They all had hugged her and said it would be okay, Skye knew it probably wouldn't, at least not for a while, but it was nice to hear it anyway. Everyone had forced Skye to get some sleep, but she only managed an hour or two before the thoughts in her mind creeped into her dreams. Skye had spent most of the remainder of the day trying to get her mind off of everything, and she had spent the time with Luken working on their earpieces. Math and science always had helped Skye take her mind off of things like that.

Jayla flipped through her closet. "Not really. Just wear your pajamas and bring a bunch of pillows and blankets.

Once all three of them had formed a pile of bedding on Jayla's floor, it was getting dark.

"Please girls, make sure you actually sleep tonight," Mentor Ariel said as they went into Jayla's room after dinner.

"Yeah, yeah. Aye, aye Captain," Jayla said, saluting her Mentor mockingly. "Have you ever even been to a sleepover?"

"Yes, Miss Payge, I have, and that's exactly why I advise you on the subject."

Jayla pulled the two girls into her room before her Mentor could ruin their night.

"I hate it when she does that," Jayla said, jumping into the pile of pillows.

"When she does what?" Skye asked sitting on the bed.

Jayla faked Mentor Ariel's crisp accent. "Miss Payge, oh Miss Payge, make sure to sleep. Here's some more homework, Jayla dear. I wish you would have the smallest pinch of respect for your elders. Jayla Payge, I am quite cross with you!"

Everyone burst into laughter at the last one.

The three made a bed big enough for them all to sit on and watch a movie. Jayla had suggested one that all of them had seen before so they could talk as they watched it. They mostly ate snacks and did each other's hair, things anyone would do at a sleepover.

"What do we do now?" Jayla asked after the movie was over.

Both girls shrugged.

Jayla started doing handstands and practiced flipping back onto her feet. After a multitude of amusing failures, she managed to land it, using the pillow pile as a crash pad. She then showed Daria and Skye her backflip, frontflip, handspring, aerial, and backhandspring.

"How did you learn to do all that?" Daria asked.

Jayla paused. "I... dunno, I just... learned it I guess."

Something about the way Jayla had said it sounded like she was lying, but Skye decided to abandon it.

"I have an idea," Skye said, needing to keep herself distracted.

Jayla perked up. "Is it prank-calling one of the boys? Cause I am *so* in."

"Uh, no. But I guess we could do that if you want."

"Oh yes, I want." Jayla grabbed her commscreen. "Who first?"

"Guys, we should leave the boys alone," Daria said.

"Geez, Dar, live a little," Jayla said. "Let's call Zaith, he'll probably be awake."

Jayla set her comm to ghost mode so Zaithrian wouldn't see her contact number and dialed. It rang for a few seconds, before they heard him answer.

"Hello?" he asked.

Jayla pinched her nose to make her voice higher. "Hello sir, this is uh… Alan Baker from…the toilet supplies company. We received a notice that you bought 1,000 orders of toilet paper. We were just checking in on you to finalize your purchase. We have your toilet paper outside your door-"

"Go to bed Jayla," Zaithrian said, hanging up.

Everyone burst into laughter.

"That was hilarious," Jayla said, wiping tears from her eyes.

"Oh my gosh, he sounded so done with you," Skye said.

"Here Skye, you do Luken," Jayla said, handing Skye her commscreen.

"Should I just do the same thing you did?" she asked, putting in Luken's number.

"No, no, I have a better idea," Daria said, shyly.

The other two girls were surprised, but when Daria explained her idea, they all agreed it would be hilarious.

Skye lowered her voice and waited for Luken to answer.

"Hello?" he answered, sounding very tired.

"I regret to inform you that-"

He yawned. "You girls are psychos. Leave me alone, I'm trying to sleep." He hung up.

Everyone burst into laughter again.

Eventually they put on another movie and by the time it was over Daria and Jayla had both fallen asleep.

Skye sat alone, wide awake and more anxious than ever. As much as she had wanted to put the whole Daken Claw mess out of the picture, she couldn't. It was huge. And it scared her. She thought of her dad, had he told her mom? Or was she just as clueless as Skye had been. Or maybe she did know and had agreed not to tell them. Skye deep down hoped her mom hadn't known, that way she couldn't have lied to her. But that was a long shot.

Her thoughts were interrupted by her commscreen's message ding. It was from Revin.

Hey kid, sorry to interrupt your sleepover, but I just got home and need to talk to you for a minute. And can you bring Jayla? This has to do with her too.

Skye glanced at the time, it was 3 in the morning. But if Revin needed her this late, it had to be urgent.

She shook Jayla awake and showed her the text.

"Hmm. Weird," Jayla said, rubbing her eyes and getting up. "Let's go, it sounds important."

"Should we tell Daria?" Skye asked.

Jayla shrugged. "I don't think we should wake her up just to talk to Mentor Revin."

The two of them tiptoed through Jayla's house and out the door. The hallway was lit with only one light, but they could easily see in the dimness.

Suddenly, the light flicked off and the hallway was pitchblack. Skye felt a hand cup over her mouth and another grip her waist. She thrust against her capturer, trying to break free from their vice-like grip. The hand over her mouth muffled her screams.

Skye felt herself being lifted off the ground. She kicked blindly at whoever was holding her. She still couldn't see in the dark, but her eyes could just make out another struggling figure a few feet from her.

She felt a blind fold going over her eyes and the person holding her removed their hand just long enough for them to shove a gag in her mouth.

Her screams were even more muffled from before. She felt herself being picked up and carried. The capturer gripped her hand and pressed her finger against a panel. She heard a door open and a faint light shone through her blindfold.

Fear rose through her body like a current. She kicked and squirmed trying to get free, but she failed.

She was brought through another door. The kidnapper gripped her wrists and released their hold on her waist, letting her fall to the floor. She felt her wrists being tied and was shoved down onto a chair. The stranger pressed her against the back of the chair and tied her waist to it. They tied her ankles to the chair legs.

Skye's heart pounded in her ears. She thrashed against the rope bonds but the knots held firm.

Who were these people? And what were they doing to her?

Skye's blindfold was suddenly ripped off and she squinted against the harsh light. When she looked up, she saw two smug-faced, arm-crossed, smirking boys. Zaithrian and Luken.

CHAPTER THIRTY-THREE

The two boys burst into laughter and high fived each other. They stood there and let Skye and Jayla stare at them in pure shock. Zaithrian pulled out Skye's gag as Luken pulled out Jayla's.

"WHAT THE SKED IS WRONG WITH YOU!" they both yelled at the same time.

The boys doubled over with laughter.

"Their faces!" Luken said. "Oh this is too good!"

Zaithrian patted him on the back and smirked approvingly.

"What is going on?" Jayla yelled, trying to break free from her chair.

"Shh, don't go waking up the whole school," Zaithrian said.

"What were you thinking!" Skye said.

"That we would beat you at your own game," Zaithrian said. "And I think we did pretty well."

"Oh my gosh. You freaking kidnapped us!" Jayla said, struggling to fight her bonds and murder both of them.

"Yes we did, and I will treasure that moment always," Luken said.

Skye glared at them. They looked so ornery, both of them standing side by side with smirks and all black clothes.

"But how did you know I was awake? And the message was from Revin-"

"And why are we still tied up!" Jayla said.

"I think if we untied you, you'd probably kill us," Luken said.

"I *definitely* would," she shot back.

"Well, after you prank called me, I messaged Luken and said to watch out for you guys," Zaithrian said. "Then we got together and planned out this."

"I made my commscreen say Mentor Revin's name, I knew you wouldn't go anywhere we told you to go in the middle of the night," Luken said. "And I temporarily knocked out the security cameras in the hallway so no one would come and shoot us."

"You guys are jerks, you know that right?" Jayla said.

"We sure do," Zaithrian said.

"Can you get us out of these chairs now?" Skye asked.

"Hmm what do you think, Luken? Should we let them out?"

"I don't know, maybe we should leave them there."

Zaithrian nodded. "Good with me."

"If you leave I'll-"

"Relax, Jayla," Luken said, cutting off her threat.

Luken untied her and Zaithrian started on Skye's wrists.

"That was dirty play boys," Jayla said, rubbing her wrists as Luken untied her feet.

"Maybe, but it was fun getting the jump on you. I was just glad Jayla didn't lick me," Luken said.

"That's why I insisted I should grab Skye," Zaithrian said, finishing up his job.

"I'm sure that was the reason," Luken said with a smirk.

"Can we go back to sleep now?" Jayla asked.

"Yeah, go ahead, go back to your girly camp out where you giggle and paint each other's nails and talk about boys all night," Zaith said.

Jayla glared at him, then walked up and punched him in the stomach. Hard.

Zaithrian bent over, coughing and trying to regain his breath. Luken jumped back a step from Jayla.

"I told you I was saving that punch, and I'm glad I did."

Zaithrian stood back up and gave a small, strained laugh. "I forgot about that."

"You totally deserved it," Luken assured him, giving Jayla a thumbs up.

Jayla rolled her eyes, trying to hide her grin. "Can it, Smart Boy, you could be next. C'mon

Skye, let's leave these pitiful males to their sad form of enjoyment."

Jayla pulled her out of the room. Skye looked back to Zaith. He stood up and clutched his stomach. He met her eyes and gave her a small, reassuring smile. Skye could tell it said, "sorry" and "it's gonna be okay" at the same time. She was almost grateful for it.

After leaving Skye's dorm, the girls went back to Jayla's room where Daria was still asleep. As soon as Skye shut the door, Jayla burst into laughter. That sent Skye over, and soon they were both caught in an endless cycle.

"That was pretty good," Skye admitted.

"Dude, Smart Boy is so much stronger than he looks, I was kicking and thrashing like crazy and he held on."

"I'm surprised you didn't lick him." Skye slid back under the blanket.

"I would've but I didn't know where that hand had been." Jayla scrunched up her nose and layed down next to Skye.

There was a long pause where no one spoke, Skye wondered if Jayla had fallen asleep.

"Are we gonna get the boys back?" Jayla asked.

Skye thought for a minute. "I don't think we can beat them at a prank war, it's probably best to leave it at this."

"I guess so. Maybe I'll figure something big out eventually."

Jayla soon fell asleep. When Skye finally drifted off, she could still feel the pressure of Zaithrian's hands gripping her.

CHAPTER THIRTY-FOUR

The next morning, Skye and Jayla slept in until noon. When they finally got up, they were told Daria had gone back to her dorm hours before.

"Oh, we should probably tell her what happened last night," Skye said as the two of them ate their breakfast for lunch.

"Eh, she'll find out eventually." Jayla slurped her milk from the bottom of the bowl.

"Good afternoon girls, how was your night?" Mentor Ariel said, walking in.

Skye and Jayla shared a look.

"It was great," Skye said. "Thanks for having me."

"You're quite welcome dear. Oh I forgot to mention, your Mentor wanted me to let you know that he got back this morning, he said he had something important to talk about."

"He's back?" Skye gave Jayla a look that told her she wanted to leave.

"Yeah, go get out of my house you imp," Jayla said with a dismissive wave of her hand. "You can get your stuff later."

Skye ran out the door and across the hall. When she opened the door, Revin was sitting on the couch, doing nothing.

His head shot up. "Hey, kid."

Skye smiled. Her eyes were just starting to fill with tears. "Hi."

Revin stood up and walked over to her. "Skye-"

Skye launched herself at him and wrapped her arms firmly around him in a hug.

Revin stood stiff for a minute, then laughed and hugged her back. "I wasn't gone *that* long was I?"

"I just... missed you."

"Missed you too, kid. Being a Beacon sure doesn't pay enough, if you know what I mean."

Skye broke off and wiped her nose. "I think I know what you mean."

His smile faded. "Skye, I have to tell you something very important." Revin made her sit down.

Skye fiddled with her fingers. "I already know."

"What? I just found out, how could you know?"

"I... saw the video on your computer, I was searching something and found out that Daken Claw is my... brother."

Revin furrowed his brow. "What? That's a joke. How is Claw your brother?"

Now it was Skye's turn to be confused. "Isn't that what you were going to tell me?"

"No...no there's-" He sighed and ran a hand through his hair. "I guess I don't need to explain this Claw mess do I?"

"Are you mad?"

"I...no. I could be, I *should* be, but I'm not. But Skye I need to tell you something." He seemed to be unsure of how to say the following words. "Daken has your father."

Skye froze. Her words came out barely above a whisper. "What?"

Revin sighed. "Yesterday afternoon Dr. Carsten Zareb left for a meeting in the Medical District to go over a new serum. Four other scientists were meeting with him. None of them showed up to the meeting." Not thirty minutes ago, The Board received a video sent from an unidentified location...it was sent from your father, and showed him and the other scientists imprisoned by Claw. He took them. We don't know why yet, but it's not a coincidence that he took five of the leading scientists in biological enhancement."

Skye sat speechless. Her eyes welled with tears. Daken had her dad. And he was going to use him.

"Can I see the video?" The words barely came out more than a whisper.

Revin nodded and led her to the computer in his room.

The video started. Skye sucked in a breath.

"This is Dr. Carsten Zareb," her dad said. The room around him was dark and the screen he was using was cutting in and out. "I was taken by Claw … there are others … we have … using for …" static took over for a few seconds. Then the audio returned, but no picture.

"What did I say about breaking protocol?" A female voice called. "You break protocol, and you suffer the con- …"

The audio cut again. This had to be a terrible camera, not the same made by Daken for sure. Had her dad put it together?

The video turned on again and her dad was huddled in front of the camera. "You have to come. He's forcing us to make… he'll kill them … our coordinates are …"

"Hiding something, Zareb?" the woman sneered.

The last thing Skye heard before the video cut completely, was the sound of a gunshot and her dad screaming.

Skye fell onto the bed and burst into sobs.

"Hey, it'll be okay." Revin sat next to her. "They need him. They won't hurt him beyond repair. And Isarn needs him, we're going to do everything we can to get him and the other scientists home. Okay?"

Skye couldn't speak. Her mind was filled with hatred, fear, worry, anger, and confusion. A wave of white heat burned in the back of her mind. How could Daken have her dad? How could he be doing that to him? She had just talked to him two days ago. And now he was being held captive by her evil half brother. This was beyond anything Skye could ever imagine.

"Does my family know? Have you told them yet?"

Revin nodded. "We have Beacons driving down to break the news to all the families."

The way he said it sounded like they were already dead. Like soldiers who'd fought valiantly and had paid the price.

When Skye finally regained her thoughts, she told Revin everything. About finding the video, about telling her Squad, and about finding out Daken was her half-brother.

Revin listened patiently, not interrupting once. When Skye finished, he wrapped an arm over her shoulder. "I'm sorry Skye, I wish it wasn't like this."

"I don't know what to do," Skye whispered, feeling like she might cry again.

"I don't know either. But we'll figure it out, we're ingenuitive, that's what we do."

Skye was silent, an idea was bubbling up in her mind. She had just maybe found a way to fix at least one of her problems.

Skye stood up from the bed. "Thank you Revin. I needed that." She ran into her room to work on her plan. She was going to figure it out. She was going to get her dad back, and she knew just how.

CHAPTER THIRTY-FIVE

Skye's commscreen hadn't stopped buzzing with messages from her mom and Locke since she sat down. She'd thought about answering them, but she just knew that if she looked at them, she would break into sobbs. She didn't have time to cry right now.

"Hey Skye, I got Mentor Ariel to get some doughnuts, figured you might need some." Jayla walked into Skye's room and tossed a small white box on her desk.

Skye looked up. "Thanks Jayla, but I'm not really hungry right now."

Jayla sat down on her desk and opened the box. Taking the swirl of fried dough and shoved it into her mouth, spraying powdered sugar all over herself.

"You've been in here for 5 hours. Eat."

Skye sighed and nibbled on the pastry.

"What happened now? You leave my dorm and don't come back. I bring you food, your favorite food I might add, and you don't eat it. And you've been in the same spot for longer than I have sat still my entire life. Something is wrong, and if you don't tell me what it is I'll pester you for the rest of the day."

Skye glared at her. "Daken Claw has my dad held captive and is forcing him to make something that will most likely destroy Isarn and kill tons of people. And if I don't figure out how to get him back, he's going to be killed. Does that suffice your curiosity?"

Jayla got quiet. "Skye, you *really* need that doughnut."

"Do you have to make this a joke? It's not funny Jayla! None of this is! You don't understand what's going through my mind right now because you don't *know*. You don't know what this is like for me. My dad is in a prison, probably chained to the wall by a maniac, who is also my brother. This isn't a joke, this is the real world Jayla. And you don't understand that."

Skye didn't know why she was yelling, but it felt good. It felt too good for her to stop. And soon they both were yelling.

Jayla's eyes filled with rage. "You think I don't know what the real world is? Well guess what Skye, I've seen more of this world's reality than you would ever begin to imagine. I've seen people claw at each other like dogs for a few crumbs. I've wrung my hands until they bled just trying to earn my keep. I've been on the verge of death and then cast out like a piece of trash. Skye, if I know one thing about this world it's that it hates me. It has beaten me over and over without mercy. So don't say I don't know what the real world is like because that's all my life has ever been."

Jayla's eyes burned with tears as she burst out the door.

Skye stared at the spot where her best friend had just stood. What had she done? How could Skye have said that to her?

She collapsed back into her chair and cried into her hands. What was she doing wrong? Her life was in ruins. It had been so good only three days ago, how had everything gone downhill so fast?

Skye wiped her eyes. She needed to focus, she could worry about Jayla later. She returned to her computer work, but she had a sick feeling in the pit of her stomach the entire time. Her mind kept wandering over to the words Jayla had said. Had all that really happened to Jayla? She really didn't know her best friend. Or maybe they weren't best friends anymore.

After a few hours of working on her computer, Skye heard Revin knock on her door. Skye quickly flicked off the screen as Revin walked in.

"Got you dinner," he said. "What's been going on in here for the past 8 hours?"

Skye shrugged. "Just doing some homework." She knew she was absolutely awful at lying, but she couldn't let Revin know what she was doing.

"Well, I'm here if you need any help. I'm going to head to bed early, I don't know if I'll get called back over to the Palace District."

"Goodnight."

"Night, kid."

Once Skye was sure Revin was asleep, she messaged her Squad to come over. Instead of texting Jayla, she decided to go ask her in person. When she knocked on Jayla's door, she was greeted by Mentor Ariel.

"Hi, is Jayla able to come over?"

"Sorry dear, Jayla went to bed a little while ago. Would you like me to wake her up?"

"No no, it's fine, I'll see her tomorrow."

As Skye walked away, she was half disappointed and half relieved. As much as she wanted to fix things with Jayla, there was still the tiniest part of her that was mad and scared and confused.

Soon Luken, Daria, and Zaithrian were all piled in Skye's room.

Skye filled them in on her dad and the other scientists' capture and showed them the video.

"What are we going to do?" Zaithrian asked, clenching his jaw.

"I'm making a plan," Skye said. "And I'm going to need all of your help to pull it off."

"Well, that obviously goes without saying," Luken said. "What about Jayla? Where is she?"

"I'll fill Jayla in later," Skye said, hoping someone would volunteer instead. No one did, so she continued.

"Revin said the Beacons and Flames are planning a mission. The thing is, that could take who knows how long, and I want... I *need* to get my father back. If I can hack into the ID tracker in his finger, we can pinpoint his location and extract him."

"Is that really a good idea?" Daria asked. "If they're going to send the Flames in we shouldn't interfere."

Skye sighed. "Look, I know it's not the best plan, but Daken has my dad and I couldn't live with myself if he gets hurt and I could have done something about it. You don't have to help, this will be dangerous, rebellious, and if we get caught we'll be in huge trouble, but I'm willing to risk it. If you don't want to, I only ask that you don't rat me out, because *I* need to do this. The choice is yours."

"Oh come on Skye, you know us, we'll stand by you till the end. No matter what." Luken said.

Zaithrian nodded. "He's right. We're with you."

Daria's gaze turned hard. "I'm with you too. We'll get them back."

"Or we'll die trying."

Everyone turned to see Jayla leaned against the door frame. She walked over to them, avoiding eye contact with Skye. "I heard everything. I'm coming too."

Skye smiled at Jayla, she only turned her gaze in return. She'd have to worry about that later. In the meantime, she had to prepare for possibly the worst idea she had ever had.

"What do you have so far?" Zaithrian asked, pulling up a chair and sitting at Skye's desk.

"Um. I've started a plan but I know you're supposed to be the Leader-"

He shook his head. "Just because I'm the Leader doesn't mean no one else can make the plans. I want to hear what you have."

Skye nodded. "Okay. I've been doing some research, we can track his ID chip, but it's difficult to get into secure records, so I'm going to access it from Revin's computer, he should have clearance since he's on the Board of Beacons."

Zaithrian nodded and rubbed his jaw. "That could work."

"What should I do?" Luken asked.

"I need you to make three more earpieces for the rest of them, all they need is the tracker and comms, but if you can make the eyescreens that would be amazing."

"So what about the rest of us?" Daria asked.

"Someone can help Luken assemble the earpieces, they aren't hard to put together if you know what to do. You can have that job, Jayla."

She nodded stiffly.

"I've already figured out the creature problem. We have a patrol mission this Tuesday at 3 pm, we can go to find my dad instead of our patrol."

"What about the trackers?" Zaithrian asked. "They'll send out a search party if we turn them off."

"I can program them on the spot to make it look like we're going on our planned route."

"Are you saying we need to finish the earpieces in two days?" Luken asked.

Skye nodded. "I know it's a lot to ask, but it's our only chance. And I'll help you as soon as I can get my dad's coordinates."

"And what should I do?" Daria asked.

Skye swallowed hard. "We're going to need weapons... just in case we do get caught."

Everyone became quiet.

Daria nodded. "I'll see what I can find."

"Zaith, if you can start on a strategy for our flight, that would be great."

He nodded. "I can do that."

"Does everyone understand their jobs?" Skye asked, looking over the group.

They all nodded and got to work.

Luken took Jayla to his dorm so they could work on the earpieces. Daria didn't tell them where she was going to get the weapons, but Skye guessed she was going to the Stealth tower where they had target practice when their Squad had Mentor Baylyne.

Zaithrian went to his room to start on a strategy. He wouldn't be able to do too much until Skye had her dad's coordinates, but he tried to get a general idea on how this was going to go.

Once everyone was gone, Skye got ready for her job. It was going to be simple enough, get onto the files from Revin's computer, download them onto a drive, and get out. The only catch was that Revin was sleeping in the room and if she woke him up… she'd be in *big* trouble.

She could possibly wait until Revin wouldn't be asleep in the room, but she didn't have time, she needed the coordinates as soon as possible.

She found a blank drive and fingered it nervously as she came to Revin's door. She knew the door squeaked like mad, so she'd have to be slow. She held her ear against the door. She could hear Revin's soft snoring.

She opened the door a crack and whispered a silent prayer to the Eagles. Her heartbeat thudded against her chest so loudly she could barely hear. Bit by bit and creek by creek, it opened slowly. The thin stream of light widened as it flowed through the crack into Revin's dark room.

Once it was wide enough for Skye to slip through she sucked in a breath and squeezed in. She tiptoed through the room, her eyes never leaving her Mentor's sleeping form.

She turned on the computer and started searching through his files. She felt sick to her stomach as she looked through private files. She knew it was wrong. She hated that she was doing something wrong. But she had to. She needed to get her dad back, and she needed him back as soon as possible. Who knew how long it would take the Beacons to get him home? They would be careful and methodical and they would plan everything out to the final detail. But they might be too late.

Revin rolled over in his sleep and Skye's heart leapt into her throat. She almost spit it out when he started mumbling.

She couldn't make out all of what he was saying in his sleep, but she heard the word 'sorry' said a few times. She wondered what kind of nightmare Revin was having.

Skye was sweating so much her fingers were slipping on the keys. What would she do if Revin woke up?

Finally, she found what she was looking for. She shoved the drive into the computer and hit download. After a few minutes of her being a nervous wreck, the green bar on the screen filled and she grabbed her drive.

She flicked off of the files and back to Revin's homescreen. She stopped when she saw that his background was a picture she had taken of the two of them. It was the day he had taken her to one of the nearby towns to celebrate the Half Year Festival. She was smiling and he was making a ridiculous face. It was the best memory they had together.

Looking at the picture only made her feel more sick for stealing off his computer. She slipped out the door. *I'm doing this for Dad*, she reminded herself.

She made her way back to her room and brought up the file. After a few minutes, she could track her dad's coordinates.

"VACA, bring up the world map."

A 3D map of the world popped up on Skye's screen. "Show me where these coordinates are." Skye typed them in and the map spun until a dot appeared on a small island in the middle of the ocean.

"What am I looking at, VACA?"

"This is the island of Dalren, it is unclaimed by any of the continents and is not known to house any intelligent life forms by the Isarnian government.

Skye chewed on her fingernail. "That's where Daken has my dad."

She turned off the screen and commed her Squad.

She updated them on what she had found, and learned that Luken and Jayla had made some progress with the earpieces, and Daria had gotten them some weapons and stashed them in her room for later.

Skye glanced at the clock. "It's pretty late, let's all get some sleep and we can work on our plan tomorrow."

Everyone left the group call except for Skye and Luken.

"I had an idea for how to add the eye screens in," Luken said.

"That's great! Can you do it?"

"I'll need your help. But I also had another idea. What if we put VACA in them?"

"You want to put VACA in the earpieces?" Skye had never thought of it, but the idea made sense.

"Well, think about it, we wouldn't need to put access buttons, we could just tell VACA to turn it on. The only concern is the time frame."

"Is it even possible?"

"Anything's possible, you know that better than anybody."

Skye rubbed her forehead. "If we want to do this before Tuesday, we need to hurry. Big time."

"How about we try it? Jayla can finish the last two earpieces tomorrow, and we can work on the VACA upgrade."

"I don't know…"

"Skye." Luken's voice came through the commscreen with a plea. "This could solve all of the problems I'm having with the eye screens. It's worth a shot at least."

"I guess that means we won't be getting any sleep?"

"The door's unlocked."

CHAPTER THIRTY-SIX

Skye's eyes opened slowly. Where was she? She looked around her. She was at Luken's desk, her work was still sprawled out in front of her, and Luken was sleeping on the other side of the desk.

They must have fallen asleep while working. Skye yawned and checked the time on her commscreen. Her eyes shot open and she jumped up from her seat.

"Luken! We have morning announcements in five minutes!"

He lifted his head up. "What?"

Skye shoved the commscreen in his face. "We're going to be late for school!"

"Sked!" He jumped up and started rummaging through his drawers for his uniform.

Skye ran to her dorm and got dressed as quickly as possible. She threw on her boots and ran out the door, pulling her hair up as she went.

The announcements had just started when Skye found the rest of her Squadron. Luken came running up a few seconds later.

"What happened to you two?" Zaithrian asked.

"We might have stayed up late working," Skye said.

"*Again*?"

Luken sighed. "Again."

"Did you make any progress?"

Skye and Luken shared a look and sighed. They hadn't made much.

The announcements lasted about fifteen minutes. Skye's Squadron was announced to have their first patrol the following day. Skye couldn't help but feel nervous about the whole mess. She was breaking a direct order, probably expel worthy, and she was making her entire Squad do it too. At least she was going to get her dad back. She hoped.

She still hadn't fixed things with Jayla, she knew she should before they left but… was she ready for that? She wanted her and Jayla to get along, but what Jayla had said about her past made Skye sick to her stomach. It almost didn't sound real, but the way she had said made Skye sure Jayla had actually gone through all of that. She had never seen Jayla like that, she'd never seen Jayla cry, yell at her, or even get mad at her. It scared her that this meant so much to Jayla.

Skye knew she needed to talk with her soon, but something in her mind wouldn't let her. Maybe it was selfishness or bitterness, she didn't know, but she hated that it was keeping her away from her best friend. Besides, she had to help Luken as soon as she was done with her classes.

"See you guys at lunch," Daria said as they made their ways to their towers.

After Skye had endured her enormous trek to her classroom floor, she slid into her desk.

"Where were you last night?" Revin asked.

Skye's stomach flipped. She probably shouldn't have stayed all night at Luken's dorm alone without telling Revin. "Sorry. Luken and I were just working on the earpieces. I've been trying to connect VACA to the earpieces, but it's going slower than I'd hoped."

He sighed and nodded. "How are you doing with...everything?"

Skye knew what he meant. She had been trying to block all of that out of her mind, she knew she wouldn't be able to focus on getting him back if she let herself worry about him. But the thought of her dad brought a flood of emotions that crashed against her heart.

She choked on her words. "I'm okay."

"I have a lesson, but if you don't feel up to it-"

"No, no. I want to do the lesson." Skye needed to keep her mind busy. A mind left free to think whatever it wanted was undoubtedly more dangerous than anything else.

He nodded and silently gave her a tablet with her lesson on it.

Skye immediately got to work. It was one of the more common things Revin had her do: a timed multi-layered puzzle.

Unlike every other puzzle Revin had given her, Skye couldn't get herself to find the solutions. She couldn't solve it.

"Aaaaand time," Revin said, calling the end of her timer.

Skye shook her head. "What did I do wrong? Why couldn't I do it?"

"Skye, you can't work on a brain like that."

She rolled her eyes. "My brain is fine, Revin."

"How late did you stay up last night?"

Skye shrugged. "Until three or four maybe."

"You see kid, you match lack of sleep with emotional distress on a maximum level, and bingo, you get failure to do the simplest things."

"I wouldn't call that a simple test," Skye said, pulling up the tablet with the unfinished puzzle.

"I would." Revin swiped a few pieces and finished the puzzle in under a minute. "Skye, I have given you problems that Professional Educators couldn't solve. But this? This is from a ten year old's Spark worksheet."

Skye stared at him blankly.

Revin sighed. "Kid, whatever happens... don't let it change you. Not in a way that counts."

The bell rang and Skye left, she wasn't sure what Revin meant, but somehow she knew he must have gone through something like what she was.

* * *

Skye found Luken and Zaithrian as soon as she stepped into the cafeteria. She filled Zaithrian in on their progress with the earpieces as they got their food.

"I was hoping you can work on the strategy now that I have the location," Skye said.

Zaithrian nodded, one of the most fundamental lessons he was being taught during Leadership training was how to form strategy. "If you can show me a map of this place I can get to work."

"He can do that as we finish up with the tech," Luken said, eyeing the greenish-blue goop that had just been slopped onto his tray.

They found Jayla and Daria seated at a nearby table, Jayla stopped talking as soon as Skye sat next to her. Skye noticed the way she slid an inch in the other direction.

They filled both girls in on all of their plans, then ate in an awkward silence.

By the time the bell had rung, Zaithrian had given Skye several questioning looks. She knew what they meant.

He ran up next to her on their way to the arena.

"What's going on with you two?" he asked quietly.

"I don't know." It was a lie, she knew exactly what was wrong with her and Jayla. They'd had a fight. A real fight. And Zaithrian was just about the last person she wanted to talk about it with.

"You okay?"

"I'm fine." Nope. More lies.

He pulled her to a stop and made her look him in the eyes. "I get it, okay? I understand how hard this is. And you have *every* right to be completely ticked off. But if we're going to be going into this, we should probably all be on the 'would definitely trust our lives with this person' page."

Skye hesitated. "Are you?"

Zaithrian nodded. "I am."

Skye was half flattered and half terrified at his answer. He trusted her with his *life*. She didn't even know if she trusted herself that much.

She swallowed hard and nodded. She broke her eyes away before she could start crying.

Zaithrian noticed and put a hand on her arm. "Skye?"

She ducked her head as tears started falling.

Zaithrian pulled her close into a firm hug. "Skye," He held her tightly as she started crying into his sleeve. "It's gonna be okay. I promise."

* * *

After creature training, Squadron 999 met up in Luken's room. Everyone was seated at the desk, Daria and Jayla sat together working on the earpieces, Zaithrian was studying a map of the island, and Luken and Skye were working on their projects.

After about two hours Jayla and Daria finished their jobs and left to get a list of supplies Zaithrian had requested.

Skye was one brain cell away from chucking her tech at the wall. She was tired, braindead, and completely out of ideas.

She closed her eyes, planted her face on the desk, and let out a loud groan.

"Do you want a break?" Luken asked.

"Nes and yo," Skye mumbled.

"Do you mean yes and no?" Zaithrian asked.

"Probably…?"

"I think you really need a break," Luken said.

Skye sat back up. "No, I should finish this first, I'm close-ish."

Luken set down his contraption which was starting to look like something straight out of a spy movie.

"Want me to try?"

Skye shrugged and swapped seats with him. "Why not, it's not like you'll get it to work."

"What's your problem with it?" Luken turned it over and examined it.

"I don't know, it should be working perfectly, everythings there, but I can't get VACA to go through."

After a minute Luken gave her a dead stare. "Skye, it's not on."

"What?"

Luken pressed the on button and the small light turned on. "VACA? You in there?"

"Voice Activated Control Algorithm loading…"

Skye blinked exactly 23 times, stood up, and screamed into her hands.

Luken attempted to hold back a laugh. "Skye, you are the most brilliant idiot I have ever met."

"I'm so stupid. I am so insainely stupid," Skye sat back down and took her modified earpiece from Luken.

"VACA, run a full test and activate into the command center chip," Skye said, putting in the earpiece.

After a few minutes a bell chimed and VACA's voice came through.

"It's working, I have access to all of the tech in here, which isn't actually all that impressive Skye, I thought you could do better than this-"

"Mute."

VACA's voice stopped and Skye took out the earpiece. She had to bite the tip of her thumb to stop herself from squealing.

"You did it?" Zaithrian asked.

Skye nodded and burst into laughter that eventually led into crying that also led into her falling asleep at the desk.

Both boys shared a look.

"You think she's going insane?" Luken asked.

Zaithrian nodded. "Oh, for sure."

CHAPTER THIRTY-SEVEN

VACA, what time is it?"

"10:08 am."

"What *day* is it?"

"It's Tuesday."

Skye groaned and jumped out of bed, ignoring her headache. She got into her school uniform and brushed her hair out as best she could before racing out into the kitchen.

"Morning kid," Revin said.

"How long have I been asleep?"

He set down his commscreen. "The boys brought you over at about 6 last night, I thought they'd killed you or something. Then you slept until 10, and well, you can do math."

Skye made herself breakfast. "What time do I have to be at the arena for my patrol?"

"Uhhh, I think 11."

Skye ate as fast as she could. "And I don't have lessons today right?"

"Nope, I get a day off. You better hurry up, the blond kid came over earlier and said your Squad was meeting up over at his place."

Skye pulled on her boots. And opened the door to leave. She cast a glance back at Revin, if their plan didn't work... she might not make it back.

"Revin-"

He gave her an earnest look. "Go kid, and remember what I told you."

Skye nodded and headed out the door. Did Revin know about their plan? She didn't have time to worry about it now, she needed to help the rest of her Squadron with the preparations. And fast.

Skye knocked on Luken's dorm and said a quick hello to Mentor Chloe. She practically ran into Luken's room where the rest of her Squad were seated.

"Look who finally decided to join the party," Zaithrian said with a smirk.

"I'm sorry about that. What have you got so far?"

"We finished all of the earpieces with VACA *and* the new eyescreens," Luken said with a look that was supposed to be smug but ended up looking like he was about to squeal.

Skye gaped at him. "Nuh uh."

"Yep."

"Shut up."

"That's rude."

Luken and Skye stared at each other for thirty seconds while everyone stared at them.

Skye ran up and hugged him as she squealed and jumped around. "Oh my gosh! You are a genius and amazing and I need to see it right now!"

Luken laughed as he stepped away from Skye to grab a finished earpiece. He handed it to her and she placed it in her left ear.

It had changed slightly so that it came out onto her cheekbone a little.

"VACA?"

"I'm here Skye."

"Tell her to open tracker on me," Luken said.

"Open tracker on Luken."

Instantly, a small blue hologram appeared in front of Skye's left eye with a satellite image of the school and a pinpoint on Luken's location.

Skye gazed in awe. This was absolutely amazing.

Luken smiled as he watched Skye go through all of the systems he'd added. "VACA, open a group call with the Squad."

Skye hadn't noticed everyone else wearing their earpieces until they were all talking using their new invention.

"This is… amazing," Skye said, not sure if the word truly did justice. "How? How did you do all of this?"

Luken ended the call. "After Zaith and I brought you home, Mentor Revin asked us about our project, and he offered to help us. He helped me figure out the retracting screen, which was my main problem."

"At about 12 last night he made us all go to bed," Zaithrian said. "He took it all back to his dorm and finished them while we were asleep, I have no idea how he did it."

"Did you... tell him?" Skye asked.

Luken shook his head. "We told him we needed them finished tomorrow for our recon mission, he doesn't know about the real one."

After Luken had shown Skye how the earpiece worked, Zaithrian talked her through the plan he had been previously discussing.

Once everyone had said their opinion of the plan, and it had been tweaked, they were ready to start preparations.

"We should all bring a pack with food, water, and some survival gear, just in case we need that," Zaithrian said, already making a list.

"What about the weapons?" Jayla asked.

"I have them in my closet, I was able to grab everyone a blade and a micro blaster, I couldn't get anything else without looking suspicious," Daria said. "We can pack them in our backpacks and get them on hand when we leave the school."

"Alright," Zaithrian said. "Then let's all get to work, we're almost ready, and we need to hurry."

They all faded from Luken's room and into their own dorms. Skye tried to ignore the loudest thought in the back of her mind. *Talk to Jayla.* She didn't want to… but she did… sort of. She needed to fix things with Jayla, they had barely spoken for the past few days, they definitely weren't on the level of trust they needed to be on.

What was she supposed to say? "Jayla." That seemed like an okay start.

Jayla turned around before she opened her door.

"What do you want?" Her tone wasn't mean, but it sure wasn't nice either.

"Can we talk?"

"Isn't that what we're doing?"

"Can we talk about what happened?"

Jayla picked at her nails. "Lots of things have happened, I don't know which one you mean."

"I think you do."

Jayla looked at Skye, her blue eyes looked like they would fill with tears at any moment. "Fine. We can talk."

Skye swallowed. She hadn't actually thought this far ahead. Maybe she should do this like an experiment, analyze the issues and target the problem. Or maybe… she should do it as a person. A person talking to her best friend.

She took a shaky breath. "I'm sorry."

Jayla's expression only faltered for a second. She still remained propped up against the wall with crossed arms, but Skye had her attention.

"Jayla, I'm really sorry. I know what I said was awful and horrible and mean, and I wish I hadn't said it. I didn't know what I was saying, and I hope you can forgive me."

Skye waited. And waited. And waited.

Jayla said nothing, she just stared at Skye with an unblinking gaze. Finally she let out a hard breath. "You don't understand."

"Then help me to." Skye took a step closer. "I'm your best friend right? You can tell me."

Jayla let out a shaky breath and laced her fingers together. She opened her mouth to speak a few times, then closed it, never letting more than the first syllable of a word break through. She bit her lip and shook her head as tears broke free. With a quick jerk, she ran inside her dorm, slamming the door behind her.

Skye followed her with her eyes. She wanted them to trust each other, she wanted them to be able to work together. She wanted her best friend back.

As much as she wanted to go to Jayla and fix their problem, she knew she needed to give her time, the only problem was that they were running dangerously low on that.

Skye sighed and went into her own home to get ready. After packing some food, bottled water, and a few tools she would need to hack the trackers, Skye got her earpiece and headed out.

Zaithrian and Daria were already waiting in the hall, both of them had a backpack and their earpieces. Daria signaled her over. She silently and secretly handed her a small sheathed dagger and a blaster.

"Once we get in the air we can keep them out with us, but until then keep both packed," Zaithrian said.

Skye nodded and put them both in her backpack. She glanced at the time, they had only about ten minutes until they needed to be at the arena.

"Any sign of the others?"

"Luken went to get Jayla a few minutes ago, I haven't heard anything from either yet," Zaithrian said.

"VACA, open a comm with Luken," Daria said. After a few minutes of a conversation, she ended the call and Luken and Jayla came out. Jayla didn't even look at Skye.

The group had to run to get to the arena in time. A soon as they ran in, they all darted to the changing rooms, got dressed, and ran over to their enclosure.

Venna ran through their rules and directions. "Sweep over the southern quadrant of the Forest District. Collect video records of any unusual activity. Don't turn off your trackers, that's one of the most fundamental rules." She continued for about three more minutes. Skye didn't bother paying attention, she would rather not know exactly how many rules she would be breaking.

After she had finished they all saddled their creatures and Venna went to open the dome.

Skye smiled as she fit herself onto Kade's saddle. Under different circumstances, this would actually have been really fun.

Once the dome was open, Skye tapped Kade's side with her heel and he lept into the air. After everyone had made a check with their earpieces, they headed into the direction of the Forest District.

Skye got to work on hacking. She spent about a minute on getting her tracker to make it look like she was on the course she was supposed to be on.

"Alright, let's land so I can hack your trackers," Skye said through the comm.

They found an area and landed. Skye had to work quickly so their stop wouldn't look suspicious. After about ten minutes, they were back in the air and headed to the island where Daken had the scientists and her dad held captive.

Skye's stomach was twisted in just about as many ways as possible. She wasn't sure what was more nerve wracking, the fact that she was sneaking into a heavily guarded facility, or that it was her evil, psycho half-brother's facility.

Zaithrian had estimated about a three hour flight, which was definitely their longest one yet. At least Kade seemed to like it.

He was twirling through the air without a care in the world, so glad to be out of his cage. Skye wished she could feel the same way.

VACA's voice started coming through her earcomm. "Jayla has requested a private commlink. Would you like to accept?"

Skye said yes and Jayla's voice came into her ear.

"Um, hey Skye," Jayla said in a very uncharistic way.

"Is everything okay?" Skye asked.

"No, I just… I needed to talk to you."

"Okay."

She took a shaky breath before starting. "I know I've been acting weird lately, and I was yelling at you the other day, and I'm sorry."

"Jayla, don't apologize, it was my fault-"

"Shut up Skye I'm trying to fix everything!"

Skye smiled a little.

"Ok look, I've decided that I want to fix things between us. There's lots of stuff you don't know about me, and I had never planned to tell you about all of it, but… I guess the best way to really trust each other is to fix the wounds and stop just covering them up."

Jayla paused before continuing.

"I told you before I don't have a mom, which wasn't exactly true. About five years ago my mom… she had a problem with drinking… and one night on her way home from the bar, she hit another hover. The crash... it killed two people. She was sent to the asylum island, and I was really mad and confused and just really full of rage that she had done that. So, I left home."

She stopped talking for an entire minute, Skye saw that she was trying to figure out how to say her next words.

"So yeah, funny enough... I ran away and joined the circus. I was only 11 at the time and I really didn't know what I had hoped to do. I guess I just really wanted to get away from my family, school, everything really."

She hesitated so long Skye thought she'd lost connection. When she started talking again, her voice was wobbly.

"Skye, what I saw while I was with the stunt show...there were people starving on the streets, blood and dirt everywhere. The places we walked through were filled with homeless and diseased people. I was an acrobat, that's how I learned to do all those tricks. I had to work hard and train all day and clean the stalls all night. The Stuntmaster told me if I didn't carry my load they'd drop me from the show as fast as they had taken me in. He was an awful man, big and fat and had an ugly face and smelled awful. It wasn't all bad there I guess, a few people were nice to me. The miniature dragon trainer was fun, we all called him Pocket 'cause he could take anything from your pocket and you wouldn't notice, no matter how hard you'd try. Then there was the other kid acrobat, no one knew where he'd come from, but we called him Squirt since he was so skinny, but he was my age, he was my aerial partner and we did plenty of tricks together. They called me Firework, you could probably guess why."

Skye could tell from the smile in her voice that she had really liked that part.

"I stayed with them for a year, but I had an accident. I fell from the trapeze and I broke half my ribs and my back. It was in the middle of the show and somebody got me to the hospital. I had 3 surgeries, and by some miracle I made it out all right. Mostly anyway. Sometimes I still feel the pain, and when I do, it's horrible… " Jayla was fighting away a sob. After a few minutes she whispered out the rest. "I woke up and my dad was there. My dad… he welcomed me back without a thought. Even after I told him about all the awful things I'd seen and even some of the bad stuff I'd done, he told me he still loved me."

Jayla started crying. She sobbed into her hands from the back of her pegasus. And Skye could only listen.

Finally, Jayla stopped crying and looked over at Skye from across the cloudy air. "I wanted to tell you…but I was scared you wouldn't want me anymore-"

"Jayla. You're my best friend. I don't care what you've done, or what's been done to you. I'll *always* be here for you."

Jayla smiled and wiped away her last tears. "Thank you Skye. You don't know how long I've wanted to tell you. Now let's go get your dad back, and maybe kick your big brother in the face while we're at it."

CHAPTER THIRTY-EIGHT

The hours passed slowly. The air was cold at their altitude, making each of them shiver. They were stuck in a storm for half an hour and when they finally came out they were soaked to the bone and freezing.

"Hey Zaith, we might want to think about taking a break, Phenton is getting pretty tired," Luken said.

"We might not be in the air much longer," Zaithrian said. "Look ahead."

Skye's stomach twisted into a knot. The island was just coming into view.

"And the fun begins," Jayla mumbled.

Everyone stared as they approached closer, no one really knew what to think. This was it. They were going in.

For a moment Skye wanted to scrap the whole idea and go home. But remembering the sound of her dad screaming was the only push she needed to find the courage.

They flew over the island multiple times and checked their maps over and over. Nothing but mountains. No buildings, structures, or anything that gave the impression that there were people living there.

"Maybe Daken cut out his chip and dropped it here?" Luken suggested.

Skye shivered at the thought. If that was true, they wouldn't be able to find her dad. The white hot spark burned in her mind. No. No. No. This wasn't supposed to happen. They were supposed to have found Dad and brought him home safely and everything would be fine. But this? This was all wrong.

She wiped the forming tears from her face. What was she going to do now?

"It's okay Skye," Jayla said, as if she was reading Skye's thoughts "We'll figure something out."

Skye pressed her face into Kade's neck, letting herself cry into his soft feathers. Kade cawed in concern and stopped flying forward. He hovered over the center of the island, flapping his wings to keep his in the air.

Skye jerked out the earpiece. "What do I do?" She whispered to herself.

Kade screeched loud and dove for the ground.

"Kade!" Skye screamed, grasping for a hold on her saddle.

He dove so fast Skye could barely see anything but a flash of his blue feathers. She braced for sure impact, but Kade slowed to a stop in mid air, fifty feet from the ground.

Skye slowly opened her eyes and peered over at the empty ground. "What are you doing, Kade?"

He cawed and bent his leg to rest in the open air. Then his other. Then he stopped flapping his wings.

Skye expected them to fall, but they stayed floating as if it were magic. "What?" Realization dawned on her and she put the earpiece back in. "Guys, I think it's a projector."

"Really?" Luken asked. A minute later he landed his griffin next to Kade, and yet again, it looked as if he were floating.

"There must be an obscured building under here," Luken said, stepping off Phenton's back and standing on an invisible platform.

"Woah, is Smart Boy a ghost? I always had my suspicions, but now I know it's true." Jayla landed next to them.

"This has gotta be a device," Luken said. "Do you think this could be how Daken got away with the dragons? He just vanished, right?"

Skye nodded. "That has to be it. Can we just...go through?"

"I think if we landed, we'd be able to see inside."

They all got back on their creatures and soared down.

Skye wasn't sure what she had expected the transition to be like, but she was sure it was nothing like how she imagined. It was quick. Like a blink of the eye. She was in blue and white air and not even a second later, she was in a forest of green and black.

The island was obviously a jungle, it had towering bright trees with leaves from the brightest greens, to ones almost black. There was a mountain in the center of the jungle, and set into its side was a silver building.

Skye took down Kade in a clearing a little ways off from the base and the rest of her Squadron followed.

Alright everyone," Zaith said. "Here's the idea. I'm going to take a sweep around the base for any entry point we could use. You stay here and get ready."

"Be careful," Skye pleaded.

"Of course I'll be careful," he said with a smirk and a wink.

Once he had left, Skye went over the rest of the plan again. "Is everyone on the same page now?"

The other three nodded and got together their supplies while they waited for Zaithrian.

Fifteen minutes later, Zaithrian came gliding back into their camp.

"What did you find?" Skye asked, running up.

He slid off of Ryo's back. "There's a point we can get in near the back, it looks unused, but I can't be sure."

Skye nodded. "I guess that'll have to work."

Zaithrian raised his voice and called everyone over. "Alright everyone, it's time. We can ride up as close as we can without getting detected, then we'll have to keep our creatures hidden. Stay alert, be quiet, and if you're ever gonna believe in the Eagles, now would be a sked of a time to do it."

They all followed Zaithrian to the tower, Skye couldn't help but shiver at the sheer sight of it.

Zaithrian led them through to a small clearing amongst the trees where they could keep their creatures hidden. He pointed to a small cave-like opening in the side of the mountain, there were some old bulbs lining the entry, unlit.

"That's our entry. I went down a little ways and it led into the castle."

"Sked, you went in there?" Jayla asked with an exaggerated shiver. "That looks like a nest for blive bats."

"I saw a few," Zaithrian told her.

"Ugh, those things are *awful*. Someone once told me that if you touch them with your bare skin, they'll-"

"Maybe don't tell us what they do," Skye said, already sure she *didn't* want to know.

"Let's get going," Zaithrian said, pushing past Jayla and taking the lead.

Skye trailed behind him followed by Luken, Daria, and finally Jayla. The walk wasn't far, but it was filled with trees, bugs, and who knew what else.

Skye tried not to trip on the sprouting roots. She'd never seen so many trees so close together before. The mud was thick along the floor of the jungle, and Skye tried to stay near the edges of the puddles.

Zaithrian was way quicker and much better at maneuvering then everyone else, Jayla kept a pretty good pace as well though. He could jump from the roots without twisting his ankles, and constantly had to wait for everyone else to catch up.

Finally they came to the base of the building.

"Watch for any security," Zaithrian said, scanning the walls for cameras. "We need to get up there." He pointed to where the opening was in the mountain about fifteen feet up the steep cliff.

"You know what?" Jayla said sarcastically. "It would be amazing if I had a creature that could literally fly right about now. Oh wait! I do. If only someone had decided to bring them with us."

"They would be much easier to detect than us," Zaithrian said, scanning the cliff for handholds. "And I knew how much you would love to climb a mountain."

Jayla stepped up to the rock and started climbing effortlessly. "Well, aren't you kind."

"Alright Luken, Can you give me a boost?" Zaithrian said.

Luken cupped his hands for Zaithrian's foot and hoisted him up. Zaithrian grasped onto a ledge and found a large enough spot to stand.

"Alright, get one of the girls up here."

Daria stepped into Luken's hands and he hoisted her up. Zaithrian grasped her hand and helped her start. Jayla effortlessly used one hand to hold onto the rock and the other to show Daria which holds to grab.

"Alright, Skye you're up," Zaithrian said.

Skye nervously stepped into Luken's folded hands and reached to grab Zaithrian's. He gripped her wrist tightly and helped her get to the ledge.

"Use these holds for your hands," he said, pointing to where rocks jutted out or where there were indents.

Skye nodded and started her ascent. Once she was far enough up, Jayla showed her the final handholds. Once she had reached the top, Daria hoisted Skye up onto the cave platform.

Luken came up next, then Zaithrian, and finally Jayla.

"Let's head in," Zaith said. "Comms on, everyone."

Zaithrian led the way through the unguarded opening. It was covered in vines and leaves that had grown over the broken entrance.

Zaithrian stayed in front, always keeping his blaster raised.

They stayed flush against the wall, keeping to the shadows as much as they could. They hadn't seen anyone yet and had to hope no one had seen them.

"Stop," Daria said suddenly.

Everyone froze. "What is it?" Zaithrian asked.

Daria pointed to a microscopic blinking red light on the bottom of the wall a few feet ahead of them. Skye hadn't even noticed it. "That's a movement detector. If you step in it's beam it will send a signal. This place is boobytraped."

Skye's breath caught in her throat.

"This complicates things," Zaithrian mumbled. "Can we get over it?"

"We can go over it, but the rest of the beam is invisible, it could go higher than we think."

Zaithrian grimaced. "Can you disable it, Skye?"

"I can try." Skye took out her commscreen. "VACA, see if you can detect a signal coming from that wall."

After a few seconds, VACA was able to get inside the system, and Skye typed on her screen the shutoff command.

Everyone let out a breath.

"I want Daria right behind me," Zaithrian said. "You can probably identify most of the traps in here."

They reorganized themselves and continued.

They came to an open room. They must be in the main section of the base. "Okay, there are probably cameras all over this place now. There's going to be a lot more people walking around. We're going to be more open out here. We're exposed, so be alert. I want Daria scanning for traps, I'll take the front and watch for people, Jayla you guard our 6 o'clock, Luken get your tracker on for Dr. Zareb and tell us where his position is. Skye, I need you ready to disable traps and cameras."

They nodded and made their way through the large open room. They stayed in the shadows of concrete support pillars lining most of the building. Skye took out a few more cameras as they made their way through the base by Luken's directions.

"Which way do we go?" Zaithrian asked as they came to another hallway that split.

"I- I can't tell, something's messing with my signal. I have to wait for it to clear up."

"We don't have time to wait," Zaithrian said, looking behind him. "I think we need to split up."

"That wasn't part of the plan," Skye said.

"Well it is now. I'll take Skye and go down the right tunel. Luken, Jayla, and Daria, you guys go down the left. Search for the scientists. The plan's the same otherwise, if you find them, get them out. Understood?"

Everyone nodded at Zaithrian's orders and got into their groups.

"Everyone stay in touch," Skye said. "And be careful."

"We will," Daria said as she led her group into the dark tunnel.

"C'mon," Zaithrian said.

Skye started down the tunnel. "VACA, show Dad's coordinates on the eyescreen."

Skye repeated the numbers to Zaithrian as he checked their current position on his eyescreen.

After a few minutes he flicked off his screen. "Looks like he's down. There's got to be another floor below us."

She nodded and they continued down the tunnel. It was lit with lightbulbs but still pretty dark. Skye made a mental note to add night vision to the eyescreens.

They continued to walk, Zaithrian made sure to keep them in the shadows, which meant they pressed to the wall a majority of the time in a single file line.

Skye started to notice a small descent in their path. "Are we going down?" She whispered to Zaithrian.

"I think so."

"Daria, what's your position?" Skye asked over comms.

"We just came out of the tunnel and we're in more of an open room. We haven't come in contact with anyone yet."

"It may be a good idea to get your blasters out everyone," Zaithrian said.

Skye shivered as she gripped her gun, she had only used it during training, and she had no faith in herself to use it properly.

"You're holding it wrong."

Skye looked up a Zaithrian.

"Your pointer finger needs to slide into that loop. Here." He moved her finger into the right position.

Skye looked up at him in the dark. "Thanks."

"Well, I can't have you missing a shot and shooting me, can I?"

"Oh come on, I'd never shoot you."

He smiled. "Isn't that nice to know." His expression hardened. "Don't move."

"What? Why?" Skye tried to turn, but Zaithrian gripped her arm tightly, pointing to the red blinking dot right where Skye had set her foot.

The walls started to shake.

"Run!" Zaithrian screamed, pulling Skye away and darting down the hall.

"Guys! Come in! Help... we ne-" Jayla's voice blasted into Skye's ear.

Skye held her finger against the comm as the floor shook "Jayla! Jayla what is it? Jayla can you hear me? Luken! Luken come in! Daria do you copy? Is anyone there?"

"Skye... We need...caught... come.... Help!"

"I can't get anything," Skye said. Everything is static."

"It's this skeding trap!" Zaithrian yelled, pulling Skye into another tunnel as she tripped on the shaking floor.

Shouts rang from somewhere in the room. Skye let out a scream as they grew louder and closer.

Zaithrian jumped behind a wall and pulled Skye next to him. "Quiet!" he hissed, holding his hand over her mouth.

Skye's ear started blasting again with static from Jayla's comm.

Zaithrian bent his head low to whisper. "We need to find them."

Just then, the thundering of boots ran past Skye and Zaithrian's hiding place. Skye gripped Zaithrian's arm tightly to steady her racing heartbeat.

The agony of knowing they could die at any moment went on for what felt like years. Skye couldn't get a signal to contact the others, and the marching of an army went on right next to where they were crouched behind a wall, reminding them that they were trapped.

Slowly, the men's footsteps subdued and Skye and Zaithrian were in the clear.

"It's okay, they're gone," he whispered as Skye let go of her death grip on his arm.

They stood up, Zaithrian using the wall as a support. There was a faint click. Both froze as Zaithrian stared at where his hand had touched a pressure panel in the wall.

"Oh, sked."

The floor started to shake and the lights went out.

"Zaith?!" Skye yelled, unable to find him in the dark.

Suddenly, the floor dropped out from under her feet. She fell into a deeper darkness than she thought was possible. She screamed as she flailed her arms, she heard Zaithrian yelling from somewhere near her, but she couldn't find him.

Out of nowhere, the darkness was replaced with a blinding light and Skye hit the ground. Then everything went black.

CHAPTER THIRTY-NINE

Skye groaned in pain. Everything hurt; her head, her muscles, all of it. She opened her eyes to find herself in a dimly lit room. She was sitting on the floor with her hands cuffed to the wall above her.

Jayla, Daria and Luken were cuffed on the other wall across from her and Zaithrian was next to her.

"Where are we?" Skye asked, lifting her sore head.

Jayla spoke up, "Daken's base still. He trapped our group in some sort of forcefield, it messed up all of our tech. Then they got the drop on us and brought us in here. And then you and Zaith just fell from the ceiling like psychos and knocked yourselves out. That was about twenty minutes ago."

"Where's Daken?"

"He hasn't come back since he chained you two up, I don't know what to do."

Skye placed her head in her knees. They had screwed up *so* badly.

"I'll think of something," Skye said, knowing she probably wouldn't, but needing to reassure herself.

A clicking of keys disturbed her thoughts. The door opened and in stepped Daken Claw. He was just as awful as Skye had thought he would be. And what was even worse, was that she saw parts of her dad in him. Parts of *her* in him. His eyes. She'd never noticed how similar they were to her own.

He was dressed in black, a thick cloak draped over his shoulders hid his frame, but she guessed he must be pretty strong. His sandy blond hair must have come from his mother, since Skye's dad had dark brown. But still, his eyes came right from her– *their*–dad.

Daken put his hands in his pockets and studied each of them.

"Can't really say I was expecting *that*," he said.

No one said anything.

"Okay then." Daken leaned back against the cold metal wall. "I'm sure you know who I am, but I don't think I've met you five before. Names maybe?"

"We know all about you. Freak," Jayla said, spitting on Daken's foot.

Daken looked down at the glob of spit on his boot, then up at Jayla. "That was a little harsh."

"So is killing a bunch of innocent people. And kidnapping scientists. And chaining kids to walls. Don't blame me for not appreciating."

"If we're being technical, *I* never killed anyone," he pointed at Jayla. "And you'd probably want to swallow that comeback before I do something you'll wish I hadn't."

Jayla was about to shoot another comment, but bit her tongue. Literally.

"I could just scan your ID chips if telling me your names is really *that* hard, but you know, time is valuable and those extra ten second you're all burning are *really* important."

Zaith's jaw tightened as he pulsed against his cuffs. "Zaithrian Erick Delainey. 9042041912. Current student at the Academy of Light training in the Leadership Guild under Mentor Lonan Cambridge. You want my former home address too?"

"Got enough attitude to last you a lifetime, Z, I'll give you that."

"That's Luken, Jayla, Daria, and Skye. Zareb." He glared at Daken.

Daken's eyes widened and he turned to Skye. "Zareb?"

Skye swallowed and nodded. "Yeah. That's my father you have locked up. I'm here to tell you that the Flames are coming, and they're going t-"

"You were the one who found me, weren't you?"

"No–we all did-"

"No, Skye, *you* were the one who figured out how to find me. That's what I mean."

"I- I guess so."

"With the signal blocker, it should have been impossible. Skye, how did *you* find me?"

Skye shrunk against the wall as Daken walked closer. "I- uh I just hacked the chip records. They showed me the coordinates for my dad's position."

Daken stood up straight and cocked his head. "That shouldn't be possible."

"It wasn't hard. I'm sure the Flames have already-"

"No, the signal should be blocked, all the rooms on the lower level are guarded for any kind of electricity. Unless..."

Jayla started yelling. "That's why he won't talk! You pig! He's deaf and you shut off his hearing aid!"

Skye's eyes immediately went to Luken. He couldn't hear without his *electronic* hearing aids.

Luken's eyes were staring directly at Daken's mouth, probably trying to read his lips, but by the look on Luken's face, he was out of practice.

Daken's eyes fixed on Jayla, and then Luken, and back to Jayla. "That's not my problem."

That sent Jayla off. "That's the most cruel thing I've ever seen in my life! That's just-"

Daken wasn't listening. "Take the prisoners in room 9, and punish them," Daken said to one of the masked men in the room with him. "They've broken protocol again and need to be dealt with."

The man nodded and left.

"What's in room 9?" Zaithrian asked mockingly.

Daken ignored him. But Skye already knew what he was talking about. Her father and the other scientists were being held in room 9, and they were about to get punished. And not lightly, by her guess.

"So," he said. "I don't have any use for the five of you. I can't let you go, obviously, and killing a bunch of kids wasn't on my agenda today. Any suggestions?"

"We have a dance off, and whoever wins gets to keep the other in jail forever?" Jayla suggested. "Because, no offence, but I could *totally* crush you in a dance off."

"Sweet land of the Eagles, does she ever shut up?"

"Nope," Zaith said. "And for once I don't mind."

Jayla glared with a wicked smile. "And since you like it so much, I'll make sure to talk the entire time I'm here."

"You know, I think I have a nice gag with your name on it somewhere," Daken said.

"Sweet. While you're at it, mind grabbing me a pillow? Oh and maybe a blanket too, you might want to look into the draft problem in here."

Daken leaned to speak to one of the guards and he ran out of the room and came back a minute later with a cloth gag.

"Woah dude, where was that thing?" Jayla said, trying to squirm away from him.

317

He grabbed her jaw and shoved the gag in her mouth. She kicked against him, but he managed to succeed.

"As I was saying, I don't need you five, you're useless to me. And while I don't want to kill you, I really don't see a better option. That's why I'm proposing that you join me."

Zaithrian scoffed. "Yeah, no thanks, I don't work with psychos."

Daken crossed his arms. "You five seem smart— maybe minus that one," he gestured to Jayla. "You managed to get into my highly secretive base. That's impressive for your age. So I offer your Squadron a seat in my rebellion. No harm will come to you, and you get to fight in the greatest battle Isarn has ever seen."

"You expect us to ally with the same man who has us locked to a wall?" Daria spoke for the first time since Daken had entered. "I can't speak for them, but I know where my allegiances lie. I will not betray the nation I swore to protect. Even if it comes at the cost of my own life. I'm loyal if nothing else."

"How old did you say you were?"

"16."

"Dar's right," Zaithrian said. "I won't betray Isarn. And even if they can't say it, I know for a fact Luken and Jayla won't either."

Daken stalked closer to Skye. "My sister. Comes down to us then? Hard choice, thrive and fight alongside your brother to regain your nation to its designed glory, or die for your Vire. Your call."

Skye wanted to glare at him, but she couldn't look into his eyes. "I'm not going to join you. And you're not my brother."

"Somehow I find that unconvincing. Your peers gave elaborate speeches of patriotism and devotion, and yet…I'm not getting the same energy from you."

Skye tilted her head up a little. "I'm here to get my dad home safe. I don't care about your rebellion."

"Don't you feel it, Skye? The pull for change? You're smart. Sked, our father is one of the greatest minds in Isarn, don't you see? It's in our blood. He's a renowned scientist, I was the prodigy of my time, and you? You've got something great in you. And I want you to use it for what's right. Making our nation the best it can be."

Skye didn't look at him. She didn't look at anyone. Her thoughts were a mess of emotions. She didn't know what she felt. Her eyes burned with tears, and yet she had no reason to be crying. The white heat that had been so frequently present the past few days rose in her mind again.

She tilted her head up and made herself look into Daken Claw's eyes. "No."

Daken nodded. "I have a feeling you can be persuaded." He turned to leave. "One hour." He left and slammed the door behind him. And they were alone.

No one spoke for minutes. No one knew what to say.

"How are we going to get out of here?" Daria asked.

"Haven't you been learning to pick locks or something?" Zaith asked hopefully.

Daria shook her head. "I have. But I didn't think to bring any wire, I can't reach anything else to use."

He sighed. "We'll figure something else out. If this room is electronic proof, that means there are no cameras."

"Where do we go if we escape?" Skye asked.

He sighed. "I don't know."

"I don't think we're getting out," Daria said.

Zaithrian sagged his head. "I don't... I don't know what to do. There isn't anything we *can* do. We're stuck down here."

Skye's hope drained. She had always known they weren't getting out, but hearing Zaithrian admit it made it feel so much more real.

She looked over at her Squadron. Jayla was unable to speak, Luken couldn't hear anything, Daria looked terrified, and Zaithrian had completely given up. What about her? She was in pain, enraged, and exhausted. She couldn't do anything but sit there and accept defeat.

CHAPTER FORTY

Ugh, that tasted *nasty*."

Skye looked up to see Jayla had managed to pry the gag out of her mouth and was now…kicking off her boot?

"What are you doing?" Zaithrian whispered.

Jayla used her feet to pry off her socks and used her bare feet to tip her boot over. A thin wire fell out.

"How are you going to-"

Jayla shushed Zaith and nodded her head to the door. Skye got the message. If they had guards outside, and they could definitely hear if they talked about a key.

"Zaith, do you know if I locked my dorm before we left?" Daria asked.

His eyebrows pressed together then relaxed. "I think so. Did you see Mentor Lonan today?"

"Yeah. I passed him in the west hallway twice. "

Why were they talking about- ohhhh. Mentor Baylyne–Daria's Mentor for the Stealth Guild–had had them develop a code system. Skye never thought they'd actually use it, but now she wished she'd memorized it better. She knew that passing

Mentor Lonan meant 'were there any guards?' and twice must mean when Daria's group was brought in, there were two guards positioned outside. She couldn't remember what locking your dorm meant.

Skye looked over at Jayla and tried not to laugh. She had the wire pinched between her toes, and was bent over with her feet in the air, her wrist cuffs holding her up.

"How are you even going to do that?" Skye whispered.

"I told you," she mumbled. "I was in the stunt show. Sometimes the magicians needed assistants. I'm good at unlocking things with my feet." She winked and turned back to her work.

Skye could only stare as she fumbled the wire between her toes into the old fashioned padlock. Completely upside down, Jayla somehow managed to get the metal strip into the keyhole. Skye's jaw dropped as Jayla fell from the wall, completely free.

She rubbed her wrists and failed to move her numb legs. "One second guys," she mumbled, trying to get her limbs to work again.

After a minute, she came to unlock Skye's cuffs. Skye dropped to the floor and rubbed her raw wrists. Her legs and arms had gone fully numb and all she could do was sit there and wait for the blood to flow again.

Jayla was sitting with Luken and was moving her hands around in all sorts of ways. Skye followed her eyes to Luken, who was using hand signals back at her.

"What are you doing?" Skye whispered.

"I'm using sign language to tell Luken about everything," she said.

"You know sign language?"

"I... decided to learn it. I'm not very good yet, but I want to be able to do it fluently. I just- I figured that if Luken's hearing aids got broken or something, we would need a way to communicate beyond just lip reading."

"Everybody good?" Zaith mumbled, holding a hand to his head.

"I've been better," Daria said. "But I think the two of you got it worse. You had to have cracked a rib or something."

Zaith nodded. "Yep, think so. Never a dull moment with her." He grinned at Skye and stood up straight. "We need a plan. We have to be out fast. Claw could come back any minute and if those guards outside get even a hint of suspicion that we're not where we're supposed to be, we're dead meat. We need an exit point. I don't know what the outside looks like, and besides the two Dar saw, we don't know how many guards will be out there. Anyone have an idea?"

Skye gazed around the room for any way to get out. The room was made of plain metal, nothing that resembled a camera or anything technical. The only vent was in the wall and was way too small for anyone to get through. There were no cracks, no breaks, and no way out besides the door heavily barred and guarded.

Her thoughts broke with Luken crossing the room and feeling around the door.

"What are you-" Zaith started, then must have realized he couldn't hear him. "Jayla, did he uh, sign what he's doing?"

Jayla pressed her brow. "He doesn't think there are guards out there. I don't know how he could tell."

Luken was feeling around the edge of the doorframe and pressed his palm up against it. He turned to Jayla and moved his hands around in positions Skye couldn't hope to understand. Some signals touched his face and some were gestures, and all of it made no sense to anyone but Jayla and Luken.

"He's saying there's no one outside the door but there could be people out in the hallway. And he thinks if we get to the floor above us our tech will start working again and we can signal the Flames and send a tracking uh ... beacon I think he said."

Zaithrian ran a hand along his jaw. "Alright. I guess if we're going to get killed anyway we might as well try to annoy some people while we're at it."

"We don't have any weapons," Jayla said.

"You're not the only one hiding stuff in their boots," Daria said, pulling off her shoes. Two sheathed blades were strapped to the sides of Daria's tall boots. "They took all the weapons in my pockets, but I have these two." She handed one to Zaithrian and took the other knife for herself. "But I couldn't store a blaster."

"What are the rest of us supposed to use?" Jayla asked, pointing to herself, Luken, and Skye.

Zaithrian sighed. "We don't have anything else, which is definitely not ideal, but we'll have to work with it. Dar and I have the most weapons training, so it'll have to do. Do we know how to get the door open?"

Skye walked up to it and looked around it for spots of weakness. "I think it's locked from the outside. We'd need an insane amount of force to break it down. You can't ram into it," she said, already knowing Zaith had started thinking that.

"I know how we can get through," Daria said, undoing her hair from her tight bun.

Everyone shared a confused look until Daria pulled a small metal disk from her hair. "I took this from the Stealth Tower. It gives off a tiny silent explosion. It should work for breaking the lock if we get it positioned right."

"Dude, I never even thought about hiding weapons in my hair," Jayla said. "Mind blown. You just changed my life, Dar."

"You sure no one will hear this?" Zaith fingered the disk.

"I'm not sure about anything, to be honest."

"That makes two of us."

"Mh, that's comforting," Jayla said.

Zaith took the position he always did when he was about to give orders. Skye liked that about him. The way he would stand tall and cross his arms, ready to take on the mission he was about to announce. Skye wished for his kind of confidence.

He gave them a small, almost mischievous grin. "Dar, you and Skye are going to bust the door down."

They set the disk in the weakest point of the lock and stood back into their positions.

"Everyone ready?" Zaith asked.

A silent spray of sparks flew from the seam of the door. With a clang of metal, it swung open, revealing a completely unguarded hallway.

CHAPTER FORTY-ONE

Jackpot," Jayla murmured, pulling a gun from the shelf.

"You only need one," Zaithrian said. "Hurry."

"Okay dude chill, you want a handheld or rifle?"

"Obviously a handgun now hurry up, I don't know how long the coast is going to stay clear."

Jayla handed Skye a small blaster from the supply shelf she'd found. Apparently it was normal to keep closets full of weapons all over the base of a rebellion.

Everyone took a handgun and ducked back into the shadows.

"Here's the plan," Zaith whispered. "Luken and Jayla need to get to the next floor. Luken should get his hearing working again and he can send a signal to tell the Beacons where we are. The rest of us are going to find the best way out and we're getting our creatures. We'll be much safer with them."

Jayla signed to Luken and the two of them left silently.

"What about my dad?" Skye blurted. "We came here for him, he's still inside- we can't just leave."

"I know," Zaith said sympathetically. "But that room is going to be guarded so heavily we'd never get in. Let alone out. We should be glad no one cared about us enough to guard us. If the Flames come, they'll get the scientists out-"

"You're completely changing the mission!" Skye said–much louder than she should have. "We came here for *my* dad, that was the whole point we even dragged ourselves out here you can't just-"

"You're going to get us killed Skye!" Zaithrian hissed in her ear. "We have a chance of surviving, we need to take it."

"You- you *promised.*"

He shook his head. "I'm sorry."

White hot anger burned in her mind. No. She was getting her dad out of the hands of her cursed brother. She was getting *all* of the scientists out. That was her objective. The reason she'd gone in the first place.

"I'm *getting* my dad home safe," Skye shot at him. "You two get out, I'm finishing the mission."

She bolted away from them before they could say anything.

CHAPTER FORTY-TWO

Skye peered around the corner and from her crouched position. She waited outside the hallway that led to room 9. Her dad was right behind that metal door. She was so close. And yet all that stood between him and her was a heavily locked door and a security guard pacing the stretch of the hallway.

There weren't any cameras on this level, which she had to be grateful for, but she had no clue how many people would be roaming through the base. She needed to be quick.

The door wouldn't be electronically locked, but it was probably more complicated than the one that had locked them in. If only she had thought to ask Daria if she had any more exploding discs. In hindsight, it probably hadn't been such a good idea to run away from them. But Zaithrian was being ridiculous. She wasn't going to just leave her dad here.

She studied the guard. He stood tall and looked strong—much too strong for her to hope she could take him out. He wore an all black suit like Daken had worn, with a hood obscuring his head and a black sleeve pulled up over his face.

Skye shrunk deeper into the shadows as another hooded figure walked up the hallway next to the guard. The new figure stopped to talk to the larger one. Skye's heartbeat was wild as she waited for one of them to turn the corner and spot her. It could all be over in no time at all.

A hand clamped over her mouth.

Skye jerked around and almost screamed until she heard the hushed voice.

"You're such an idiot," Zaith whispered, removing his hand from her mouth.

"You shouldn't be here," Skye hissed, hitting him in the arm. "You're going to get me caught."

"You're going to get yourself caught," he said. "You're the one sitting out in the open without a disguise."

Skye finally noticed that he was wearing all black clothes that looked exactly like the one's the guard was wearing.

"I'm not leaving him here," she said. "You can't make me leave."

He laughed a little. "Skye, I could knock you out and drag your unconscious body out of here and you wouldn't be able to stop me. But we're here to help you. But you need to promise me if things get messy, we can run. I know it's hard, but you can't just throw out the safety of your entire Squadron if things don't go to plan."

Skye swallowed. "Fine."

"You're not convincing me."

Skye wanted to glare at him and run again, but her mind remembered their training exercise from months ago. She'd been the reason they'd been shot out that day. She had been impulsive and she'd gotten her whole team taken out.

"Alright," she swallowed. "If it gets messy I'll pull out."

He gave her a reassuring nod. "Get ready to run for the door when he drops."

"What?"

Zaith pointed over her shoulder and she whipped around just in time to see the figure deadleg the guard and nail him in the head with the butt of their gun.

"Go," he hissed, pushing her from her sitting position.

Before Skye could think, she was running to the door of room 9. The hooded figure who'd taken down the guard whipped off their hood and mask.

"Daria?"

She grabbed the key from the unconscious man's belt as Zaithrian ran to drag him out of the hallway.

"We have to hurry," Daria said, working on the locks. "We have a stash of uniforms to disguise them hidden not far from where we found the guns. But we need to be quick or we'll be spotted. Luken and Jayla are on their way over too."

Zaithrian ran up and Daria undid the last lock. The door swung open and the three of them ran inside.

Skye spotted her dad right away and ran across the cluttered cell to him.

"Skye?" he asked. "What are you- you need to get out of here!"

"We're getting you out!" she said, looking around at the faces of the other scientists. Everyone was sullen.

Skye looked back at her dad, who's face had gone pale. "What's wrong?"

"Skye, get behind me."

Skye turned to see Daken standing in the doorway. Guns in both hands and a smirk on his terrible face.

"They're just kids, Daken!" her dad screamed, grabbing Skye's arm and holding her behind him. "You don't want them!"

"Not really, no," he said, pointing the guns straight at Skye's dad. "But they can't leave now, can they?" He put his guns away. "Throw the other two in and gas them all."

"They've been gassed today already," a female figure said from next to Daken. "Effects will increase from an extra dose."

Daken shrugged. "We don't need them too much longer anyway."

He turned from the room and Luken and Jayla were thrown on the floor. The door locked, and white gas started pouring from the ceiling.

"Cover your mouth!" Dad screamed.

But it was too late. Skye had already inhaled a deep breath and collapsed to the floor.

CHAPTER FORTY-THREE

Skye woke to the sound of groaning. Regained consciousness would probably be a better term, since she could hardly count getting knocked out by gas a good night's sleep.

Her eyes opened just in time to see Jayla vomit all over the floor. That woke her up all the way.

"Jayla?" she asked. "You okay?"

She bent over and put her head in her knees. "It hurts," she mumbled.

"What does?"

"My *head*." She looked up with a pale face. "Doesn't yours?"

Skye shook her head slightly. She felt fine. Apart from the cracked rib she was sure she had from falling down the trap, her head didn't hurt. She wouldn't say normal since there was a strange cool breeze feeling flowing through her head. It almost felt nice, definitely not normal though.

"Where are we?" Jayla mumbled. "Can you tell?"

Skye looked up. They were in a new room. It was small with harsh lighting coming from the ceiling. And apart from Jayla's pile of vomit, it was empty.

"I don't know where we are. But I think we're on a different floor since the lights are working."

"Do you think they let Luken keep his earpiece?"

Skye's hand went to her ear. "I still have mine. I don't think it works, but it's there. So, they might have left Luken's in too."

Jayla nodded and crawled to the other side of the room to lay on her side and clutch her head. "Sorry I barfed on the floor."

"It's fine." Skye walked over to the door. "Do you think the others are in the same kind of cell?"

Jayla only moaned something that sounded like, "I don't know."

Skye turned back to inspect the door. It was electronically locked–she could tell easily from the red light signals. She could hack it, but would need VACA and with her glitchy earpiece and no commscreen, there was no way to access her.

"Does your earpiece still work?" Skye asked.

Jayla sat up a little. "Skye...if you're planning a big escape again, I'm...I'm not sure I want to."

"What?"

"Where do we go? We can't get out of here. And definitely not with everyone else. If we try to get out and go home, they'll catch us and kill us on the spot. It's a work of the Eagles we aren't dead right now."

"What are you saying, Jayla?" Skye asked. That was so not like her. Jayla didn't just *give up*.

"Skye, don't make this harder than it needs to be," she mumbled. "I'm sorry okay?"

"You don't want to go home? What about your dad? And your sisters? And Zeno? What about your Squad? Your *life*? You're just going to leave all that behind?"

"You think I want to die?" she snapped. Then her voice dropped to a whimper. "Of course I want my life...I just can't. We lost, Skye. Can't we just leave it at that?"

"No. We can't leave it at that." Anger burned in Skye's throat. Not anger at Jayla, this was anger at Daken. He'd broken Jayla down to the point where she had given up. He'd done something to her.

"I'm not going to let us *die* here!" Skye yelled.

The lights in the ceiling started to dim. Then they brightened.

"Skye, calm down."

"I can't calm down!" Skye yelled. "He took my dad from me, he's not going to take you too!" Her limbs felt numb. Cold.

"Skye, you're scaring me."

Skye froze. Jayla's words felt like a cold slap of water. "I- I'm sorry."

337

Jayla pressed her hands against her head. "I don't want to give up. Really. I hate quitting." She let out a small whimper. "I'm just scared."

"I know," Skye said, sitting next to her. "I am too."

Jayla looked up at her. Her face was pale and covered in sweat. "You really don't feel it?"

Skye shook her head. It didn't make any sense. She *should* be feeling the effects of the gas. But she wasn't.

Jayla's head sagged and leaned on Skye.

"Jayla?" Her eyes were closed, but she was breathing.

Skye eased against the wall. She wished she could sleep. Her mind was too loud. If this gas had done all that to Jayla in one dose, what was it doing to her dad after a week's worth?

* * *

"Locked us up and didn't even bother to clean the cell. Gross."

Skye looked up from where she had been almost asleep. Jayla was standing up and walking over to the door.

"Are you...feeling better?" Skye sat up straight. "Huh?"

Skye cocked her head. "You were saying you had a headache a few hours ago? You threw up-"

338

"What are you talking about?" Jayla looked as confused as Skye felt. "I *just* woke up. Luken and I got thrown into that room and they sprayed us with gas."

"Yeah, and you woke up already." Skye's frown deepened. "Don't you remember?"

"I...I don't know what you're talking about." She looked around the room in confusion. "Skye, you're making no sense!"

Skye held her hand up in defense. "That's what happened. You really don't remember? You asked about Luken and you said you didn't want to try to get out and-"

"I said that? I would never say that." She held a hand to her head. "Skye, what did they do to me?" Fear flooded her eyes.

"Is there anything else you don't remember?"

"How am I supposed to know!"

She had a point.

"Calm down, it's okay, we'll figure it out."

Jayla started breathing hard. "What if I forget you? Or Luken? Or my dad? What if I forget who *I* am?"

"Jayla." Skye placed her hands on Jayla's arms. "Breathe. You didn't forget us. I think it's just from when you took the gas in until you passed out."

Her breathing seemed to calm. "So, I'm going to be okay?"

Skye nodded. "I think so."

She hesitated. "Why are you fine? Didn't he gas you too?"

"He did. I don't know why I'm not reacting to it." Skye placed a hand to her head. "It feels weird though. I don't feel normal."

Jayla started looking at the door. "When we get out of here, remind me to punch Claw in the face. Hard."

"You don't need me to remind you, because *you're* not going to forget."

Jayla nodded. "We're gonna get out of here."

"How?"

The door opened, and two hooded figures stepped into the room. "Claw wants to speak with you."

CHAPTER FORTY-FOUR

"Where are we going?" Jayla snapped as the guard clapped a thick metal lock over her wrists.

"We already told you, Claw wants you," the guard said with palpable annoyance.

That was pretty unfortunate for Daken, since Jayla *really* didn't want to see him for any other reason than to punch his teeth out.

Jayla gave Skye a quick glance that she instantly knew asked, "You want me to take her out?" and she hastily shook her head. There was no point getting out without everyone else.

The cuffs were slid onto Skye's wrists and each of the guards gripped one of the girls by their arm. The door opened and they were led out into a bright hallway.

The two guards lead them silently through the hallways and then into an elevator. They stepped into the box and started a strangely awkward ride.

"No music?" Jayla mumbled.

"Jayla," Skye warned.

"What? You'd think there would be some, like, creepy orchestra music playing to match the vibe."

Skye couldn't see much more than her guard's eyes, but it almost looked like she was smiling. Skye noticed she looked young, probably not much older than the two of them–maybe just graduated from Light. The thought seemed so foriegn that there would be people so young working for Daken.

The woman's expression turned blank again as the elevator gave an unfittingly cheerful ding and they were led into another room. This one was huge and the most decorative place in the whole base. Her dad and two other scientists stood at one side, and the last three members of her Squadron at the other. Between them both was Daken.

"Glad you could join me," Daken said, looking over at the two of them.

They both just glared as they were all pushed into a line next to the rest of their Squad.

"You five have caused me an unnatural amount of annoyance today," Daken said, walking so that he looked at each of them. He stopped in front of Skye. "But I see something in you that I think could help me. Especially you, *sister*."

Skye squirmed at the way he said it. "I'm not your sister."

"No? That's where you're wrong Skye. You are my sister, and you are going to join me and help me take over the Vire because you're the missing piece I need. Those scientists?" He waved a hand at the cuffed adults. "They're nowhere near as smart as you could be. You could be the game changer. You and that brilliant little mind of yours."

"My mind is not yours to play with," Skye spat. She looked over at her dad and the other two scientists. "And neither are theirs."

Daken stood up straight again. "We could do this all day long, but I've got more important things to do, so I'm giving you the chance to live. You just have to help me."

"I would never."

He walked back over to the center of the room and started pacing again. Skye looked around the room for a place to escape from. There were guards stationed at each exit of the dome shaped room. The ceiling was too high for climbing out of, and she couldn't see anything else that could get her out of the building.

Jayla leaned over slightly and whispered into Skye's ear. "I think we can make it out of that window. If we climb those edges and use some of the jutting bricks, I think we could make it up to the window and smash it. I'm sure I can make it, maybe Zaith and Luken too, but I don't know if the adults are strong enough."

Skye looked up at the decorative window about 15 feet up in the wall. She could tell easily that she wouldn't be able to make it, but Jayla might have a shot. And if she got out she could find the creatures and they could escape.

She was about to whisper back at Jayla when Daken turned back around.

"You five are a Squadron? Interesting. When I was a Light, I was only 12 years old. People said I was a prodigy child, a genius. I don't know about all that. But, I became a Flame when I was about your age. I'm sure you know the story of what happened with the election. They do teach that in schools don't they?"

Jayla spoke up. "Oh yeah, they have been teaching all the kids in Isarn about how crazy you are. They say you're a politician gone mad and everything. I see why they do, you're just as creepy as they said you were."

Skye turned her eyes to the window. If Jayla was going to make a move she was going to need a distraction.

She made eye contact with Jayla. Jayla turned slightly to show Skye that she had undone her handcuffs, then gave her a small metal wire she must have used to get out of her cuffs.

Skye made the silent exchange and started to work the metal into the hole.

Daken scoffed. "I hate how that government thinks that they can just control every person in Isarn by filling their heads with lies. It needs to change. They're brainwashing the next generation. Don't you five see you could change that?"

"Not to be that person," Jayla said. "But I'm pretty sure the only person here that needs a good brainwashing is you. What kind of creepy dark thoughts are going on in that evil mind of yours?"

Daken held a hand to the bridge of his nose. "I'm just going to ignore everything you say from now on."

Skye made a loud cough to hide the noise of the handcuffs unlocking. She had to hold them in place to make it look like she was still cuffed, and passed the pin back to Jayla.

"Alright, Skye, here's a question," he said.

"What do you want now?" she asked harshly.

"I'm just interested to know what our father has told you about me."

Skye looked across the room to her dad. His face was turned down to the floor, not meeting her eyes.

"He didn't." Her voice was cold, and she wasn't sure which of them it was meant to be cold to.

Daken laughed and walked over to Skye's dad. He finally looked up to meet his eyes. "You really think I would tell my kids their brother is a murderer?"

"I thought you'd at least give them the truth. Or is that too much to ask from a father?"

That seemed to hit him hard.

"He was just trying to protect us," Skye said, cutting in.

"Was he? Or was he ashamed of the fact that *I'm* his son?"

He paused and looked over at Skye's dad–their dad.

"Come on, Zareb, you can talk. Answer the question."

Skye felt a tap on her foot, Jayla was signalling her.

She looked to her dad. She wanted to hear him talk. She wanted the answer to the question that had burned itself into her heart for the past week. Why had he lied?

Dad met her gaze once and opened his mouth to speak.

Jayla tapped Skye's foot again.

"I didn't want to- I- Skye, I'm sorry I didn't want to hurt you."

"Well, you did," she shot, not bothering to add any sympathy to her voice.

"Okay, so I know this is important and all," Zaithrian cut in. "But could we maybe be having this conversation when we're *not* chained and waiting to be killed by a murderer? No offence, of course."

"You're starting to sound like Jayla," Luken mumbled with a laugh.

So he did have his hearing aids. At least that was one good thing.

"*The point is,*" Daken said with a raised voice. "Is that, Skye, you can't trust him. You can't trust your own dad for sked's sake. He lied to you your whole life. I never did. What does that tell you?"

"I don't know who to trust anymore, but it certainly can't be the man who kidnaped my dad for his own selfish gain." Skye made eye contact with Jayla for a second and that was all they needed.

Jayla broke out of her cuffs and made a mad dash for the wall.

Skye and Daria ran to the scientists as the boys rushed Daken and Zaith landed a solid blow to his jaw.

Then chaos erupted.

Skye started unlocking the cuffs of the scientists, just as the guards ran in.

"Run!" Dad screamed at her pulling himself away.

"I'm not going to leave you!"

Daria grabbed her arm and dragged her to the exit before she could protest.

"Split up!" Zaithrian yelled, darting to a hallway.

Skye bolted to the nearest exit, where armed men started rushing forward. Skye dodged around them. They must have been caught off guard, since she managed–somehow–to get out of the room. She didn't know where she was running, but she needed to get away.

Then the shots started to rain.

Skye dove behind a pillar and army-crawled into the darkness.

She held a finger to her comm. "Can anyone hear me?!"

There was a line of static, but a hint of Zaithrian's voice came through. "...re you? ...s...one? ...ain roo...pty for now so...urry ba...ck!"

The dots connected almost instantly in Skye's brain. The main room was empty and she needed to get back. Maybe Jayla had gotten out and could get their creatures. Was Dad okay?

She didn't have time to think of it, she needed to get out. Lucky for her, her hiding place had worked and the guards footsteps had passed.

She got up, clutching her sore chest and rib. She ran.

Her lungs screamed for more air, but she never let herself slow. Skye was only a little farther from the main room where everyone would be waiting.

"Abort! Abort! Don't come- Daken's-"

Zaithrian's voice blasted into her ear just as she ran into the room.

Hands immediately grabbed her arms. Skye thrust herself away at them, unable to break free.

Daken twisted her arm behind her back and landed a knee into her stomach. She crumpled to the ground.

"What did I say would happen?"

Skye struggled to crawl away from him, she was exhausted, and her air wouldn't come due to Daken's blow.

"Hey, freak."

Jayla jumped from a ledge above them and landed on top of Daken. He fell over and Jayla pinned him in a neck lock against the ground. Daken thrust around, trying to break free. Jayla nailed her fist into his face.

Luken and Zaithrian jumped down, both had blasters they'd had to have stolen pointed at Daken's face.

"I wouldn't try that if I were you," Zaithrian said, charging the gun.

Daken stopped struggling. "Smart choice," Jayla said, getting up.

She cuffed his wrists. "Don't try anything, buddy. I can snap your neck using only my feet if I wanted to." Jayla gave him her most innocent smile, then ran over to check on Skye.

"Are you okay?" she asked, grabbing her arm to steady her.

"Where's my dad?"

"Up on the edge with Dar," she pointed to where the room went in for the ceiling. "I tried the window, it's way too thick to break out. We need to find a different exit. Fast."

The boys shoved the chained Daken to the ground.

"You know my men will be here any second now, they won't hesitate to kill kids."

Zaithrian placed the gun against Daken's temple. "That's why you're going to tell us how to get out of here. Now."

"I'll help you leave, just remove my cuffs."

Jayla scoffed. "Only an idiot would do that." She grabbed the gun from Luken and shot Daken's foot.

He screamed in pain.

Everyone stared at Jayla. She scrunched her eyebrows. "What? You gotta establish authority." She held the gun out for Luken.

His eyebrows were still raised in shock. "Um, why don't you keep that."

Daken groaned in pain.

"Where's the exit?" Zaithrian said. "Or she'll shoot you again."

"Oh, I will."

He laughed, his breathing still heavy. "Skeding kids. You can't win."

50 men charged into the room, each one with a loaded gun pointing at one of the Squadron.

CHAPTER FORTY-FIVE

I'm really ticked off now."

Daken stared Skye down. She stood against the wall. Across from her, Zaithrian, Daria, Jayla, Luken, and the three scientists were kneeling against the ground, tied at the wrists, each one had a gun pointed at their heads.

"I wanted to work with you. You could have saved your nation, Skye. Now you're all going to die. One more chance since I truly think you can make the right choice. Agree to help me, or I shoot them all, one by one, then you."

Skye leaned against the wall, her heart thundering inside her chest. Tears rolled down her cheeks. She couldn't look at them. Any of them.

"I'm going to count to ten, and if you don't answer by then…"

A gun cocked and was pressed against Jayla's head.

"No! You can't… you- Jayla-"

She gave Skye a sad smile, one that broke Skye's heart.

"Do me instead!" Luken screamed. "You can't- you can't kill Jayla. Put the gun on me instead."

351

"Luken-" Jayla pleaded, her eyes brimmed with tears.

"How touching," Daken said. "But you don't understand how this works. No one will die if only Skye agrees to help me. Otherwise..." He shrugged, "you can both die first."

A gun was pressed to Luken's head at the same time.

"If you're going to kill them, you better put one on me too," Zaithrian said, giving Skye a determined look. "If they die, then I want to go with them."

"Me too," Daria said holding her head up.

"Oh shut up everyone!" Daken yelled, holding his hands up. " I'm going to start counting and we'll see what my sister does. One... "

Skye's sobbs echoed through the eerie base, bouncing off the walls and back at her tauntingly. What was she supposed to do? She couldn't join Daken, but there was no way she could let everyone die.

She stopped crying and took a steadying breath. She knew what she needed to do. Just before Daken could say 'ten', Skye raised her voice. "I'll do it."

"Skye don't you dare-" Dad started, but was kicked in the stomach before he could finish.

"Wise choice, Skye," Daken said, limping over to her. He placed a hand on her shoulder, Skye stiffened at his touch. "You are going to become my greatest asset."

Skye's eyes filled with tears, these ones for herself. "Now let them go, that was the deal."

Daken laughed, his grip tightening. "You didn't actually expect me to let them go, right? Skye, use your brain, they know too much." He turned to the gunmen. "Kill the kids."

CHAPTER FORTY-SIX

No!" Skye ripped herself from Daken's hold as a sharp sensation raced from the back of her neck to her fingertips.

A solid bolt of lightning shot from her hands and collided against each of the gunmen.

Skye did the only thing she could think of. She screamed.

She looked down at her arms. Bright white lines wove in her skin like veins. They felt cold and yet warm at the same time, and definitely *not* normal.

Daken grabbed her shoulder. "You're a Channeler!"

Before she knew what happened, another bolt of lightning shot from her fingertips and blasted Daken in the chest.

Skye leaped away from him as his body went into cardiac arrest. Skye's body trembled as the voices around her erupted into screams.

Skye heard a massive crash, then the mighty cry she had become so familiar with. Her eyes shot up to the sky. Kade.

The blue thunderbird had destroyed the roof over their heads, a cloud of darkness surrounded him.

His eyes glowed white. Lightning seemed to wrap around his wings in streams of fingering light. His wings were spread wide in the air. He was controlling lightning.

With a screech, his wings flapped and a bright bolt of lightning shot from him. It struck the ground and sent some of the charging men into the air.

The ground next to her exploded from another blast of Kade's lightning. Chunks of the stone floor shot into the air.

"Kade!" Skye screamed, trying to get his attention.

Another rush of soldiers came running through the doors, yelling and trying to shoot the thunderbird with their guns.

Kade broke each shot with a blast of lightning, sending the force back at the shooters.

Skye ran for cover and hid against the wall. She looked back down at her arms where the glowing veins had once been. They were back to normal, and all feeling had returned to them.

Skye leaned against the wall, trying to catch her breath and let her heartbeat return to normal. She closed her eyes, and instead of darkness, she saw what looked like a faded view from what was happening from above the fight.

She jerked her eyes open. WHAT THE SKED WAS HAPPENING.

Then she remembered her friends. She held a finger to her earcomm. "Can anyone hear me?"

She was replied with a horrible static.

She looked around for any of her friends or her dad, but there was no way to make out any shapes amongst the firing.

A blast of lightning shot near her. She shielded her eyes from the bright light. "Kade!" she screamed.

The thunderbird only continued to screech wildly and shoot the overflowing amounts of soldiers.

She dove away from the blasts, eyes screaming for sight of anyone.

There. Zaithrian was struggling to crawl away from the chaos. He caught her eye and started to make his way over to her. Just as he had reached her, Skye felt the racing sensation again.

She looked up at Zaithrian's shocked face. Her veins shifted to icey blue and a rush filled her fingers.

"RUN!" An uncontrollable blast of lightning shot from her hands.

The ground under them exploded from the blast and sent them flying across the room and smashing into a wall.

Skye screamed in pain as a piece of shrapnel dug itself into her leg. The rush of lightning faded from her skin again.

She clutched her leg and sat up. Where was Zaithrian?

He was lying on his side against the wall, blood smeared on his face. He coughed and started to crawl into a sitting position. He bit back a scream as he put weight on his arm.

He looked over at Skye, his gaze was filled with pain, confusion, fear, and maybe even a little awe. "How did you do that?" he breathed.

"I don't know." Skye said, hauling heavy breaths. What was happening?

Skye heard a massive screech. Her head whipped around to see over a dozen dragons flowing through the broken roof. Riders were on them. Oh no. Did Daken have more men?

No wait.

"The Flames are here!" Zaithrian gaped.

She looked over at Zaithrian. He leaned his head against the wall behind them, tears of relief sliding down his face, leaving streaks on his dirty cheeks.

A massive caw sounded. Kade. He was going to break the rest of the building. Most of it was already on fire. Skye knew she needed to do something. But what could she do? She closed her eyes, focusing her mind. She felt a strong voice coming from somewhere in her mind. It repeated one word over and over. *Protect.*

Skye tried to connect to it. She knew it was Kade's voice. She found one word in her mind and sent it back at him. *Calm.*

With one more screech the lightning began to fade. The clouds rolled away and Kade descended. It was suddenly a beautiful day again, no storm at all.

Just as sudden as it had started, it was over.

Skye sank back farther into the cold stone, her body limp, and her mind exhausted.

Zaithrian coughed. "Now how did you do *that*."

Skye gave him the smallest smile. "I still don't know."

Shouts rose higher as the Flames started seizing prisoners. Daken was among them. He looked like he was unconscious, but she hadn't killed him, that was a good thing at least.

Skye let her eyes close, her mind and body begged for rest. She could have kept them closed forever if it wasn't for a sharp shake of her arm.

Her eyes opened. "Revin?" She must be seeing things. But it looked so real, Revin kneeling in front of her, he was wearing a strange uniform. His face was full of... fear.

"Kid, wake up! It's me."

It really was him. Her tired eyes opened slowly, then they shot open when she realized she was definitely *not* supposed to be here.

"Revin-"

He cut her off by scooping her up and wrapping her in a hug. Skye hugged him back, not realizing she had started crying.

He let go and looked her dead in the eye. *He* was crying. *"Never* do that to me again."

Skye sunk back into his embrace, crying into his strong shoulder. Once she let go, she gripped onto his arm and he helped her up.

A woman next to him took her arm as Revin helped Zaithrian up. The woman led her to a cluster of her friends. Jayla ran up and hugged Skye, almost knocking her over. Besides from a few cuts, she looked okay.

"I'm so sorry Jayla," she said.

"Sweet Eagles Skye, would you stop apologizing for once in your life! We're all alive because of you, and Kade, and you doing something to Kade, and you shooting lightning out of your skeding hands- never mind. Look, we did it. We got your dad back, and Daken is captured. Let's go home."

CHAPTER FORTY-SEVEN

Stark white walls greeted Skye as she opened her eyes the next morning. The smell of cleaners and fake scents filled her nose. It all came flooding back. Daken's base, Kade, the Flames coming.

"How do you feel?"

Skye turned the other way and saw Revin, seated next to her in a chair. She sunk into the thin pillow. "I'm okay. Feeling better. Ish. Better than yesterday."

As soon as they'd landed after their flight home, she'd been rushed to a hospital and hadn't gotten any news on what had happened to Daken or her friends. She'd had surgery on her leg to remove the smaller pieces of shrapnel, and hadn't woken up since.

"Everyone's safe. Your dad and the last two scientists had to be flown to the Medical District for a more serious treatment, but they'll be okay. Your dad got a bullet to the leg and it never got properly cleaned or bandaged so there's an infection. They think it'll heal though. Dr. Bellis and Dr. Ervan–the other two scientists–were killed by Daken in captivity. Your friends were pretty banged up,

Luken, Jayla, and Daria were treated and they're all home resting. You and Z got the worst of it, the doctors say you'll both be fine, but he's still in the other room. The Flames took Daken back to Isarn and we have a patrol going around his base at the moment."

Skye said nothing. "How did you know I was out there?"

"Kid, I know you well enough to know that there isn't one thing more important to you than family. Plus, you're an impulsive idiot if I've ever met one. You didn't actually think I would help you finish those earpieces and *not* put a way to intercept your conversations, did you?"

"You bugged our comms?" Skye gaped.

"Guilty." He put his hands up. "You should be glad I did."

"Is that why were you with the Flames?"

Revin sighed. "I convinced them to move the mission to yesterday when I found out you had left. It was supposed to just be them, but an... old friend of mine *made* me go with them. And... I needed to be the one to bring you home. You scared me to death kid, I thought you were... "

Skye looked at her hands. "I'm still sorry I scared you, I know I shouldn't have gone down there. But I don't regret what I did."

"I know. The only problem with that, is now you're in big trouble, I'm in big trouble, and your

Squad is in big trouble. And I have to get everyone out of it or we'll get kicked out of the Academy."

Skye paused. "Did we at least help the situation?"

Revin leaned back in his chair. "I'm not sure if 'helped' is the right word."

"Did we make it worse?"

"Not worse… I don't know. The Flames had a reason for not going…but you found a way to track them before we could. So… maybe you helped a little."

There was another long pause. Skye finally spoke. "Revin, when I was back there, I was… *shooting lightning*. It was coming out of my hands and I have no idea what was happening, I couldn't control it, and I almost shot Zaithrian. It's how I took out Daken, and it was just...*what happened to me*?"

Revin was silent, Skye could see that he was thinking.

"Do you know?"

Revin rubbed his chin. "You ever heard of Channeling?"

She shook her head, then stopped. "I think- I think Daken said something about it."

"It's where a rider and their creature share an unbreakable bond, so strong that their minds almost…connect. So when you were using lightning, it was Kade using it *through* you. It's

362

extremely rare, only a handful of people have ever been able to do it."

She placed a hand on the back of her neck. Now that she thought about it, the lightning *had* seemed to come from her mind. "That doesn't make sense," she said.

Revin gave a small laugh. "No, not really. But think of it this way, everyone shares a bond with their creature, right? Well someone who's bond with their creature has so much of a mental connection, that their minds can start to become so familiar with each other, that they almost connect. And I know how weird this sounds, but when two minds, a human's and a creature's, have a strong enough mental connection, they can send signals to each other. So when Kade is sending a message to his brain to use lightning, he can redirect it to your mind and it will physically... work."

Skye stared at him. "That seems so... wrong."

Revin laughed. "I know what you mean. But it's actually an amazing connection to have, and it's crazy that you achieved it in just a few months. You never cease to amaze me, kid."

Skye stared at her hands. "Will I be able to control it?"

"Sort of. You yourself can't call on Kade's lightning, he gets to choose when he gives it to you, but you can learn to control him."

Skye let it all rattle around in her brain for a minute. She could use lightning. She couldn't wrap her head around it. But... it almost did make sense in a really weird way.

"How do you know so much about it?"

"What do you think I did during Beacon training? I know more useless knowledge than I could ever tell you about."

Just then, a doctor came in and ran a few tests on Skye. He gave Revin some instructions on how long she'd be on bedrest, and a few things along those lines. He said they should wait an hour, then they could go home.

After the doctor left, a woman stepped inside the room, Skye was pretty sure she was the same one who had been with Revin when they were at Daken's base.

"Rev, someone out here needs a word with you," she said.

He got up. "Keep an eye on her." He walked out the door and the woman sat in his chair.

"So you're Revin's Light?"

She nodded. "I'm Skye."

"I'm Carli, an old friend of Revin's." The girl had to be Revin's age, mid twenties, with short, blonde hair. Skye could tell by her uniform she was a flame; a black suit made of thick cargo material and a bronze armband.

Skye paused. "Were you the one who got him to go on the mission?"

Carli laughed. "Yeah, that was me alright. And it was a good thing I brought him too, he's still one of the best Flames I've ever met."

"Wait. Revin was a Flame?"

Carli pulled her leg up onto the chair. "He never told you about what happened, did he? I guess I can't really blame him for not. Revin used to be a Flame. He and his twin sister both became Flames when they came out of the academy, I had been in their Squadron as a Light so we were pretty close. We flew with D-Squad 7 for a few years, Revin was one of the best Flames anyone had ever seen, he's won a few medals even. But his sister Amie, now she was amazing. She was the best female Flame of our era. She was the bravest, smartest, and the most disciplined Flame I'd ever met. And she flew with her dragon with such ease, they had the tightest bond."

Carli's voice got quiet. "We were flying a mission about four years ago, something happened, and Amie was shot down and killed. No one was sure what happened, but Revin said that it was all his fault. She had told him it was a trap, and he hadn't listened. We all took it hard, but Rev worst of all. He quit the Flames and left everything to do with it, including all of his friends. Revin told me that after he left, he trained to become a Beacon to

keep himself busy and take his mind off Amie, he'd
been there a few years when he said he couldn't
distract himself enough. He decided to take on a
Light to keep him busier. It must have helped him,
since he seems so much better since last time I saw
him.

"He called me and asked for me to move the
mission up because his Light was being stupid and
going to get herself killed. I've tried to get in touch
with him before, but he's never even answered his
comm. I think you've really helped him. It's pretty
amazing actually."

Skye didn't know what to say. But as she thought
about it, Revin did seem more like a Flame than a
Beacon, and the thought of him flying in the
military made her smile. It was definitely something
Revin must have loved. And she could see him
being good at it too.

"Do you think he'd ever become a Flame again?"
Skye asked as she used her arms to push herself into
a sitting position.

Carli thought for a moment. "I don't know. He
might, but he's very important on the Board of
Beacons, he has an extremely high position there,
but I can tell by the way he's been telling me about
it that he doesn't like it much. On the other hand, he
would be more at risk, being a Flame is dangerous
work, I think he'd have a hard time doing that full

time. Plus, he has something to lose again." She pointed at Skye.

"Me?"

"He adores you. He's told me all about you, you're like his little sister. I don't know if he would want to leave you to become a Flame."

Skye smiled to herself.

"But as much as I hope he comes back, it's his own choice, and it's a hard one."

Carli told Skye some of the missions she had flown with Revin, and made sure to stress the parts where Revin's awful ideas somehow ended up working. Skye loved hearing about Revin's life, she could tell Carli loved to tell her about it too. She was also pretty sure Carli loved Revin, she wondered if he knew that.

Revin came back into the room a little while later and said Skye was allowed to leave. She was given a pair of crutches to use for a few days when she would need to get out of bed, and she was discharged.

"Are you sure you don't want any help?" Revin asked as they walked through the parking lot.

Skye shook her head as she used her crutches to walk. "I'm fine. I need to learn to use them myself."

She slid into the backseat of Revin's hover and propped her leg up on the side seat.

After Revin had said a *very* lengthy goodbye to Carli–one that ended in a hug–he got in the hovercar and they started the drive back to the Academy.

They both said nothing. They drove for about fifteen minutes in silence, before Skye had to break it.

"Am I grounded?"

"Obviously."

"Okay, but from what? I barely go anywhere besides the school."

"I'll figure that out later. But I have something much bigger to worry about until then. You're in deep trouble, and not from me."

Skye winced. "The school?"

"Yep, I was talking with the principal today, she wants direct word with you and your Squad as soon as you're all well enough. You better pray to the Eagles they don't kick you out."

Skye had known they'd get in trouble for what they'd done, but she *really* hadn't thought about the risks enough.

"Do you know if Zaithrian's been released from the hospital yet?" Skye asked.

"I'm pretty sure he was, if not, he will be soon. He was pretty banged up. What happened down there with you guys?"

Skye told him everything, from sneaking into his files, to hacking the trackers, getting caught, breaking out, getting caught *again,* Daken threatening to kill them, and her using lightning.

By the time she had finished, they were almost to the campus. Revin didn't say anything the entire time. Skye couldn't see his face very well from the back of the car, but she could tell he was *mad*.

He pulled into the parking lot and shut off the engine. He just sat there for a moment, staring down at the dashboard. Finally, he shook his head and stepped out.

He helped Skye out of the car and led her through the campus. Students milled around, most of them whispering to each other, and some talked as loudly as ever. Obviously they had heard about their adventure.

Skye made a slow trip up to her dorm, and was exhausted by the time she had made it inside.

"Bed. Now," Revin said, walking into the kitchen and throwing his keys on the counter.

Skye got in bed and Revin brought her one of the pills she was supposed to take.

Revin sat down in her chair and thought silently. He broke from his trance and spoke. "What am I supposed to do with you?"

Skye stayed silent.

Revin shook his head and stood up. "Get some rest." He shut out the lights and closed the door.

"Revin," Skye called.

He came back into the room. "Yeah?"

"I love you."

He gave her a tired smile. "Love you too, kid."

CHAPTER FORTY-EIGHT

Why do I have to dress up so fancy? Revin doesn't care what I wear," Skye said as Jayla tied the back of her dress.

"Two reasons. One, we were invited to the Eagle Celebration by the Vire himself and you need to look nice at the biggest event in all of Isarn. And two, Mentor Ariel is making me dress up so that means you have to."

Skye sighed, Jayla was right about the first part. The Eagle Celebration was Isarn's biggest holiday and the Vire always held a special ball in his palace to celebrate. Their Squadron had been personally invited, which was an insane honor. But Skye really hadn't wanted to go, since she knew exactly why they had been invited. She knew people wouldn't be happy about their being there. They had committed crimes. Skye didn't truly understand why the Vire would want them there.

She was surprised they were even being allowed to go, they had been pretty much grounded from any outside interaction by their Mentors, and even more by the school.

They had a list of punishments, but at least none of them was getting expelled. Sure, they had to help the Arena Hands clean the stables for the rest of the year, they had to have someone accompany them on all of their recons, and about ten other things, but at least they got to stay.

The five of them also were getting punishments from their Mentors, some had it worse than others, but Skye knew they deserved it all.

She was glad to be off crutches, her leg still hurt occasionally, but Isarn was known for its advanced medical treatment, so she was doing well. She still hadn't gotten back to her regular creature and Squad training yet, but Revin had given her *plenty* of work to do while on bedrest–another of her punishments.

The rest of the Squad had recovered too, physically anyway. Aside from some broken ribs, cuts, and bruises, they hadn't been seriously injured, and had all healed fine. Zaithrian had broken his arm when he hit the wall, and had recently gotten his cast off, so they were all doing much better.

It was already over a month since her dad had been rescued, and Skye had finally talked with her dad. It had gone how she would expect, he told her and Locke that he had just been trying to protect them. Skye was still slightly mad at him for keeping it a secret, but at least they were on decent terms. Her dad was doing well physically, but he wasn't back to normal. He had told them that Daken had given them daily doses of a weird gas, and now he and the other two scientists were having a strange memory loss–none of them could remember much from when they'd been captured to when they'd been rescued. It meant they couldn't remember *why* Daken had taken them in the first place. It must have been a safety precaution. It was bad news for the Beacons, but her dad wasn't having any other effects from it, which was a relief.

Everything had actually been going back to normal, and Skye was hoping it would stay that way.

"Okay stand up, let me see," Jayla said as soon as she finished with the back of Skye's dress.

She stood up in front of the mirror and looked at her reflection.

Her dress was dark blue and went just above her knees. The top of it went to her neck where it was tied, leaving the back of the dress open. Her hair was done with small braids on the side of her head that went into a ponytail and faded into curls. Daria had done her makeup minimally, and it made her eyes stand out.

Jayla had worn her dark hair loose and had pinned up one side so it left her ear exposed. Her dark green dress was short with long sleeves made of colored lace that went to her hands. She was also wearing a necklace Skye had never seen before, it was a thin silver chain with a small circle pendant.

Skye hadn't gotten a good look at what was carved on the circle, but it looked like an exploding firework. She didn't ask her where she had gotten it, but she could guess.

Daria was wearing a light pink dress with short lace sleeves. Her bright blue hair was twisted into an intricate braid with wisps of hair framing her face. Daria was usually so stiff and minimal, it was nice to see her loosen up a bit.

The three of them all pinned an Eagle Blossom into their hair. The flower was a sign of Isarn's freedom and it was a tradition to wear one on the holiday. The flower had five round, white petals with blue ombre starting in the very center and coming out into the edges.

"I think we look *good*," Jayla said, making a face in front of the mirror.

Skye laughed and pulled her out of the room. "Come on, we've got to get going."

All Beacons and Flames were invited, so Carli had offered to give the girls a ride and Revin was taking the boys.

Carli was waiting out in the hallway. She was wearing a simple white dress with a bronze sash that symbolized that she was a Flame.

"Come on girls, we're going to be late."

"You can't rush this," Jayla said, gesturing to herself as she walked.

The drive to the Vire's Tower was about an hour. As they neared the actual palace, the houses turned to buildings and skyscrapers. But the tallest building was the Vire's home.

Skye was in awe of the colossal building. The building was made of white stone bricks with lots of clear windows along the sides of the tower. There were two shorter towers on either side of the larger one, and both had domed roofs made of glass.

Carli pulled up to a gate and told the guard who she was and he let her into the parking lot. The parking garage was underneath the building and it was full of hovercars.

They went up an elevator to their floor where a woman was at a counter. They each scanned their finger on the pad, and were admitted into the ballroom.

Skye gasped as she walked through the doors. The white walls went high into the sky with a glass dome. Golden arches lined the walls, and balconies were placed around the outsides. Hundreds of people milled around the room, each of them wearing a suit or gown more decorated than the last. Tables scattered the edges of the room, some had delicacies from across the world, and the rest were filled with seated guests. The floor she stood on had swirls of marble with hints of gold mixed in. Chandeliers hung from the top of the dome, they were filled with gems of blues and clear.

"Woah," Jayla breathed.

"I know, it's really beautiful," Skye said.

"Oh, I meant the food. But yeah, the room's pretty too I guess."

Skye laughed. "You can eat later, we need to find our table."

Skye and Daria led her away from the food and to the tables which were marked with the names of the guests who would sit there.

They found their table near the back of the room. Revin was sitting there and eating some sort of desert. He had a sharp black suit, but his hair was still in its usual sloppy state. His silver sash addressed that he was a Beacon, Skye noticed he had two bronze pins fastened to it.

"Hi Revin, where are the boys at?" Skye asked, taking her marked seat.

He looked up at her. "You look nice, kid. I'm not sure where those two went, probably trying to find a dance partner. Or causing havoc. You can all go get food if you want, but don't eat too much, we're going to be here a while."

Jayla jumped up and ran off to get her dinner, Daria followed her timidly, but Skye stayed.

"How many of these have you been to?"

Revin shrugged. "I've been to a few, I haven't gone the past few years though."

"Why not?" As soon as Skye had asked the question, she knew the answer.

He stopped chewing for a little bit. "Stuff happened, and this didn't really seem important anymore. There were some people I didn't want to see, and...well, I guess Carli probably told you everything, didn't she?"

Skye nodded, regretting having asked the question.

Revin got quiet.

"Are you okay?" Skye asked.

He gave her a small smile. "Not really. But maybe I am a little more than I thought I was."

Jayla and Daria came back a minute later, Jayla holding three plates somehow, each piled with food.

She slid into her chair next to Skye. "These are so good, here take some. I got you a plate." She placed a plate in front of Skye with small candies on them.

She stuck the pink ball in her mouth and instantly it started to fizzle in her mouth. She nearly spit it out.

Jayla started cracking up, earning herself a few head turns. "That's what I did!"

Soon the fizz wore off and the hard candy melted into a creamy sweet liquid. Skye pushed the plate away. "It's great, but it's going to rot my teeth out."

Jayla rolled her eyes and stuck four candies in her mouth at once. "Okay, Grandma." Her face scrunched up for a few seconds.

Revin shook his head with a sigh. "I'll be around, feel free to leave the table whenever." He got up and walked into the crowd of silk and skirts.

"What are we supposed to do?" Skye asked, picking around at the other items Jayla had brought back.

"They're going to start dancing soon," Daria said. "But I don't see many boys our age."

"Where are our boys?" Jayla asked, looking around the room. "I'm pretty sure Smart Boy owes me a dance for that kidnapping prank."

She stood up from her chair. "I'm gonna go find them."

Skye sighed. "I feel sorry for Luken, he has Jayla jumping all over him."

"I don't know, maybe he likes her," Daria said. "After all he did try to get Daken to shoot him instead of her."

Skye's stomach flipped with nausea. Her heartbeat thundered in her ears.

"Sorry, I forgot-"

"It's fine." Ever since they'd come home, Skye felt sick any time anyone mentioned *that* part of their capture. She hated thinking about it, the way she had seen each one of her closest friends seconds from death, and each of their fates in her hands.

"I'll be right back," she said, needing air. She stumbled her way to one of the balconies.

She leaned against the rail overlooking the city. She took a few slow breaths until her heartbeat was back to normal and her hands had stopped shaking. The cool air smelled of summer, the wisps of wind tickled her back and arms, blowing her ponytail.

Skye felt so at peace. It reminded her of when she was flying. When she flew with Kade she forgot all of her troubles with Daken.

"It seems you had the same idea as me."

Skye turned around to see none other than Vire Malco leaning against the rail behind her.

"I- I didn't know- I'm sorry," Skye stammered.

"There's nothing to be sorry for at all, my dear. It's nice to get away from the crowd every once in a while, even if it's just out here."

Skye swallowed, unsure of what to say. "Thank you for your invitation, sir, it's a great honor to be here."

He smiled. "It's not often I meet someone like you, Miss Zareb."

"I'm sorry, sir?" Skye asked, unsure of what he meant.

"You risked your lives to take on Daken and retrieve your father, I admire you for that. Not many people have the courage and the bravery to do that."

Skye tried to get her palms to stop sweating. "Thank you sir, but I don't really deserve any praise for my actions, I couldn't have done anything without my Squadron. And we would have never made it back without the Flames."

"I appreciate your honesty, Miss Zareb, and your humility is rare for someone your age. I believe I will see many more great things from you. And you're a Channeler? Like I said before, the Eagles surely fly with you." He stepped away from the railing and left the balcony, leaving Skye alone.

Skye gazed over the city, smiling at the Vire's words. If someone had told her six months ago that she would personally have a conversation with the Vire in his palace, she would have laughed. But here she was, leaning over the railing, letting the beautiful sight leave a permanent golden memory in her mind.

"Well, look who I found."

Skye turned to see Zaithrian coming up next to her. His honey brown eyes glowed golden in the fading light of the day. He was in a dark blue suit with his Eagle Blossom pinned to his shirt. His dark hair was in its usually spikey mess.

The corners of her mouth twitched up. "Hi, Zaith."

He smiled and leaned on the rail next to her. "How are you enjoying the party life?"

She gave him a look.

He gave a small laugh. "Yeah, I figured you'd feel that way."

Skye looked back over the fading sunset. "What about you?"

"I'm not a big fan of parties," he said, shrugging. "At least not this kind. I'd much rather spend today the way everyone else does. The parade has always been one of my favorite things about moving to the City District. One year, one of my younger brothers and I stayed out until dawn with the paraders. It made my mom so mad." He smiled small and thoughtfully. "How about you? Ever done the parade?"

Skye thought of all of the years she'd watched the City District's Eagle Celebration parade. People from all over Isarn made the trip to spend the night parading through the streets wearing painted paper wings like the Eagles. Skye had done it once or twice, but the crowd always overwhelmed her. She'd started staying home, and Locke had never asked to do it without her. Ever since then, the two of them watched the colorful crowd pass by their house from the balcony in Skye's room. Then her mom and dad had started watching with them and it had become a family tradition.

Skye told Zaithrian about the years she had spent doing this with her family.

He stared out over the golden glow of sunset. "I'm glad he's home–your dad. I… can't imagine what that was like for you."

Skye picked at her dress, carefully avoiding his eyes as she tried to fight the sharp tears threatening to break free. "It was pretty horrible. I still think about what would have happened if I- we didn't go."

Zaithrian stared at her hands, as if he was deciding whether or not he should take them in his. He decided against it. "You're strong, Skye. Don't forget that. And don't forget that If you ever need us, we'll be there for you, I'll be the first one." He met her eyes. "But I don't think you'd need me when you've got that power in you."

Skye let a smile touch her lips. "I'll always need you guys."

"Ooooh, look what's going on out here," Jayla said, coming out on the balcony, she was pulling Luken by the hand and Daria was following behind, trying to act proper, but looking like she wanted to laugh. "I miss anything?"

"Not much. Are you going to dance?" Skye asked as Jayla leaned against the rail next to her.

"Oh yeah, I just wanted you to be out there to watch me rule the floor."

"I'm pretty sure it's ballroom dancing," Daria said.

"I can rule *any* floor."

"I'm sure that would be interesting to watch," Luken said. His dark green suit was almost the same as Zaithrian's, and his Eagle Blossom was tucked behind his ear–probably Jayla's doing.

"So what are you doing out here?" Jayla asked quietly, scooting closer to Skye.

Skye fiddled with her dress. "I just needed to get out of the crowd."

Jayla looked up at her and gave her hand a reassuring squeeze. "I'm here for you, I always will be."

Before Skye could answer, a loud booming voice thundered over the noise of the party. "Welcome fine guests of this year's Eagle Celebration." Applause made its way through the crowd.

A man stood on the slightly elevated stage where the band had been playing. "I would like to hand the stage over to our esteemed Vire Malco."

There was more applause as the Vire took the microphone from the announcer and stood in front of the crowd. Skye's group made their way back inside and stood next to Revin and Carli.

"Firstly, I would like to thank each one of you for coming to this wonderful celebration. Isarn is built on its great people and we wouldn't be the nation we are without you. This year has truly taken an unexpected turn as we have officially taken Daken Claw into custody."

Another loud cheer burst from the crowd, Skye couldn't help but join in.

"As you know, Claw has poisoned our world for almost a decade, and now that he is finally captured, Isarn can return to being a fully peaceful nation. I had the honor of meeting the young Lights who took him down, and I must say that I am forever grateful to them. These five young students have shaped our world for the better, and I am proud to call them Lights of Isarn."

More cheering rippled through the crowd, some of it wasn't gratitude, but it sounded like most of the people there were glad that they had taken down Claw, and that was all that Skye could ask for.

The Vire continued, "I was talking to one of those Lights earlier tonight, and she had one request for me. So here you go, Jayla Payge, and I thank Light Squadron 999 and Flame Squadron Dragon-7 again for their service."

The Vire stepped down as the speakers started playing *actual* dance party music.

Luken, Daria, Zaithrian, and Skye all turned to Jayla, who was smirking.

"You got the *Vire of Isarn* to grant *you* a favor?" Skye asked in disbelief.

"What? He was talking to me a little bit ago, and he said that if I ever needed anything to ask him, so I asked him to play some music that I could actually dance to since I was missing the parade, and he did."

"Whoever decided that you didn't get into the Intelligence Guild was horrible at their job," Luken said. "You're obviously the smartest one here."

Jayla changed her voice to sound like a circus announcer. "Alright boys and girls we have one last act for you tonight, the grand finale." She dramatically gestured her hands toward the empty dance floor where elegant people stood around awkwardly, unsure of what to do. "Okay, well, not much of a 'grand finale' yet then."

"Alright Jayla, enough stalling," Zaith said. "Let's see those incredible dance moves you keep bragging about."

"Come on Skye, let's go do this!"

Skye looked over at the faces of her Squad, an overwhelming surge of joy filled her as she thought of how much each of them had changed her life for the better.

"Alright," she said, laughing and taking Jayla's hand. "Lead the way."

ACKNOWLEDGMENTS

Here we are. The end of the book. Wow, I don't even know where to start with this, there were SO many people who made this book happen. I seriously couldn't have done it without any of you. So here's a big THANKYOU to:

-My parents for their overwhelming amount of love and support throughout this crazy writing journey. You both have always been just as passionate about my dreams as I am, and your interest in my career has really kept me going. Mommy, I definitely couldn't have made this book happen without your input and advice. Daddy, your constant reminder that you want me to follow my passion means so much to me. Skye and her Dad's relationship is completely based on the relationship we have and I hope that shows a sliver of how much that has meant to me.

-Josh for the constant motivation to prove you wrong. When I asked for your help with draft one, I didn't mean tell me there's no point. But I guess

387

that's what I get for asking my older brother for help.

-All my younger siblings for your motivation and weird ideas when it comes to solving problems. You make some pretty good beta readers. And Eli, I hope this lives up to your love of Raven Rose.

-My friends for whom this book is dedicated. You guys mean the world to me. Whether I've known you since we were little kids, or if I've met you online through the indie author community, you all have inspired this story and the characters so much.

Also, I totally just used the word 'whom' *self high five*

-Grace for being my best friend in the entire world and being the original Jayla. She's completely based on you.

-My wonderful and extraordinary beta readers because this story would belong in the toilet without you. Maddy, Becca, Nova, and Lauren–you guys are literally the best. Your input means so much. The fact that you all actually made it through my cringey villain monologue is *impressive*. You guys are so encouraging and kept me motivated when I was sure my book was the worst piece of writing that ever came out of anyone's brain. Thank you for loving my characters as much (or more, in Lauren's case) as I do. You're all awesome.

-Pedro<3 If you know, you know.

-You! The fact that there is a real person holding this book right now just blows me away. The fact that you chose to spend your time reading this weird little story of mine is just- THANK YOU.

-And last, but *certainly* not least, I need to thank my Heavenly Father. Jesus, without You I could have never made it through this journey. The nights I spent stressing and crying over this book would have made me shut this project down a long time ago if You hadn't helped me through it.

You all have made my life so much better and I feel so blessed to have all of you in my life. Here's to you. And doughnuts. Cheers.

May the Eagles fly with each one of you.

Made in the USA
Middletown, DE
13 November 2022

14743905R00231